LAYING VENEER by
American know-how mi
challenge it couldn't beat in a place where the
land seemed to have a life of its own. . . .

I, MONSTER by Henry Slesar—When he tried to turn down the case, he never imagined the curse his would-be client would place upon him. . . .

MISTS by Kristine Kathryn Rusch and Dean Wesley Smith—Was he being haunted by some creature of the mist—or by a horror out of his own conscience. . . .

ON HARPER'S ROAD by William F. Nolan—She'd never believed in fortune tellers until she found herself living out a prophecy from which there seemed to be no escape. . . .

These are just four of the pulse-pounding tales of the imagination that await you on these unforgettable—

JOURNEYS TO THE TWILIGHT ZONE

JOURNEYS TO
THE
TWILIGHT
ZONE

Edited by Carol Serling

DAW BOOKS, INC.
DONALD A. WOLLHEIM, FOUNDER
375 Hudson Street, New York, NY 10014

ELIZABETH R. WOLLHEIM
SHEILA E. GILBERT
PUBLISHERS

DAW Book Collectors No. 900.

First Printing, January 1993

1 2 3 4 5 6 7 8 9

DAW TRADEMARK REGISTERED
U.S. PAT. OFF. AND FOREIGN
COUNTRIES
—MARCA REGISTRADA
HECHO EN U.S.A.

PRINTED IN THE U.S.A.

CONTENTS

INTRODUCTION:
BREACHING THE BARRIERS   7
by Carol Serling

THE FIELD TRIP   9
by Elizabeth Ann Scarborough

GOODFOOD   15
by W. Warren Wagar

LAYING VENEER   33
by Alan Dean Foster

I, MONSTER   43
by Henry Slesar

GOOD BOY   63
by Jane M. Lindskold

MISTS   76
*by Kristine Kathryn Rusch and
Dean Wesley Smith*

ANOTHER KIND OF
ENCHANTED COTTAGE   90
by Hugh B. Cave

ON HARPER'S ROAD   111
by William F. Nolan

OUTSIDE THE WINDOWS   128
by Pamela Sargent

THE EXTRA   144
by Jack Dann

INSIDE OUT   156
by Karen Haber

SOUL TO TAKE   190
by Vanessa Crouther

STANDING ORDERS   219
by Barry N. Malzberg

COMING OF AGE   226
by Susan Casper

WAIFS AND STRAYS   235
by Charles de Lint

SUGGESTION   275
by Rod Serling

INTRODUCTION: BREACHING THE BARRIERS

by Carol Serling

Almost everyone over twelve has some idea of what the TWILIGHT ZONE means. The dictionary describes it as "an indefinite boundary, a place between fantasy and reality" but that seems rather perfunctory . . . without imagination. Rod Serling, who first breached the barriers to the ZONE undoubtedly knew it best. His description, familiar to many of you, bears repeating here, I think:

"a middle ground between light and shadow, between science and superstition. . . a place between the pit of man's fears and the summit of his knowledge."

Rod wrote about people, ordinary people, who found themselves in extraordinary circumstances dealing with problems of their own or fate's making.

The master storytellers whose yarns and fables you will find in this book have also "breached the barriers." There are exciting and highly original tales of alternate worlds of people, places, and events, in a world gone slightly askew. But there are familiar signposts of our own real world too . . . as it is . . . or as it may become.

Along the way. . . .

You'll be taken to the underground by W. Warren

Wagar where the Food Freedom Fighters battle it out with the Goodfood Bureau of Investigation and deal in Big Macs and Hershey Bars . . . and if you've just bought a new house, Hugh Cave's story will serve as a reminder that you had really better check the deed . . . or journey back in time with Bill Nolan's odyssey of a young woman's frightening return to her home town, the kind of story that Rod would have loved.

These and the other stories in this book will make you chuckle, make you sad, and some will even scare you.

Enjoy your journey.

THE FIELD TRIP

by Elizabeth Ann Scarborough

Yesterday we went on a field trip to the new Natural History Museum. It was very interesting.

The food was good, too. It was just right—ripe and squishy and full of good smells. There is food throughout the museum, all along the way, lining the corridors, so you can just eat whenever you feel like it. Our teacher said we smeared the food even farther.

There are mostly dee-o-ramas in the museum. Dee-o-ramas are scenes made with dead animals and plants and things to make it look like they're still alive, even though they're really dead. The oil companies paid for all the dee-o-ramas and they paid for the auto-tours, too, where guides talk to you from boxes and can even answer questions when you press a button. Wasn't that nice of the oil companies? They also paid for making the booklets and transcripts in the museum shop.

I bought a transcript of what the voices at the displays said and I am giving credit here so this is not play-ger-ism, which our teacher says is bad to do.

"Our true history began millions of years ago, after the onset of the fire age, during which all life was radically altered. The gigantic beasts which had previously stalked the earth, grazing and preying on lesser forms, died during this time, oddly fragile for such huge creatures.

"Our own ancestors existed during this time, too,

though they were naturally not as advanced as we who descended from them. Scientific studies show that we are larger, stronger, and with more brain capacity, have better sensory systems and are able to digest foods that they would have found unpalatable.

"Part of what has enabled us to progress to our present advanced form, however, is the very catastrophe that killed the ancient lords of the earth who were, from our viewpoint, predators."

"You mean they *ate* us?" one of my sibs asked. I thought it was a silly question especially as he will eat anything.

"Oh, no, they were far more savage than that," the voice-box told him. "They did not kill us for food. They merely killed us. Scientists have not discovered why. Perhaps in some sort of ritual sacrifice. These ancient creatures were a superstitious and fearful lot. We have discovered from recent translations of ancient records saved by our ancestors that they feared many things."

"*I* wouldn't have saved anything about such mean old monsters," I told the voice. "Who cares about them anyway if they murdered us?"

"All knowledge is useful, young patron," the voice said. "And actually, our ancestors probably did not intentionally save the records, but rather found them wrapped around food and in piles to which these creatures consigned food they did not wish to consume."

"Didn't they come back and eat it later?" my teacher asked. She sounded shocked. I bet she would have made those wasteful creatures write "Waste not, want not" a thousand times if she got hold of them.

"No. That was another of their strange customs. They feared food that grew too old. They feared many of the processes of their own bodies and perhaps, considering the monsters they were, they were correct to do so."

"Were they real scary looking?" one of my sibs asked.

"You may judge for yourself in a moment, young patron. I'm sure it was not their own appearance they found frightening, however. They no doubt found themselves and their peers as attractive as all of us find one another, and no doubt their family groups were fond of each other to some degree. No, they feared the deterioration of their bodies and had many strange beliefs about what brought it about. You will see in this next tableau a recreation of a scene in which these creatures are studying the hapless objects of their fear."

The next dee-o-rama was really strange. It didn't have plants or anything, just this big machine with a tower on it, like the towers on the oil derricks outside the colony. The tower pointed down at a piece of glass. In a puddle on the piece of glass, as if they were ice skating, a whole bunch of little creatures seemed to be scampering around. I was sad to realize they were dead. They were about the size of my younger sibs and kind of cute.

"The ancients were mortally afraid of the rather adorable little life-forms you see in the dee-o-rama. They were also afraid of things that they had already and things that they did not have. They were very afraid, for instance, of not having enough oil."

"Uh-oh, here comes the commercial," my eldest sib groaned.

"Shhh," the teacher said.

"This, as we all know, is a groundless fear. Today oil is still the cheapest, most reliable source of fuel we have. What exactly the ancients used it for, we can't be sure, but records show photographs of large dwellings and transport devices quite different from the ones we enjoy today. As you know, the Oil Companies today can power devices that move whole colonies from feeding ground to feeding ground."

"Why did they think the oil would run out?" I asked. I was kind of worried. Where would we be without oil to run the transports and heat our houses and age the food? How would the world run without such an important thing as oil? I think I will do my science fair project about that.

"Young patron, these were ancient creatures and as I've said, their brain capacity was very tiny compared to the enormous size of their bodies. You'll see next what we believe to be some of the devices they attempted to use to avoid using oil."

There weren't any explanations with the big pieces of glass, the lumps of black stuff that looked like solid oil, the pieces of unaged wood. It all looked pretty silly to me.

"I don't understand," I told the box. "Why did they think this stuff would be better than oil? Wood comes from trees and I don't see how glass could be any help—how about that black stuff? Is that where oil comes from, maybe?"

"No, young patron," the voice laughed. "Although it is similar in composition. That is coal and it, too, is an ultimate product of decomposition. Oil, however, is more durable, though it is, like coal, a fossil fuel."

"What's a fossil?"

"A fossil, young patron, is a remnant or trace of an organism of a past geological age embedded in the earth's crust. Coal is the solidified remains of plant material."

"So what's oil?"

"Oil comes from the fossils of animals. It is the oldest and most lasting of fuels. The ancients are believed to have obtained their oil from beasts even older and larger than they were. Perhaps these beasts were not so numerous, however, as the source from which we derive all of the benefits the Oil Companies bring to your lives today. In the next diorama, you will see a reconstruction of one of the skeletons we found near our easternmost colony on the continent, on a small but rich island. Note the oddly rounded skull. You will be surprised to learn that only about half of it was occupied by the brain. The feelers were believed to be at the end of the upper and lower limbs and no antennae of any sort have been found, although some scientists claim that millions of fine hairs grew to great length from the top of the skull and even more hairs, though smaller ones covered the rest of the beast. We believe they gave birth to live larvae, and did not produce eggs . . ."

It was a real neat thing to see the skeleton. It had long long legs near the head and even longer ones coming off the bottom of the trunk, with flat things with lots of bones in it and that funny looking round skull. Curved bones made a huge arch bigger than any tunnel I've ever seen at the top of the trunk and a funny-shaped bone attached by a long one seemed to be there just to keep the legs on.

"Oooh, gross," my youngest sib said. "What *is* that thing?"

"Nothing to be afraid of, young patron. They're now long dead and cannot hurt you and far from being disgusting, these bones are very useful. Bones just like this make the fuel to carry you from place to place, warm and cool your dwellings, and help prepare your food. And just think, you have creatures like this one to thank for it."

"But what *is* it?" she insisted. She is only little and I don't think she knew it was rude to talk back to a box.

"Why, young patron, that is the skeletal remains of those ancient fearful beings, the humans."

My teacher spoke up then. "As the guide says, children, there's nothing to fear now that these behemoths are extinct. Still, without them, we would have no oil, heat, or transport fuel. Neither would we have had this lovely and educational museum and tour. Shall we have a round of applause for the poor old things?"

We all clapped very loud, but I clapped loudest because I was glad they were dead and good for something now.

GOODFOOD

by W. Warren Wagar

I don't pretend to be anybody special or important, but until yesterday I had my self-respect. You know what I mean? A guy needs to believe he's worth something. Up until yesterday I always thought I was. Now, I'm not sure.

Don't get me wrong. I'm not saying I did anything I'm ashamed of. It's more like I'm confused. One side of me is glad, the other side of me is sad. Put it all together, you got a guy who doesn't know his mouth from his asshole.

It's a fucked-up world we live in. I don't guess anybody could have predicted it. My granddad never got used to it. If a cop came up to him and asked him what he thought of eating meat, he'd have rattled off all the right lines. He knew how to stay alive.

But he didn't really believe it, you know, in his gut.

He was raised different. Until he was nine or ten, his folks used to take him to Wendy's or Roy Rogers for burgers and roast beef sandwiches and that shit. The places were right out on the parkways, lit up as big as life.

You've seen clips from old videos. You know what everything looked like, but it's not the same, hearing how it was from somebody who really lived it.

"I used to get so damned hungry," he told me lots of times. "I'd be in school and I could just taste those hot greasy fries loaded with salt and those big thick

piled-up sandwiches, with all the slabs of fat meat—
we called 'em 'patties'—and the pickles and onions
and mustard. They put so much junk in 'em, it'd ooze
out all over your face and run down on the table, and
your mom would make a pass at you with a paper
napkin, and it was like the best meal you ever had in
your life. Until the next time."

Then Granddad would wink at me, and grin.

"When you're stoking in your bulgur and broiled
eggplant tonight or your pita and veggies, just imagine
it's 1995 again. Have a Big Mac on me, boy. Sin a
little, for the old guy."

I almost always got sick after hearing that story. A
couple times, I excused myself and went to the bathroom and threw up.

Maybe Granddad would be proud of me, for what
I do these days. I don't usually think about it. The
way I figure, a man has to make a dollar, one way or
another. Nobody else will do it for him.

I don't ask my customers to eat anything bad. What
they swallow is their business. I just think everybody
should get their kicks any way they want. If it's dope,
or if it's dice, or if it's hanging out at grillers eating
bacon and eggs, what's it to me?

The problem is the fucking law.

You know how it goes. No fats, no flesh, no sugars.
For the Sake of Your Life!

Sure, people live longer since the Goodfood Laws
were passed. Heart attacks and strokes are mostly
stuff you get when you're long past retirement age.
Hardly anybody dies of cancer. I know it didn't used
to be like that.

But I say, if you want to eat slow poison, it's your
privilege. Why should some skinny-assed bureaucrat
in Washington do your thinking for you?

I've seen guys in the grillers fall dead on the floor,

all rotted away with their red faces and pot bellies, but damn, they died happy.

What's more important?

You tell me.

So, like I say, I'm not ashamed of what I do for a living. If it wasn't for the dealer, nobody would have a choice in this lousy country. The actors on the video spots, all those bright-eyed beanpoles loving up their oatmeal and running marathons at ninety-nine, would be the whole fucking story.

Dealers make the difference.

Only there's some stunts nobody has a God-given right to pull. That's what has me mixed up. Since yesterday.

It all started when I saw this ladybird. She was tall and maybe thirty-five, and she walked like she owned the world. She never looked at me or anything, but you always know who's who and who's what in this business. She had to be tailing me.

The hackers in the Goodfood Bureau ought to know better than to put ladybirds built like that on the streets. They just don't blend in.

I was on my way from Giancarlo's place to a griller on the south side, to set up a delivery of cheese. She must've picked me up right after I left Giancarlo's. The food narcs have had his digs staked out for a couple weeks, so I wasn't exactly surprised.

I dodged into a pool hall I know on East Third and slipped out the back door into an alley, but when I hit the main drag again, she was still right behind me. Not bad for a ladybird.

So I detoured to Reagan Park and mingled with a crowd listening to some Goodfood preacher. He had a team of pals handing out samples of a new kind of nosh made from chestnuts and garbanzo beans, called Chest-Nuggets.

It was the usual spiel, about how much healthier

and happier everybody was nowadays, and how they were always coming up with tasty shit for you and me and, of course—

"For the Sake of Your Life!"

People in the crowd were gnawing on the Chest-Nuggets, but they got a kind of silly look in their eyes when he said that, and pretty soon a food leader was whipping them up real good.

"For—the—Sake—of—Your—Life!" they yelled.

"Tell me again!"

"FOR—THE—SAKE—OF—YOUR—LIFE!!!"

I joined in, just to stay inconspicuous, and kept working through the crowd, till I saw an opening and moseyed into a stand of trees at the edge of the park.

Then I ran like hell. When I got back out on the street and headed south, I thought my troubles were over.

But a couple blocks later, there she was again. Sexy legs like a race horse, skirt a little shorter than regular, wearing those new sandals with just enough heel to tilt her sweet ass. She even had long hair, long and red and fluffy, catching the breeze as she cantered in my direction.

So what was I supposed to do?

Well, I don't quit easy. I saw a taxi out of the corner of my eye, going north. I flagged it down, got in, and threw her a wink as I took off.

Even champion fillies can't keep up with a genuine fifty-horse electric engine.

I figured like I won the first lap anyway.

At the griller everything was normal. Security was good, nobody was getting in without a square voiceprint, and they had closed circuit TV at all the right places. No sign of the ladybird or any other narc outside. In other words, I felt real comfortable.

Manny tried his usual crap about how he could get his cheese from the Lombardi organization for half what we ask. And not just Swiss and cheddar. Lombardi even had Monterey Jack now, and some crazy goat cheese from France, and hot pepper cheeses bootlegged out of Mexico.

I had to explain the facts of life and death all over again.

Manny looked at me like I was Adolf Hitler or something, but then I threw him a bone about a new supplier we got. This guy claims he can deliver a thousand chickens and ten hogs a week for as long as we want. Also real butter.

"No marge?" asked Manny. "Not one fucking percent of marge?"

"No marge," I said, with a slow grin.

His piggy little eyes almost popped out of his skull. The quickest way to lose a customer in a griller is to cut the butter.

"Okay, you got a deal!" he said, and offered me a bacon cheeseburger with all the trimmings, on the house.

"You know I can't eat that garbage," I said. "I get nauseous just taking a deep breath in a place like this."

The rooms were all heavy with the stale smell of animal fat. It's hard to ventilate a griller, because the narcs have odor meters they carry around with them. Most people don't know it, but they do random sweeps of neighborhoods and the meters can spot any building where somebody's cooking funny food.

Anyway, all I'm trying to say is that my little visit to the griller went real nice. I came out through the trapdoor feeling like I've felt thousands of times before. You know, job done, no sweat, everything copacetic. Eight c's in my pocket, and Manny drooling over all that farm-fresh butter we might let him have.

So of course what do I find in the alleyway?

Some dumb street pusher trying to sell a candy bar?

Kids sharing a rat-meat sausage back behind a row of trash barrels?

Anything like I might expect?

You got it. No way. I'm not ten steps down the alley when out of the shadows ahead of me comes two long legs and a cloud of ruby-red hair.

I juke and make to turn left, but this time she's not following. She's leading.

"Arnie Saperstein?" she said, in a husky voice.

"Yeah, but you can call me Mr. Saperstein." I didn't want her getting too sure of herself.

"I'm Mindy MacGregor."

"You have to be somebody."

"Got a few minutes?" She flashed a big smile which hit me right in the knees.

I stood there looking pained, with all kinds of shit hopping around in my head. I mean, like I wanted to lay this ladybird, I wanted to get the hell out, I wanted to put a knife in her ribs, I didn't know what I wanted.

"You G.B.I.?" I asked, after a while.

She smiled again. "Does it matter?"

I shrugged.

She came up real close, so I could smell the scent in her hair.

"Want to see my badge?"

"Won't do you no good," I said, staring deep into her baby blues. "I'm a clean, law-abiding citizen. You must've seen me whooping it up at the Goodfood rally in Reagan Park."

"You were magnificent," she said. "An inspiration to us all."

So she had a sense of humor.

"Yeah," I said back to her, not missing a beat. "You people need all the help you can get."

"Do I detect a hint of antisocial feeling in your voice, Arnie?" she asked, but from her eyes I could tell she wasn't trying to hassle me.

"It's Mr. Saperstein."

"Of course. Mr. Saperstein. I'll remember."

"Look, what do you want? I ain't got all day." I stopped looking at her, because she was just too much woman, especially that early in the morning.

"I was hoping we could go somewhere cozy and have a heart-to-heart talk about life," she said.

I tried to push by her, but she jumped right in my way, and we collided, which is not exactly the worst thing that can happen to a guy. She's about my height, so we were making close contact, chest to chest and hip to hip.

"You don't really want to leave me here in this dark alley," she said, with her lips close enough to kiss.

"Holy shit, lady," I said after we disentangled. "What do you want from me? Like I told you, I'm clean! I got nothing to tell you."

She got businesslike. "Mr. Saperstein, the Bureau is starting a new policy this month. Instead of tracking down every suspected dealer and arresting them, we're picking out a few that we think have some real potential and we're giving them options."

I blinked. "Like I don't know double-talk when I hear it?"

"I'm sure you do. But this isn't it."

"Then what is it?"

She took me by the hand and we went back out on the street, while she explained.

The whole thing sounded crazy. The Bureau thinks a lot of soldiers in the food rackets want out. Guys like me who can't stomach the junk we sell, who would rather make an honest buck if we only knew how.

"It's just a question of meeting the right people, making the right connections," she said.

I tried to pin her down, but she wouldn't bite.

"I have to give you time to think this over," she

said. "I want you to make changes for your sake, not ours."

I let go of her hand because mine was starting to sweat.

She gave me a solid gold smile and told me to meet her tomorrow noon, at the statue of Nathan Pritikin in front of the courthouse.

I didn't say anything.

"Be there," she purred.

"Maybe I will," I coughed out. "But don't make any big plans for me."

So that's how it went, the first time I met Mindy MacGregor.

I have to tell you, I hiked to my place and lay down on the sofa and didn't move for three hours.

A ladybird like that, she shakes you up. She makes you wonder.

Don't get me wrong, she didn't come on to me, or anyway not for sure. I mean, I couldn't tell what was cooking in that gorgeous head, but I knew one thing. She wasn't futzing around.

She had an idea.

Trouble is, she was also G.B.I. Do I have to spell it out? Ladybird worked for the Goodfood Bureau of Investigation. The same pricks that lock guys in the slammer for dealing heavy cream or baked ham. They got a cousin of mine, a nice kid, for possession of one fucking kielbasa sausage. So he was dumb. But six months? Six months of hard time for a sausage?

I thought of calling Giancarlo. I mean, your capo has a right to know what the hell is coming down.

But my hand got heavy every time I reached for the phone. I decided to put it off, maybe find out a little more.

To tell the truth, I didn't know what the shit I was doing.

All I could see in front of me was legs. Long, prancing legs. The track was dry and fast, and I had a hundred bucks on a filly with an ass as round as the full moon.

It was painful, I'll tell you that.

Ladybirds are nothing but pain.

I never knew a good soldier who gave a ladybird more than ten minutes attention in a whole stinking day.

So what was I doing, sacked out for three hours with a redhead from the G.B.I. on my brain? Finally I laughed. You got to hand it to those bastards! They keep you guessing. If they can't grab you one way, they'll grab you another. It's all the same to them.

But I figured, what can I lose? She already had me on her list. She already knew pretty much where the griller was on the south side. If I went to see her, I didn't have to tell her a Goddamned thing. In fact, why not let her do all the talking? I might be the salesman, but this time the only sucker with something to sell was a certain ladybird.

Anyway, tomorrow was yesterday. I mean, the day I was supposed to meet Mizz MacGregor was yesterday.

Christ, I still can't dope out what happened.

I knew what I had to do. She didn't make it hard, either. No setup, no fuzz-buddies waiting to jump me around a corner, no mikes in her earrings. I always carry a buster with me, so I know if somebody's miking me.

But somehow or other, I blew it.

It wasn't clean, it wasn't simple, it wasn't smart.

So how do I tell Giancarlo?

What am I talking about? I can't tell Giancarlo shit.

Okay, I was there at the Pritikin statue at noon. Or close enough. I hung around across the street in a seed shop for a couple minutes to check her out.

She was wearing the same kind of skirt as before, only maybe shorter, and, like, bright green, with a matching scarf. I don't usually notice what ladybirds wear, but Mizz MacGregor was different.

With the flying red hair and all the green, she was decked out like a Christmas tree.

She got to the statue one minute before noon, and just stood there, cool as ice, not looking around or anything. I wondered what she was thinking.

I felt sorry for her, too. Those creeps in the G.B.I. would use their own mothers for shark bait.

Well, that was their business. I got enough problems without feeling guilty on their account.

So finally I sauntered out of the seed shop, crossed the street, and flipped her a little smile.

"Mizz MacGregor," I said. "You're looking real nice."

"Thanks, Mr. Saperstein," she answered. "I try."

"Yeah, well, you don't look like you have to."

She gave her eyebrows a quick lift, made a funny face, and took my arm like it was nothing.

"Look, Mr. Saper—"

I cut in. "Hell, call me Arnie. Now that we're old friends."

"I thought you'd never realize. Okay, Arnie, let's go to a saladeria and have some lunch. You hungry?"

"I could eat a horse."

"Don't be vulgar. My favorite place is just two blocks away." She paused. "And it's safe. I mean that, Arnie. No tricks."

The saladeria was packed, but we found a little booth at the dim end, parked our stuff, and got in line.

She was a big girl. She had an appetite to match.

She took a jumbo bowl and piled up the veggies. Cauliflower, sliced peppers, alfalfa sprouts, chickpeas, Boston lettuce, blueberries, and plenty of yogurt dressing. We both grabbed a cup of soup with buckwheat kreplach and a hunk of corn bread.

"Arnie," she said, when we were back in our booth, "how long have you been dealing?"

"Don't you want to hear about my wife and kids?" I countered.

"Maybe later. They're one of the reasons you need to review your options."

I studied her face. She was beautiful, all right, but a lot of it was I.Q. College grad, for sure, and probably more. Half the agents have a Ph.D. nowadays.

You know, even I had two years of college. I sort of wanted a degree in business.

But you don't need a degree to deal.

"Like I told you yesterday, I'm pure. I know some dealers, understand, but I wouldn't do any of that shit myself."

"Why not?"

"Because I could get busted, and the wife and kids would have to go on welfare."

"Arnie, you're a hero. You're also a liar."

She tucked away three or four forkfuls of veggies, dabbed her mouth, and went back on the attack. "So how long has it been?"

"Let's put it this way, beautiful. I've known a few dealers for, like, ten years. Just out of curiosity. Always been interested in how the other guy lives. Sometimes you pick up hints."

She finished her salad and took my hand. "Look, Arnie, cut the crap. You've been dealing since '58, which makes thirteen years if I haven't forgotten my higher math. Yesterday, I saw you leave a griller we've been staking out on the south side, where you sold the proprietor one hundred pounds of Swiss and cheddar, mixed, and promised to deliver chicken and pork every week when your family winds up a deal with some cave farmers upstate. Am I reaching you?"

I took a deep breath. "Go on. You got the floor."

"You also fed him a line of bull about some uncut butter you don't have. And he won't get a bite of the chicken or pork unless he agrees to take a couple of barrels of mystery-meat franks at twelve dollars a pound. Am I right?"

"You're a regular fountain of wisdom," I said.

"You better believe it. The only thing I don't know for sure is what you bastards put in those franks."

I shrugged. "It's mostly ground-up tits and asses from G.B.I. agents that get too curious," I said. "If you must know."

"Hmm. I'll remember that."

I think she turned just a little gray under that glowing ivory skin of hers, but I couldn't swear to it.

The waiter brought us our desserts, ginger pears with raisins. The ladybird took my hand again.

"Arnie, look at this food. Isn't it, well, isn't it good?"

"What do you mean?"

"I mean would you ever eat any of that trash you sell?"

"What other guys sell?"

"What any dealer sells."

"You got to know the answer. It makes me sick."

"And you wouldn't join the F.F.F.?"

I turned up my nose. "Those sons-of-bitches?"

Nothing turns me off faster than thinking about the turds in the F.F.F. Food Freedom Fighters! They torch saladerias, plant bombs at Goodfood rallies, cut the heads off Pritikin statues, force-feed hot dogs to little kids in schoolyards. All for what they call freedom.

It's one thing to make a buck, even if you have to apply a little muscle when somebody misses the point.

It's something else to raise hell for the sake of a fucking word.

Anyway, I don't guess the people fried in a salad-eria fire think they're getting liberated.

I told Mizz MacGregor exactly what I thought about Freedom Fighters. Her head bobbed up and down while I was talking, and her hair, all those fiery locks and curls, jiggled and danced. She was one fantastic ladybird.

"I hear the F.F.F. has just organized a new brigade in this town," she said, when I was done.

"Yeah," I said. "They get in touch now and then. But my pals, they couldn't care less. Dealers and fighters don't work the same streets."

"I hear they call it the Julia Child Brigade."

"Julia something. I forget."

"Do you know who she was?"

"Nope. I was never good at history."

"She was probably the greatest mass murderer of the second half of the twentieth century. A chef who wrote cook books and gave lessons on television. She smothered every entrée she cooked in heavy cream and butter. And her desserts! Her chocolate soufflé alone, well, read the recipe some time. It'd curdle your blood. Literally."

I laughed. "Don't be dumb. How could I get hold of a book by somebody like that?"

"Easy. Didn't you know there's a locked section in every major city library, where they stow culinary porn from the old days? If the librarian thinks you're a serious reader, and old enough to know right from wrong, you can get a pass."

"I never knew."

"Anyway, why do you keep pushing the food Julia Child used to cook?"

"I don't."

"Sure, Arnie, sure. But if you did, why would you?"

"I have to level with you, Mizz—uh, Mindy." It was

hard saying her first name. "I'm not convinced you guys have the right to tell people how to feed their faces. The laws are okay, I guess. But people need a little breathing space. You know? You got to make room for other ways of looking at things."

"You do understand why the laws were enacted?"

"Yeah, yeah."

"You say you're not good at history, but you must know the basic facts about the twentieth century. Before then, most people, the common people anyway, ate sound, nutritious diets. Mostly whole grains, fresh vegetables, and fruits, with just an occasional fling on Sundays or holidays.

"But in the twentieth century, the standard of living went steeply up in the so-called developed countries. Suddenly everybody, even working class people, could afford cheese, eggs, milk, cream, meat, seafood every day, three times a day. They'd have bacon and eggs for breakfast, salami sandwiches with mayonnaise for lunch, and pork chops for dinner. They'd load sour cream on their baked potatoes and cheese sauce on their broccoli. And top it all off with a chocolate ice cream sundae or a piece of cheesecake for dessert."

I felt my stomach start to turn. In my line of work, you get to know what that sewage tastes and smells like.

"Take it easy, Mindy," I said. "I visited a griller once or twice. I know all about it."

"But imagine, everybody eating like that, every day! By the middle of the century there was an epidemic of heart disease, strokes, and cancer, most of it caused by a diet that was forty, forty-five, even fifty percent fat by calories. Young men were paving their coronary arteries with cholesterol and calcium deposits, and dropping from heart attacks before they hit fifty. By the millions. Not to mention the tons of salt everybody ate with their food, which caused high blood pressure, and the colon cancers and—"

"I've heard it!" I yelled. "I know, I know. It was death by food poisoning. Worse than the Holocaust. I know."

She took a sip of her linden tea, and looked a little sad.

"But did you know that couples applying for a marriage license weren't even required to have their blood tested for serum cholesterol?"

She had me that time. "You're kidding," I said.

"I wish I were. Believe it or not, they did have a blood test requirement, but it was for syphilis, a disease that had been almost wiped out."

"Never heard of it."

"A venereal disease. Nasty, if you got it. Anyway, by the end of the century, people didn't need Julia Child's help any more. Mostly, they stopped cooking at home and ate their meals at 'fast food' chain restaurants staffed by armies of teenagers working for minimum wage. And the fast foods turned out to be nothing but fat foods.

"Doughnuts and croissants. Fried chicken and hamburgers. Milk shakes thick with coconut oil. For breakfast, you had a choice: ham and egg on a muffin or a buttered biscuit stuffed with sausage and cheese. My God!"

She was really bringing me down.

"Some of them used to deep-fry their food in lard," she said, with a shudder.

"My granddad told me," I said. "He was a little kid before they passed the Goodfood Laws."

"If the followers of the great dietitian Nathan Pritikin hadn't organized the Goodfood Society, hadn't battled the chains in the courts, hadn't infiltrated both political parties, hadn't lobbied in Congress day and night for years, the world we live in today would be your world."

"My world?"

"The griller world. There'd be grillers lining every highway. Instead of a few thousand people dying every year of premature heart disease, there'd be millions."

"You trying to make me feel guilty?"

"I don't have to. You already do."

"No way. Like I told you in the first place, I'm not—"

She slapped my face. Hard.

"You are! You are! You are a dealer, Arnie Saperstein!"

I just sat there.

"But you have a choice. You can get out. I can help you."

I looked around, wondering if anybody had noticed us, but they were all minding their own business.

Then I stared at the wall just behind her, to keep from colliding with those soft blue eyes. For the first time I saw the Goodfood slogan in the pattern of the wallpaper. Mostly it was big fruits and leaves and vines, but in and around and everywhere, the designer had written, "For the Sake of Your Life! For the Sake of Your Life!"

Some of the writing was little, some of it was pretty good-sized. There must've been a couple hundred slogans on just the part I could see. But at first you didn't spot even one. Only peaches and grapes and stuff.

"For the sake of your life," I mumbled to myself.

"Yes," she said, quietly. "For the sake of *your* life, Arnie. And the lives of your wife and kids. And everybody in this town."

I couldn't think what to say.

"I'm not asking you to stop dealing today."

I finished my own tea. I felt jumpy. It was getting to be that time.

"So tell me about it," I said, still looking over her shoulder at the peaches and grapes in the wallpaper.

"If you came in with us," she said, keeping her voice low and even, "we'd want you to stay in the organization a while, help us make more contacts, keep us informed of deliveries."

"You want me to shiv my pals."

"Mostly bring them over to our side."

"Shit."

I took out my trick pen, the one with the poison dart. My hands were sweating so bad, it slipped onto the floor.

"You dropped something," she said.

"Yeah."

I picked up the pen and started playing with it.

"Please, Arnie."

I stole a look at her. She was so fucking gorgeous.

"I'm putting my own life in your hands," she added. "I know the organization doesn't have much use for food narcs."

All I had to do was take aim and push the stud at the top of the pen. Pffft!

It takes maybe three seconds for the person to croak.

They sort of crumple up, like they're having an attack of heartburn or gas. They never know what hit them.

Then you just stroll out the door and melt into the crowds. Neat, quick, safe.

I mean, every once in a while you have to deliver a message to the Bureau. When they get too wise-assed, when they come on too strong, it doesn't matter, jack or jill, old or young, white or black, you can't afford to play favorites.

"Please, Arnie. Come over to us. Come over to me."

Her voice kept getting lower and lower.

They don't have the right. A guy should eat what he wants. Next thing, it'll be sex they go after. Or religion.

Who knows where it'll end?

So I did it. I aimed the pen.

I pushed the stud.

It went pffft.

I saw her eyes shut tight as she screamed and dove for the floor.

Now here it is the next day. I'm sitting in my room, writing all this down. Waiting for the knock.

The way I see it, either way, I would've been a shithead. Sign on with the Bureau, you break your blood oath and sell out your brothers and help Uncle Sam tighten the screws.

Do your duty as a soldier, and you let people poison themselves and keep some fat capo rich and waste a ladybird so beautiful it would make you ache.

So tell me, why did I aim the pen at the wallpaper?

What good did it do to shoot a Goddamned fruit?

LAYING VENEER

by Alan Dean Foster

"Take it easy, mate. Have a beer."

Harbison was not mollified. "National Highway, my ass! National disgrace is more like it."

The foreman was not insulted. "You won't get any argument from me. Maybe that's why they decided to try bringing in some people from the States." He proffered a cold can.

The engineer deliberately pushed it aside. "Frankly I'm not surprised. I've driven over a thousand miles this past week and I didn't see one road crew that wasn't squatting on their butts guzzling that stuff. When they weren't drinking beer, they were swilling wine for lunch and hard liquor for dinner and after. No wonder your so-called National Highway is falling apart."

Kent glanced out the window. Moreton Bay was clear of clouds. That meant it would be calm out on the reef. Good fishing. With an effort he forced himself to turn back to the American engineer.

"Your first time Down Under, isn't it?"

"So?"

Kent sipped brew. "Despite what you've seen and what you may think, we can build roads, Mr. Harbison. Look around Sydney or Melbourne."

"I have. The roads there are fine. That's not why I was sent for." He stared unforgivingly at the foreman. "If you can build there, why not every place else?"

Kent looked away. "It's this country. You get out away from the cities, there's nothing. I mean, you're talking five million people scattered over empty territory the size of the continental U.S. The Outback isn't kind to men, machinery, or plans. It doesn't matter who you put on a job; pretty soon things start to slow down. Work gets sloppy. Machinery starts to act up, break down. So do men, if they're not careful. Why do you think most of our roads outside the cities are still dirt? Because we like it that way?"

"Because of lack of determination. Because somebody hasn't been doing their job."

"They do what they can," Kent argued. "You don't know what it's like out there, what you have to deal with. But you'll find out. The Outback gets to everyone. It'll get to you, too."

"Bullshit. I've built roads in the Amazon, in Africa, all over the world. There's nothing special about the terrain here. I know. I've just driven a thousand miles of it. All I found was lousy work and excuses." He smiled humorlessly. "That will change."

Kent shrugged. "That's what you've been hired for. Believe me, I wish you the best of luck. The best. I don't like driving that road in the condition it's in any more than you did. Neither does anyone else."

"Then why haven't you fixed it? Why go all the way to the States to find a supervisor?"

The foreman eyed him over his beer. "Mate, don't you think we've tried?"

It was hot, but it had been hotter in Brazil. Harbison felt a stabbing pain in his leg, slapped fast, and saw the march fly tumble to the ground. He jammed it into the earth with the heel of his boot, looked up through his sunshades.

They were twenty kilometers north of Rockhampton, working on the middle of the highway. Not far to the east was the portion of the Pacific aptly named the Coral Sea. To the west lay the mountains of the coast range and beyond, nothing. Nothing all the way to the Indian Ocean save sand and dry plains and gravel.

It was bad enough here. Scattered gum trees (eucalyptus back home), a few bushes, desultory grasses, all bathed in sunlight that tinted everything beige.

Ahead the road stretched north to Townsville, the next community of any real size and the beginnings of the true tropics. Behind lay Rockhampton, an undistinguished, extraordinarily humid community built on cattle and commerce.

Harbison had three crews going: one south near Caboolture, one working down from Cairns, and this one, in the center. He'd chosen to spend most of his time here, where it would be easiest to deal with all three crews and any problems they might encounter. He watched the men work; good-natured, broad-shouldered, muscular. As competent as any road crew back home, but slow. It puzzled him. They seemed capable enough, but there was no enthusiasm, no desire. They shuffled through their work; the asphalt spreaders, the men on the heavy equipment, all of them.

The only time they showed any spirit was during their regular breaks, which were inevitably accompanied by the opening of coolers full of the ubiquitous, high-alcohol beer. He'd remonstrated with them personally about drinking so heavily on the job but to no avail. The breaks, and the beer, were sacrosanct.

He'd tried putting his foot down with the northern crew, only to have them go out on strike. When he threatened to fire the lot of them, they simply smiled and shrugged, as though it didn't matter if he did or not. Any new men he hired would act exactly the same.

The road stretched northward, a black arrow pierc-

ing the baked landscape. The National Highway. He
snorted. Back home it wouldn't pass muster as a farm
road. Two narrow lanes full of potholes, with no
shoulders, crumbling into dust at the edges. How eigh-
teen-wheelers and cross-country buses managed to
navigate the disintegrating course without smashing
into one another was nothing short of a miracle. Back
home the entire thousand miles would've stood a good
chance of being condemned.

It made no sense. Sure the conditions were harsh,
but no more so than in Arizona or Florida. He'd ordered repeated checks of the materials, had the bitu-
men exhaustively analyzed. Standard paving asphalt.
The road base had been properly prepared, packed
and leveled. It ought not to be crumbling this fast.
After several months of work he was beginning to
think there might be something in the ground rather
than in the asphalt that was failing.

So he'd had the earth itself analyzed, to no avail.
It was neither unusually acidic nor alkaline. It should
be holding up far better than it was. Kent had shown
him stretches which had been repaved only the year
before. Already the edges were cracking, breaking off
in big chunks, turning to gravel and dirt.

He removed his wide-brimmed hat and wiped sweat
from his forehead. Someone in the crew, sitting in the
shade with his mates, waved a beer in his direction.
Irritably he shook his head and looked away. Kent
had been right. The beer wasn't the problem. There
was something else going on here, something he
couldn't put a finger on. But he would. It was what
he was getting paid to do.

He looked sharply to his right. There were several
aborigines on the road crew. They sat with their white
mates, race relations having progressed further out in
the country than in the city. One of them was clapping
a pair of sticks together, beating time to an ancient

unknown rhythm. His companion was playing that long tube, what was it called? A digereedoo. Except it wasn't an actual digeree he was playing. He was cycle-breathing on a four-foot long section of plastic pvc pipe. Remarkably, the sound was the same as that produced by the traditional wooden native instrument.

The music hung like a fog above and around the gum trees, as if some massive fantastical creature lay sleeping just beneath the surface. Sometimes Harbison found himself hearing it at night, which bothered him. It did not sound quite like anything else he'd ever heard. It tickled his brain.

When he'd asked Kent about it, the foreman had smiled and explained that some of the men on the road crews, isolated in the Outback, believed that the music of the digereedoo kept away the quinka, the evil spirits of the land that snatched men's souls from the real world.

He stared. The white roadworkers seemed to be enjoying the music as much as their darker colleagues. It was the kind of camaraderie he'd rarely observed in the cities, where the only aborigines he'd encountered were aimless groups of drunken men and women who spent their time arguing in city centers or sprawled tiredly in public parks. Here, out in the country, on the fringes of civilization, it was different.

He'd seen that elsewhere. In rough country there was no time for such absurdities as racial prejudice. All of them were too dependent on one another, too busy trying to survive, to worry about inconsequentialities like the color of a neighbor's skin. You were much more interested in what kind of a mechanic he was.

The break stretched on. Several of the blonder workers had shed their shirts in defiance of the tropical sun. They wore shorts and shoes only. Their bodies, Harbison mused. If they wanted to burn, let them burn, so long as they kept working.

He drove himself hard. He was the first one on site in the morning and the last to leave. He meant the two-kilometer section north of Rockhampton to be an example, a demonstration of what could be achieved with American know-how and determination. It would be a real highway; four lanes with divider and paved shoulders both directions. A proper piece of Interstate.

It took longer than he'd anticipated, but once the last asphalt had been laid and smoothed, he was able to content himself with the look of it. Beautiful it was, like reflective obsidian under the relentless sunshine, a straight dark path through the gum forest. Only a dead kangaroo, hit by a car the previous night after the new section had been opened to the public, marred the ebony perfection.

Even Kent was impressed. He stared at the roadway and nodded. "Well, I have to admit, you did it. Didn't think you could, but you did. She's a beaut, that's for sure."

"Three years." Harbison surveyed his work with satisfaction. "Three years and the whole highway from Brisbane to Mossman can look like this. All it needs is money and the right attitude."

"Maybe so," Kent agreed. He straightened. "Care for a beer?"

Harbison almost, but not quite, smiled. "I told you when I got here and I've been telling you all along, I don't drink. Especially not that stuff you call beer. Too strong."

"Suit yourself." The foreman turned toward his car. "Need a ride?"

"No. I want to run a final check here. Then I'm moving up to Cairns. They're still having trouble with their section up there."

"So I heard. They need you, Harbison." Kent smiled admiringly, climbed into his car.

Harbison lingered, not wanting to leave, enjoying the looks on the faces of motorists as they shot past him at a hundred kph plus. For a little while, for the first time in hundreds of kilometers, they could actually relax and enjoy driving.

The sun was going down. He slid behind the wheel of his big Holden, almost headed off down the right side of the road before remembering where he was and correcting. On the way south he passed the striping crew, knocking off early as usual. He shook his head. It was a wonder they ever finished anything. Without him driving them, they never would have.

The onset of evening brought with it only a slight break in the heat. The gum trees closed in tightly around him, separated only by the four lane roadway. A brush fire burned unattended to the very edges of the road. It would be ignored, he knew, left to burn itself out. Valuable wood and forage left to burn, as though nobody cared. No doubt the members of the local fire department were already gathering at their favorite pub, he knew, and wouldn't wish to be disturbed. Social activity in every little Outback town centered around its pubs, or the bottle shops where liquor could be purchased for takeout.

Near the southernmost part of the new section he slowed, pulling over onto the neat, wide paved shoulder. Frowning as he climbed out, he walked around the front of the car and knelt by the side of the road. He pushed with a hand and stared as a section of asphalt the size of his fist broke free and crumbled into powder.

It was like that all along the shoulder, on both sides of the roadbed: big pieces breaking free, crumbling, the neatly laid edge already being taken over by eager grasses and weeds. It made no sense. This section was less than three months old. It should be solid, impervious, yet it was coming apart as though made of sand. The asphalt that had been used had been rigorously checked prior to application. The surface was designed to hold up without maintenance for a minimum of two years.

He straightened and stared into the forest. The gum trees stood silent, their pale slick bark peeling like his workers' skin. It was dead quiet; no birds, no insects whining in the brush. Only there; a cluster of roos, traveling noiselessly in great leaping bounds at the limits of his vision.

He blinked. There were no roos. Quinka? Digereedoo music drifted through his brain, hypnotic and unsettling. Suddenly conscious of the age of the land around him, of his isolation, he found himself backing toward the car, his eyes trying to focus on suspected movement in the brush. He tried to think of something else, anything else, except the inescapable fact of his aloneness in a vast and inhospitable land.

It was hot, so very damn hot. The heat seemed to come not from the sun but out of the earth itself. Dust hung suspended in the air like talcum, making breathing difficult. The moan of the digereedoo was a pounding in his temples.

A march fly landed on his arm and he smashed it before it could bite. It spiraled indifferently to the ground, as though its death didn't matter even to itself.

As he fumbled with the door handle of the car he stared wide-eyed at the road, brand new but crumbling, unable to resist something he could not fathom, could not analyze. It ran north through the fringes of the Outback, a feeble lifeline stretching from the cities of the south toward the hostile tropics. Stretched too thin?

Bad place for a road, he decided. The problem was

simple enough. It wasn't wanted here. The country, the land didn't want it. Yet as he was wont to do, man persisted in trying to defy the obvious, to bend to his will a part of nature too ancient to know it had no choice in the matter.

A growling sound made him whirl, but it was only a truck coming toward him. A dozen men rode in the open bed. As it slowed to pull over, several of them eyed him knowingly.

"Car trouble, mate?" one of them asked.

"No," Harbison replied slowly. He gestured. "There's something wrong with the road here. There shouldn't be."

Several of the crew exchanged glances. One of them smiled down at him. "Don't worry, mate. She'll be right. You worry too much, I think." He squinted at the silent, suggestive gum forest through the beige-tinted heat. "Can't worry too much out here. Gets to ya."

"Not a good place to be standin' about alone," the man next to him said. "Hang about too long and a bloke's liable to go troppo. Start seein' things, know what I mean? This ain't Bondi Beach." His tone was sympathetic, understanding. "Care to join us in a beer?"

A new image filled Harbison's brain, shoving aside the cloying, suffocating silence which pressed tight around the intruding road. A cool dark room surrounded by thick walls which shut out the oppressive heat, the dust and the flies. Shut out the hum of the digeree and hallucinated roos. Kept the quinka at bay.

Better to drink than to think. Thinking was wasted in this place. Ambition was excess baggage. This country battled both, all the way. It always had. No wonder the aborigines had never developed much of a civilization like other primitive peoples.

Man had spread his highways, his parking lots, his

civic centers and shopping malls across the face of the planet. Everywhere the land had accepted the insult in silence. Except here. Here the land fought back, fought every incursion, every attempt to domesticate it. Not with violence, but with ennui. It wore you out, just as it wore out the roads.

There was a reason why people here kept tight to their few cities, clung to the cool southern coasts. Up here, in the north, in the great center, the Dreamtime still held sway, still dictated the pace of life and decay, of people and of roads. It sucked the drive out of a man, and if one wasn't careful, the life.

He understood the drinking now, the intensity and the frequency of it. It held the land at bay, kept it out of a man's mind, kept him from thinking too much about the vast open empty spaces. Prevented them from invading one's spirit and taking over.

God, he was tired.

His shirt was soaked through. He pulled it over his head, threw it up into the truck.

"Yeah, sure," he mumbled, accepting a hand up. "I'd like a beer."

Someone could pick up the car later. It didn't matter. Nothing mattered now, except getting to the pub.

The truck drove off. Once more the shiny new section of road was silent and empty. A beetle struggled out from beneath a bush, to be snatched up by a silent, watching magpie. Already the black sheen of the newly laid asphalt was fading, turning to a tired gray.

A foot-long crack appeared in the southbound lanes. Soon it would widen.

I, MONSTER

by Henry Slesar

I thought it was one of my better ideas, baptizing the company with my first name instead of my last. My name is Aaron Zachary, and I had a choice of appearing early or late in the Yellow Pages under "Detective Agencies." Aaron Associates is listed second (There's an AAA agency in every town) but I still didn't get any of the finger-walking business until I broke the piggy bank for a small ad which read: "Divorce Evidence, Personal and Domestic Investigations, Missing Persons." Then I got my first potential customer, and another kind of baptism. . . .

It's not easy for someone who spent two years in Security training to admit that he can't describe a person, especially a man who might have been bringing him his inaugural case. But despite the fact that my office wasn't big enough for an eye-chart examination, despite getting close enough to wrap my hand around his elbow, all I can recall is that there wasn't much *heft* to him. I remember thinking that his face had an unfinished look, but even though he had two eyes, a nose, and a mouth, there was no way I could pluck them out of an Ident-A-Kit if my life depended on it. I mentioned his elbow. Why did I grab it? I was steering the guy out of my office. Who wouldn't, after hearing what he wanted?

"I'd like you to find someone," he said. "A woman."

"All right," I answered cordially, feeling good at the prospect of an easy initiation into private practice. A lot of missing persons cases could be solved by one phone call to the Motor Vehicle Bureau. I drew up a nice fresh notepad and asked the usual questions.

I got unusual answers.

"I don't know her name," he said. "She isn't related to me. And I'm afraid I don't know what she looks like."

"There must be something you can tell me about her."

"I'm afraid not."

"Maybe if you told me the circumstances, the reasons you want to locate this woman . . ."

"I really can't do that, either," he said.

I didn't get steamed. I assumed he was nervous. Maybe it was his first time, too. I leaned back and waited for him to tell the story his own way, but his unfinished face remained as blank and uninformative as the empty file folders in my cabinet.

"Is that it?" I said. "Is that all you have to say?"

"I'm sorry," he answered evenly. "But it will have to do."

So much for second-place in the Yellow Pages. I thought of suggesting psychiatric help, but decided it was none of my business. Instead, I murmured something about being too busy at the moment and recommended the AAA Agency. Then I walked him to the exit.

The problem was, he didn't want to walk.

"You really must help me," he said. "I think you *can* help me."

"I don't see how, with so little to go on."

"I can tell you one thing," he said. "The woman is in this neighborhood. I'm quite sure of that. In fact, that's why I chose your agency. You're bound to run into her, sooner or later."

"I'm afraid that isn't enough."

That was when I put my hand on his elbow. It wasn't an aggressive gesture. It was only a light, suggestive move, conveying my desire for him to be on the other side of the door. But his reaction surprised me. Astonished is a better word. Despite his air of insubstantiality, his body became monolithic, an intractable piece of stone. Except that it moved. He put his hand on my chest, with only the slightest pressure, and I found myself flung backward with such force that I slammed into the filing case behind me. I hit it so hard that every drawer label from A to Z must have been tattooed on my spine. That was my last thought before the world shut down for the next three hours.

I knew how much time had gone by when I opened my eyes and saw that the narrow strips of light between my venetian blinds were gone. Despite low back pain, and a natural chagrin at being karated into unconsciousness, my first concern was about Bobbi. It had taken me three weeks to convince her to accept a key to my studio apartment; she shared her own place with a couch potato who was a powerful deterrent to romance. Bobbi was coming by that evening to cook me a steak dinner, and was that promising or what? I looked at my claw to see what time it was.

I'm telling this wrong. I didn't know it was *my* claw, not right away. I thought it belonged to some creature that had been left behind by my lunatic visitor, a baby alligator he had nurtured to full size in his basement. Only I've never seen an alligator claw close up, and I sure as hell never saw one wearing a Seiko.

Even if my powers of description had failed me before, I can recall every detail of the hideous extremity that was sticking out of my gabardine sleeve. Its six talons were lime green. Its fingernails were yellow, and so long that they curled up underneath the horny

palm. The leathery skin was beaded with wartlike protuberances. But the worst discovery I made was this.
There were two of them.

When I saw the second claw where my left hand
should have been, I scrambled to my feet in uncontrolled panic. With one claw, I tried to rip off the
other one, hoping they were only some kind of
glovelike coverings, but it was useless, and the dry,
raspy sound made me sick to my stomach. Not as
sick I was going to be. Because a really nasty thought
occurred to me. What if this Kafka-esque metamorphosis didn't stop at my hands?

There was no bathroom in my little office; such
amenities weren't included in the lease. But there was
a cracked mirror hanging on the inside door of the
coat closet, and I managed to open it despite my unfa-
miliarity with six-digited manipulation. I soon wished
I hadn't. What I saw in the mirror was worse than a
compilation of all the nightmares of my life. I was
looking at a face that made me wish my alligator anal-
ogy had been correct. Alligators were handsome by
comparison. Rhinos were dashing. Lizards were
lovely. My new features had many of the aspects of
all three, but assembled with the finesse of a three-
year-old with a lump of Play-Doh.

A scream started in my throat, but I choked it off
in fear that flames might shoot out of my dragonlike
jaws. The last thing I needed was to set the office on
fire and let a crowd see me crawling out of the burning
building like some giant salamander. Then I had
something else to worry about. The front door was
opening.

It was only the cleaning woman. She clattered into
the room with her mop and pail, muttering Baltic
curses, and I instinctively dived into the small closet
and pulled the door shut after me. I knew that the
sight of me might unhinge her; she was likely to throw

a bottle of industrial strength cleaner in my face, and it was grotesque enough the way it was. Fortunately, she never took more than a minute to clean my premises. She emptied my wastebasket, sloshed some dirty water on the linoleum floor, and went out again, unaware of how close she had come to a glimpse of hell.

I was supposed to have a good, logical mind. That's what they told me at Detective School. But what was the use of a logical mind in the body of a creature? I looked in the mirror again, praying fervently that the metamorphosis had reversed itself, but there was the same abominable image staring back at me, just as it had before. Except now I became aware of the badly-knotted tie around my scaly throat and the baggy brown suit covering up God knows what kind of loathsome body. For all I knew, I had a prehensile tail sticking out my rear end.

I needed help, that was obvious, but I wasn't going to find any here. I had only one impulse, the desire to get myself into familiar surroundings, behind the safety of a locked door. I had to get home.

There was a raincoat in the closet. The weather had been dry for two weeks, but I put it on, grateful for its oversized collar and deep pockets. At least I could conceal my claws and my wart-covered neck, but it wouldn't be enough to hide my monstrous face. I needed a hat, but I never wore hats. Without a hat, I had no chance of escaping attention. One look at me and the villagers would be coming after me with torches. *I needed a hat!*

In desperation, I looked in every desk drawer and even into the filing cabinet, ignoring the fact that I had moved in only two weeks ago and there was nothing on hand but pencils, pads, candy wrappers, and a two-day-old newspaper. Good logical mind, right? Then Fate, perhaps aware that it had dealt me the worst hand in its deck, decided to give me a usable card. I heard a pattering noise against the window, and yanked up the blinds. Sure enough, there were raindrops on the glass. I grabbed the newspaper, prepared to use it as a makeshift umbrella.

Of course, I had to get to the parking lot first. Fortunately, the Seiko on my claw told me it was after seven, and few people worked late in a building occupied by failing entrepreneurs and their part-time secretaries. There was one bad moment at the elevator when I heard a man's footsteps in the corridor. I managed to outrace him and pushed the Close button before he reached the doors. He doesn't know how lucky he was. Even I wouldn't have liked to have shared that small space with me.

My Toyota was the only car left in the lot. I jumped inside, avoiding a glance at the rearview mirror. I must have become adjusted to my six-fingered hand, because I had no trouble inserting the key and firing up the ignition. I merged into the traffic on the rain-blackened street, driving cautiously to avoid any chance of a violation. This was no time to be stopped by a cop. For one thing, the face on my license no longer matched my own.

It wasn't a long drive to the fern-infested stucco building on Santa Monica where I lived in what Bobbi, the real estate agent who found it for me, called a Stud. Apartment. Living in one room hadn't seemed objectionable to me before, but as I let myself in that night the limited space revived the panic I had experienced in the office. I felt even more trapped in my hideous new body by not being able to escape to another space. Then I remembered that there *was* another space, and I had the masochistic impulse to make use of one of its features. The full-length mirror.

Slowly, I began to remove my clothing. I shut my eyes and kicked off my shoes. Then, like shedding skins, I removed coat, pants, shirt, and underwear, and headed for the bathroom. My single greatest act of courage may have been pushing that rocker light switch to "on."

There I was. In full-length, full-color monstrousness. A waistless expanse of skin like the outside of a cucumber. Rubbery arms and legs that were like the stalks of an alien tree. No tail, and no genital organs. Ludicrously, I felt an additional pang of bitter resentment at the latter deprivation. Then I noticed a ring of convex protuberances where my "hips" were, each one shaped like a baby's pacifier, and wondered if they were connected with procreation. I had no time for further reflection, because I heard, through the open bathroom door, the distinct sound of a key turning in the lock.

Bobbi had kept her word.

Of course, I pulled the door shut at once and even snapped off the bathroom light, but there was no way I could deny my presence. For one thing, my clothes were scattered all over the rug. The fact didn't escape her notice, but it brought her to a more reasonable conclusion.

"Aaron?" she said. "You taking a shower?"

"Yes," I answered, realizing for the first time that my transformation hadn't included my voice. "I got home late, on account of the rain."

"Do you always throw your clothes on the floor?"

"They were wet," I said. Then I decided sound effects were in order and unstuck the faucet to send water splashing into the tub. The noise drowned out her next speech, but it didn't matter. I lowered the toilet seat and sat down with my face in my hands—I mean my snout in my claws—and tried to decide what to do next. There was no way I was going to get rid of Bobbi. Even if I couldn't hear her own sound effects, I knew she must be yanking up the aluminum blinds that concealed the alcove kitchen, and would soon be banging pots and saucers in a ferocious display of domesticity. I was her prisoner, and there was no recourse but a full confession. I turned off the tap, and pressed my dragon's head against the bathroom door.

"Bobbi," I said. "There's something I have to tell you."

"I know," she responded cheerfully. "You hate broccoli. Well, you're going to love it the way I fix it. It's a souffle."

"That isn't it," I said. "It's about something that happened to me today. Something pretty horrible."

I heard her coming closer, and knew I had her attention.

"You're not going to believe this," I continued. "But this afternoon a man came into my office . . . I don't know who he was, or what he did to me, but— I've changed, Bobbi. I've been turned into . . . something else. Something not human. I mean, I'm like this six-foot lizard, only worse."

There was a momentary silence, and then she said: "You told me you were six-one."

"I'm not kidding," I whimpered. "I'd open the door and show you, but you'd just scream or faint or God knows what, hit me with a frying pan or something. I'm going to need help, a doctor, a priest maybe, I just don't know . . . Bobbi, are you there?"

Another silence, broken by a giggle.

"Boy, I've heard excuses for not eating my cooking, but this is the best one yet. Okay, Lizard Man, come out of there and let's hear the punchline."

"I'm not coming out. I can't come out!"

"Oh, I get it," she said, with a new level of amusement. "You want me to come in *there*. A little fun and games before dinner. Sorry, Aaron. I'm not sure about f. and g. *after* dinner, either." Adding seductively, "It all depends on how much you like my broccoli souffle."

It was an obvious stalemate. I had to make the deciding move. I had to show myself, and hope that Bobbi could survive the onslaught to her senses, at least long enough to get me help.

I wrapped a bath towel around my middle, concealing what may or may not have been my new set of family jewels, an instinctive act of delicacy and consideration.

Then I opened the bathroom door.

Bobbi stared back at me.

I waited for a Fay Wrayish scream of primal terror.

Instead, she said, "Is this how you always dress for dinner?"

My heart did a triple gainer of happiness and relief. The enchantment was ended! The spell had been lifted, perhaps by the pure love of a Maiden! Well, a female, anyway. If the bath towel had been knotted, I would have clasped Bobbi in my arms, swearing oaths of eternal fealty—as you can tell, I was thinking in medieval locutions. But then I saw myself in that same full-length mirror, and realized that the towel was still covering one-third of a Thing.

It was a bafflement almost as horrendous as the first discovery of my metamorphosis. But when Bobbi continued to look at me without the slightest sign of shock or surprise, I knew my conclusion had to be correct. *She didn't see what I saw.*

"Gee, what a cute towel," she said. "But don't look so worried. I was only kidding about the broccoli. I mean, I do make a gorgeous souffle, but it's too much trouble after a hard day's work, you know what I mean?"

I wanted to clamp my claw over her mouth, but all I did was shout my next sentence.

"Bobbi, for Chrissake, don't you see anything different about me?"

"Well, you do look pretty terrible," she said primly. "But considering what time you get to bed every night, and how you carry on *before* bedtime, it's amazing that you don't look worse than you do. Anyway, lizard face, I'll forgive you if you'll forgive me."

"For what?" I managed to say, surprised that I could utter anything in the way of normal conversation.

"It's not just the broccoli. The truth is, I didn't have time to shop for *anything* today—the office went bezonkers with all the new listings coming in— What's happening in this town, anyway, is everybody moving out? Anyway, I *promise* to cook you that steak Diane some other time, only would you mind eating out tonight? I've already made a reservation, that new Tex-Mex place I told you about, where I take my really hot clients? Aaron, what is it? You're not angry at me?"

She kissed me on the snout, and I knew it was true.

It wasn't a metamorphosis.

It was a hallucination.

I should have felt relief, but in the next thirty minutes, I felt nothing but revulsion and disgust. I showered my green body under a full spray of water that seemed to bead right off my thick, scaly hide. I doused myself with cologne, but it only intensified the fetid swampy smell surrounding me. I would have sprayed deodorant under my arms except that I was certain that my sweat glands, if I possessed any, were located in some other part of my body. But shaving was the real problem. I knew I had to shave the face that Bobbi, and perhaps the rest of the world, could see. But how do you shave a hairless snout with warty protuberances and strange contours? The answer was: very carefully.

Getting dressed was just as bad. I pulled on a pair of Jockey briefs whose support was totally unnecessary. The only clean socks available were brand new, and I winced as I pulled them over the long curving nails on my elongated toes; there were only four of those, probably to make up for my six-digited claws. I didn't think the new Tex-Mex place had a dress code, so I skipped the tie and reached for the first sports shirt in my drawer. I changed my mind when I saw the little alligator sewn over the left breast. There's a time and a place for irony, and this was neither of them.

When I was finally assembled, I looked in the bathroom mirror and was awed at the sight of the natty monster I had become.

The effect didn't displease Bobbi, apparently. She slipped her arms around me and bestowed still another kiss on my saurian mouth, this one wet and probing. All I could feel was disgust at her lack of discrimination, and all I could think of was, Lips that kiss Lizard would never kiss mine. I know my reaction was bizarre, but so were the circumstances. I actually resented the fact that Bobbi would date such an odious Creature, even though it was myself.

I made one discovery as we left the building: there *were* sweat glands somewhere on my loathsome person, because I felt perspiration dripping down my side as we encountered a group of early revelers on the sidewalk. I knew that Bobbi still saw Aaron Zachary in his Armani blazer, but could she be the only one? I was quickly reassured. There were no shrieks or gasps or the obligatory Oh-my-Gods one expects from the horror flicks. I was alone in my delusion, but the fact didn't ease my suffering.

It was the same at the Tex-Mex restaurant. Nobody noticed me. I mean nobody. We waited so long for a table that I almost wished my Magnificent Monstrosity

was visible, at least long enough to catch the eye of
the head waiter. By the time we were finally seated,
I had imbibed so many salty margaritas that I was in
equal danger of alcoholic stupor and high blood pressure. I drank enough to almost forget what I had seen
in the mirrors that terrible day, but there was always
a reminder in front of me, reaching for the tortilla
chips: my green, scaly, six-fingered claw.

I'm usually an amiable drunk, prone to slobby senti-
ment and the lyrics of old songs, but that was before
the Change. Now I felt hostile and pugnacious, beginning to resent the fact that nobody in the crowded
restaurant was aware of my mythical ugliness. They
went right on chomping on their enchiladas and re-
fried beans, completely oblivious to my Petrifying
Presence. I wanted to rear up on my green hind legs
and roar my defiance at their human inadequacy, their
thin pathetic pink and brown flesh, their small teeth
and smooth faces, their short fingernails. I wanted to
see them scream and scurry the way the Japanese did
in the Godzilla movies. I also wanted to go to the
bathroom, but I wasn't sure about what to do when I
got there.

I began to feel sick, and decided it was time to go
home. Bobbi quickly agreed, but for a reason I didn't
suspect until we returned to the apartment house on
Santa Monica. The same salty tequila that had made
me ill was an aphrodisiac to her, and she assumed I
was just as eager to drop my clothes back on the floor
of my Stud. Apartment. We were both in for a great
disappointment.

There was no way I could explain my squeamish
behavior. When the front door closed behind us,
Bobbi flung herself against me with inebriated aban-
don and crushed her lips against my snout. Her tongue
darted between my jagged teeth and her hands began
sliding around my waist as if she sensed a need to

excite that disgusting ring of baby pacifers that were now part of my basic equipment. Then she started working on the buttons of my shirt, and when her hand slid underneath the cloth, I heard and felt the rasp of my warty skin against her palm, and I could no longer keep my stomach in operating order. With a strangled apology, I stumbled into the bathroom and did what I had to do.

I was vaguely aware of Bobbi's questioning voice on the other side of the door, but I didn't answer. I sat on the cold bathroom tiles and undid the rest of my shirt buttons, my claw rubbing at the burning pain inside my rubbery green chest. Tears rolled down my snout as a great tsunami of self-pity washed over me. I don't know how long it lasted, but by the time I emerged from its depths, Bobbi was gone.

There was a note on the middle cushion of the sofa. It read: SEE A SHRINK.

It was, of course, good advice, but I didn't do anything about it until the following day. I flopped onto my bed without undressing, and spent a night in a thicket of dreams I'd rather not recall even now. There was one in which I was rooting about in some kind of brackish swamp, and something that looked like five pounds of raw liver with eyes on celery stalks swam into view, filling me with unimaginable, lip-smacking delight. I opened my cavernous jaws and— woke up, thank God. I quickly shook off my disgust in favor of overwhelming gratitude, because obviously yesterday's events had also been a dream. I sprang out of my bed and welcomed the daylight with all the joyousness of Scrooge on Christmas morning, What the daylight did in return was illuminate the two green claws clutching the cord of the venetian blind.

I didn't have to go far for professional help. On the day Bobbi showed me the Stud. Apartment I now called home she had boasted of the quality of the tenants, giving specific mention to a Dr. Marcus, a psychiatrist who occupied a professional suite on the first floor. I had encountered Marcus more than once at poolside, and he was one of those shrinks who was determined not to appear intimidating; he smiled a lot and talked about movies and baseball. I called his office, and there must have been enough urgency in my voice to get me an immediate appointment. By ten a.m. I was stretched out on his leather sofa, and heard myself admitting that I was not merely his neighbor, but that I was also the tenant of a body more suitable to a Mesozoic jungle than present day Santa Monica.

I'll give the doctor credit; he didn't throw a net over me. He merely leaned back and asked me for details. Admiring my own rational presentation, I told him about my office visitor of the day before, a man I couldn't describe looking for a woman *he* couldn't describe; there was obviously some connection between him and what happened to me. I assumed that Marcus wouldn't buy the idea of an Evil Enchanter, so I suggested that I might have experienced a concussion following his violent reaction to my refusal to handle his case. That would explain it all nicely, I said, with growing enthusiasm for my own diagnosis. I must have hit my head and damaged some area of the brain marked off for Monster Mirages. Now if I could get the right prescription, one of those psychotropic medications you read about in TIME, I'd probably get over it in a couple of days; in fact, just *recognizing* what caused the problem has been a big help, Doc, I'm feeling perfectly normal right this minute, even though my claw— I mean my hand—doesn't really look any different than it did when I walked in here. . . .

I was babbling, of course, but Marcus let me wind down before he cleared his throat and said, "Tell me about your father, Mr. Zachary."

My heart began to sink lower and lower in my reptilian body as I realized the direction Marcus was taking. Did this "visitor" resemble my Daddy? Was Daddy impossible to please? Did Daddy make me feel worthless when I was growing up? Like something unwanted, something repulsive, something loathsome? Like a cockroach, maybe? A rat? A lizard? A vermin of some kind?

I tried to tell him that he was mistaken. The man didn't resemble my father in the slightest. My father was a burly police sergeant who thought everything I did was terrific. This metamorphosis didn't spring from some poisoned childhood well. It wasn't traumatic. It was *real*. It was only too damned real! But Marcus, with Buddha-like serenity, paddled his fingers on the desk, and asked me about my mother.

It was too much for me. I dug my talons into my horny palms. I gnashed my fangs together so hard that my prognathous jaw ached. I wanted to roar like a tyrannosaurus, I wanted to belch flames, I wanted to ravage the office, the apartment house, the countryside! I wanted to trample buildings with my splayed feet and tear down power lines in great crackling bursts of energy! But all I did was sit up with a movement so rapid that my right claw knocked over the box of tissues on the coffee table. When I bent to pick it up, my jointless knee caught the underside of the table and toppled it over, smashing a blue Chinese vase and spilling bluebells and murky water over the doctor's Oriental carpet. His expression went from toleration to alarm, and I found myself enjoying the effect.

"I'm a *monster*, Doctor, don't you understand? It's not my imagination. I can see it. I can feel it! And if you really had any insight into people—you'd see it, too!" I waved both arms at him, causing him to slide his armchair back against the wall, crashing into his diplomas. "Claws!" I shouted. "These aren't hands any more, they're claws!"

"Yes, yes!" he said. "I do understand—"

"And these," I said, pointing to my jagged teeth. "These are fangs, Doctor. Fangs!"

I was still holding the box of tissues, and on a mad impulse, I bit into it savagely, shook it ferociously from side to side, growling all the time, and then hurled the mangled box into a corner. Marcus came out from behind the desk with his arms extended, thinking he could calm the Beast by the laying on of hands. I pushed him away so violently that he tripped over the overturned table. Then I slammed out of the office, using the wrong exit, the one where patients were still waiting. There was one nice blue-haired lady and a thin little man who looked as if he had been cowering all his life. I waited for their bleats of terror, but they obviously refused to see what I really was. I had traumatized the whole human race.

I walked blindly for the next half hour, not sure whether I was seeking calm or stoking my anger. I knew there was no hope for me in conventional therapies; no medicines or medicine men could cure this disorder, with possibly one exception: the man who had inflicted it upon me. But how would I find him? There was no use phoning the Motor Vehicle Bureau, that was for sure. I had no name, no useful description, nothing but the fact of his appearance at the agency. The thought gave me a sense of badly needed purpose. I decided to return to my office, in the slim hope of another encounter.

An encounter was awaiting me, but not the one I was hoping for. There was a uniformed policeman lounging near my office door, and I had the key in the lock before I realized that his presence was connected with me.

"Mr. Zachary?" he said, with a forced smile I recognized as humorless, or rather, humoring. "I'd like to talk to you for a few minutes, if you don't mind."

"Did Marcus call you?"

"The doctor's a little worried about you, Mr. Zachary, that's all."

"Tell him I'm sorry about his table," I said. "It was just an accident."

"You had more than one accident," he said.

"I'm also sorry about his Kleenex. Tell him it was delicious." I tried to slip past him into the office, but then I saw a second cop coming from the opposite corridor, and realized that the pincer movement had only one purpose, to get me into a psych ward. "Oh, gee," I said. "I forgot my briefcase in the car."

I slammed my door shut again and took off in the only unobstructed direction, heading hastily for a part of the building that was served only by a freight elevator. The officer shouted something at me and the second cop shouted at him, and then they were both lumbering at my heels. I made a panicky turn, and it was the wrong one, a dead end leading to an office whose double doors proclaimed it to be the world headquarters of Fiore Film Processing. I knew I was entering another cul-de-sac, but I had no choice. I barged into the reception area, and saw a vaguely familiar face at the front desk, the doll-like features distorted in surprise. Her name was either Eileen or Irene and we'd broken croissants together in the coffee shop downstairs. "Bill collectors," I said, and hurtled through the open doorway on the other side. There was a long stretch of offices like an endless railroad car, and I raced all the way to the end, hoping it would lead to an escape route, a fire exit, anything. All I spotted was an unmarked door, and I flung it open and pulled it shut behind me.

There was a Xerox machine chattering away as it cheerfully spewed out copies of some document extol-

ling the services of Fiore Film Processing. There was
a young woman attending the machine, a slim, not-
too-shapely young woman with mousy hair and nondescript features that nevertheless embedded themselves
forever in my brain. Because the nondescript eyes
widened into apertures just the right size for Horrified
Recognition. Her nondescript mouth became a gaping
oval, and her swollen throat emitted a sirenlike scream
of pure terror whose echo bounded from wall to wall
until I thought my eardrums were going to disintegrate
inside my head.

I took one step toward her, raising my hands in the
universal gesture of peace, but that only increased the
volume and frequency of her screams. Then I realized
that she, too, didn't see "hands" in front of her. She
saw *claws*. She didn't see my pleading expression. She
saw the pitiless physiognomy of a scaly green creature.
She didn't see Me, Aaron Zachary. She saw the
Monster!

In a way, it was almost gratifying. But I was just as
happy when the shrieking stopped, especially when I
learned the reason why. Behind me, the door had
opened quietly, and *he* was there.

"You see?" my would-be client said, moving his
unfinished features into what might have been a smile.
"I told you you could do it, didn't I?"

"Do *what*?" I answered, in a scream of my own.
"What's this all about? What did you to do to me
yesterday?"

"Why, I just let you do your job," the man said.
"I let you find my poor missing Dreeth."

The woman swallowed a sob and covered her face,
as if not wanting to look at either one of us.

"I knew it wouldn't be easy," he said. "I knew I
would have to resort to unconventional methods, since
I had no idea what sort of humanoid form Dreeth

would adopt. All I had to work with were the coordinates of her landfall on your planet."

"*My* planet?"

"Our measurements were quite precise, but I still required some kind of identifying procedure." He went to the girl and put his arm around her. "Dreeth is my intended mate, you see. She was a scientist on our world—most of our scientists are female. But she was so terribly career-minded, that . . . well, she hesitated about Uniting with me, even though she admitted to an abiding affection." As if to illustrate the point, the woman rested her head against his shoulder. "When she was faced with the actual Uniting time— you call it a wedding here—she decided to use a certain transporter device and flee to your planet, assuming the aspect of one of its inhabitants. It isn't as difficult for us as you might imagine. Of course, I followed her. But I quickly realized that the only way to make her reveal her presence was to do what I did. Only a native of our world would have recognized one of her own. And now that you've accomplished your mission, Mr. Zachary, I give you back your earthly form."

He reached out and put his hand flat on my chest. That was all. There was no blinding flash of light. I felt no sensation beyond a slight tingling in my fingers and toes. Did I say fingers? Yes! I lifted my right hand and counted them. One, two, three, four, five! Smooth pink fingers with short pink nails. Puny little things, really, but it didn't matter. They were mine, and they were human, and I was back among my own kind! I went looking for a mirror and found one hanging over a small sink in the corner, and there was my old serviceable face, grinning back at me, looking happier than I had ever seen it in my life.

I turned just in time to see Dreeth go into the man's arms and mumble something about being sorry. "Obviously, it was just a case of bridal jitters," she said, "and now I'm ready to come home." He smiled at her fondly, and said:

"Let's get into something more comfortable."

I knew it was time for me to leave, but I wasn't quick enough. In the blink of second, they were gone, replaced by two lizardy creatures pressing their snouts together, and I could swear I heard him say, "My God you're beautiful."

GOOD BOY

by Jane M. Lindskold

Running. Eyes on the spinning thing above, hard to keep track of in the growing twilight. Joy in muscles bunching for the leap and snap. Leaping, ground gone from under pads before I hear the approaching car and the boy's shrill cry, "Rover!"

As my teeth close on the plastic, I feel a thud and something breaking in me as a beef bone does in my teeth. There is pain and falling. Then there is nothing.

Next knowing comes slow and hurting. I am on my side; beneath is hard. Sharp bitter scents sting my nose, almost masking the Joey scent, the Mom scent, and one other. The pain and stink helps me to know this one—the hurting man. I try to raise my head to run, but it is too heavy.

I settle for opening my eyes and hear Joey's voice and my name. His voice is happy, but when he comes near I can smell that he has been crying. I want to lick at the tears, but I cannot make my head go up. I whimper instead, and Joey pats me, gently, not touching the side that hurts so much.

"Good boy," he says, over and over. "Good Rover."

There are more words, fast, to the Mom, but I cannot follow. I manage to lick the boy's hand when it comes close and taste salt.

The hurting man pushes the table then and it moves. Scared, I whimper again, louder when the

Mom pats me and then takes Joey away. The place the table stops in is brighter and the acrid scent is stronger.

I am not awake, not asleep, but somewhere in both—I smell soap and hear voices, all unfamiliar except for the hurting man's. I feel pressing on my broken side but cannot growl to warn them away. They say the words that Joey says, but not the same.

I tremble. Then a young man comes into this place, holding something carefully. He smells of blood—dog or human? In this place I cannot tell. The hurting man touches me with his thorn hand. I feel the sharp puncture. Then I sleep.

When slow waking comes, I smell dogs and much sickness. Sharp barks and whimpers, some close, some muffled by distance, fill my ears. I don't move for a long time. Then I smell water and am thirsty. More awake, I realize that I am not at home, not in the kitchen on my rug or on Joey's floor. But there is water, tasting of metal from the bowl. I drink.

Looking about, I see bigger and smaller kennels, and in them more dogs than even in the Park on a warm day. Next to me, in one of the big kennels, is a heavily built dog with thick, dark fur. His eyes are light and watch me. I stare back, my hackles rising as I scent him. His scent is wrong, not dog—something like dog but wilder, rougher, dangerous to me. Wolf. And mingled in with the wolf scent is that of a human.

I find that I can roll without so much hurt, so turn to watch this dangerous one, my head resting on my paws. Other of the dogs watch him too, I see, but he watches only me. Much time passes and sleep takes me again.

Waking, I find a man outside of my kennel. The wolf's kennel is empty and the man has light eyes and smells of wolf. I growl and he laughs, an unfriendly sound.

"Good boy. Good Rover."

Then he turns and goes out a door. Behind him, all the dogs join me in furious barking.

People come in time, but none is Joey or the Mom or the Dad. I eat and drink. Stiffly, I go outside and smell many dogs, but no wolf.

I remember sleeping times when I caught the squirrel before it reached the tree and Joey and I ate hot squirrel together. Perhaps the wolf is like the caught squirrel. Unreal.

I forget it all when Joey comes with the Mom. I try to wriggle and romp, but I am yet too stiff and the pain bites sharp. I still my body and bark loudly in greeting instead.

I am too long in the kennel, the lair of the hurting man, before I am free to go home with Joey. The pain is less now, too, so I am happy. At home, the Mom and Dad let me sleep in Joey's room instead of in the kitchen. We are both happy. My rug is on the floor, but when the door is closed, Joey lets me on the bed.

Pain is nearly a memory when cold wakes me one night. I try to curl my tail around my nose and paws, but it does not listen. My belly fur is also not there when I try to nestle my nose into its warmth. Sleepily, I thump at one ear with my hind foot and kick myself hard with a knee into my nose.

My nose? Knee? I awake and try to shake and find myself sitting upright on the foot of Joey's bed. A full moon shines through the window and I am cold because a boy doesn't have any fur.

I want to hide under the bed like I do when the crashing rain gets too loud, but my legs are hinged wrong and I tumble down in a heap and Joey wakes up.

"Rover?"

His voice sounds a bit different, but it is his. I try

to wag my tail, but there is not a tail. The moonlight is enough, though, for Joey to see that I am different.

He asks something. Frustrated because I do not know the words, I lie there and hope that he will help me. He says something else. The inflection is curious, not angry or afraid. When he turns on the bedside light, I blink and then I shriek and my voice is a boy's, but I cover my eyes with my hands, instinctive action coming easily. I must guard from the too many colors that the light has revealed. Something in me recognizes them as normal, but I am afraid.

Joey speaks and I hear two words I know, "Rover's collar." It seems to be a question and I hear my tags jingle and feel the warmth of Joey near. His hand is on my shoulder, then on my head fur.

"This is Rover's collar," he says, his voice quiet like he speaks when he does not want the Mom to hear. "Where is Rover?"

I know this phrase, from a game, and I peep out from under my hands. These human eyes sort the colors into shapes and I can see Joey is crouched next to me on the bed. He is looking at my side where, without fur, the fresh scars from my accident are easy to see—pink and red against pale flesh. His face is wrinkled with concern.

"Where is Rover?" he repeats.

I look at him and try to yap, like I would in the game. It comes out funny, but he understands.

"Rover?"

I yap and try to smile; the tongue won't loll out right, but he smiles hesitantly back.

"Rover?"

He says too many words, too fast; all I know is "boy." He waits, when I cannot answer, he sighs and says "Good boy" and awkwardly pats me.

I cannot tell if he is afraid—this human nose is dead to all but heavy scents, but he does not run. Instead he reaches for the cloth he keeps with his slippers. He fits my paws through the cloth and ties it around me. I am almost as warm as if I had fur and when he comes close, I lick his face. He giggles and puts the slippers on my feet.

"Good boy," he says, "Slippers. Robe. Collar."

I know most of the words and am content.

He gets up, "Stay, boy. Stay, Rover."

He leaves the room, carefully closing the door. I stay and look about. I find that, as with color, if I let my human senses work I am less afraid. I can see and even hear fairly well. Smell is gone, but there is color.

My nose itches and my hand moves to scratch it. The motion reveals my fingers to me and I play with them—absorbed in discovering how they move, picking up and dropping one of the slippers, wishing I did not have to "Stay" because I wanted my ball.

Joey comes back when the moon has moved only a little. He carries a paper bag which is bulging full. Happy, I leap off of the bed, stumbling only a little.

"Stay, boy," he cautions softly and I freeze, glad for the moment to test my balance and new orientation.

Joey closes the door and pushes his desk chair against it. When he walks over to me, I realize that we are nearly the same height, though he is still the taller. I look into his light eyes and tremble when I remember the wolf, but Joey comforts me.

"Good Rover. Sit."

I try, and manage to lower myself halfway. Joey laughs softly and untangles my legs so that I am comfortable.

"I said 'sit,' not hunker," he chuckles.

I don't know all the words, but his tone is comforting. Since I can't thump my tail on the floor, I try smiling again. It works easier without the tongue and Joey smiles back.

Joey digs into his bag, pulling out many things.

Most are people things, but he has brought my ball and something that even the human nose can tell is roast beef.

I whine.

"Quiet, boy," Joey orders. Then he places the ball in my hand and holds out a slice of roast beef.

I have trouble snatching the treat, but he feeds it to me.

"Stay, Rover. Sit. Quiet."

I sit and play with the ball. Fingers are better than mouth for this—boy mouth won't open enough and the head is too high.

Joey plays with the things from his bag. One thing flashes and makes a noise. Another leaves my finger pads dirty. Joey puts soap and water on them. He looks out the window at the moon a lot and says some words that I don't know.

We eat roast beef.

Joey is excited. I realize this from the noises that he makes, but it is night and finally he gets sleepy. The moon is almost gone when he buries his toys in the bag and buries the bag under the bed.

Then he takes away the slippers and the "robe" and puts the leash on my collar.

"Up, boy," he says, pointing to the bed and I jump clumsily up, "Good boy. Stay."

He puts a blanket on me and I am warm and tired. Joey yawns and, still holding the leash, gets under his blankets and turns out the lights.

"Good night, Rover."

I can't thump my tail, so I smile. Before I fall asleep I think I see pale eyes at the window, but I am too tired and too full of roast beef to care. Besides, Joey is there and already asleep.

When morning comes, I am a dog and I shake happily. Joey wakes up, too. Sometimes he goes away all day, but since it got warm he hasn't. Now that it is warm, we go to the Park or for Walks. I like this.

The Mom and the Dad leave and the Mrs. Peters comes soon. She guards the house and moves things. Joey likes her so I do, too, even if her voice is high and she talks to me in a different voice than she uses for anyone else.

While Joey eats, I go outside. Running in the yard on legs that work, I suddenly catch a scent that makes my hackles rise. The man/wolf scent. It starts by the gate from the alley and goes to Joey's window. I growl and pee all over the scent, scratching dirt to make it go away.

Mrs. Peters shrieks at me, scolding, so Joey takes me to the Park. I chase a stick and swim in the Pond, almost forgetting the night before. Joey plays with me. He calls me "boy" a lot and laughs.

A few times, I smell the man/wolf scent and stop to destroy it, leaving my mark over the stranger's.

Days pass and get warmer. I remain a dog. Joey teaches me to find things when he hides them: ball, stick, slippers, robe, shoe, bone, newspaper. I can remember many things, so he teaches me the names of hiding places: closet, garage, Joey's room, kitchen. The Mom, the Dad, the Mrs. Peters are very pleased. They call me "good boy" and "clever dog."

The moon gets fuller in the sky. In my sleep I chase gray squirrels under green trees and swim with Joey in blue water. Sometimes I am a dog. Sometimes I am a boy. Sometimes a wolf with yellows eyes watches me. Sometimes it is a man with yellow eyes who watches. Always when I see him, I am afraid.

As the moon gets fuller, Joey gets more excited. When it is full, I can feel it below the horizon even when the day is still bright and hot. Joey knows, too— he is wise. He is yawning before full dark comes, but he does not smell tired. The Mom and the Dad smile at us when we go to Joey's room and Joey makes noises as if he is going to sleep.

They smell tired and something else—I do not think that they will leave their room tonight. I feel relieved, as if I had dug a hole and Mrs. Peters did not find it. Becoming a boy may be worse than digging a hole. I don't know.

Joey has buried many things in his room. He takes them out and lines them up. We get sleepy and I think we must sleep because when I next notice I am a boy, the same as before I think when I raise my hand and sniff it. Joey's blue eyes are wide and he laughs with excitement—reaching out and touching my collar.

"Oh, Rover!" He hugs me, "Oh, boy!"

I shiver and try to bark, but it doesn't work well. Joey lets me go.

"Quiet, boy," he warns. Then he gets the robe and the slippers and helps me put them on, "Here, boy."

I come when he calls and go to where he stands in front of a dresser. The colors make people who move on the wall. Two boys. One is Joey—light golden hair tumbling into blue eyes. One has the robe and my collar; his hair is brown, so are his eyes. I shake and the boy shakes and the tags on my collar jingle.

Confused, I whine and Joey pats me. He goes to the bed and climbs on.

"Here, Rover," he says, "Up!"

I try, but the bed is unsteady and I fall. Joey laughs, not unkindly.

"Easy, boy. Sit."

I do. It is easier this time. I remember how it is done. I smile. We eat ham and Joey shows me things and says the words. Some I know. Others are new. But I remember easier—color helps and boy seems to do this like dog makes history from smells.

Some things I do not like and will not touch. These

are metal and their shine seems like a menacing scent. Joey calls them "silver." I want to bury them.

We play this way until I get tired. Then Joey shows me more about fingers and feet. We are playing catch with something like a ball that Joey calls a "nerf" when a tap startles us both.

Joey darts to the door, but I have heard better and growl as I look at the window where two pairs of yellow eyes reflect back the light.

Joey turns at my growl and sees the eyes and I do not need scent to know that he is afraid. My guard dog soul sparks and I get between Joey and the strangers, my growls roughing my throat.

I cannot smell man/wolf, but the hands that remove the screen and then push up the window are not human like Joey's and mine. They are covered with fur and the fingers end in heavy claws. As soon as the window is open a bit, a gray and black wolf leaps in, more easily than I could, even as a dog.

I start to lunge forward, but Joey's hand grabs my collar. I feel him trembling, but his grip is strong.

"No, boy. Stay." The rest of his words mean nothing to me, but his tone is firm.

The window opens enough to let in a man. Or is it a wolf? I am confused. He walks almost like a man, but he has heavy fur and his teeth are fangs. His eyes are the yellow of a wolf.

Joey has let go of my collar and now he runs to his toys. He picks up a silver knife—I had not liked it before—and holds it before him.

"Stay," he tells the wolf and the man/wolf. There are more words. I only know "silver" and "knife," but I can hear the threat in his tone even though he keeps his voice low. I growl.

The intruders sit and stay.

I am proud of Joey. For lack of a tail I smile, but

I do not stop growling, though my boy throat hurts. I move to stand in front of Joey—away from the silver.

Man Wolf speaks to Joey. I know "boy," "dog," "silver," "Rover." Joey answers. I understand "Joey," "knife," "silver." There are many words I do not know. They talk for a long time. I glare at the wolf who stretches lazily on Joey's floor. His pose is not one of threat. In fact, I detect only alertness and amusement.

The talking stops and Joey says, motioning to his right side, "Rover, sit."

I am hesitant, but he sits on the floor, putting the knife in front of him. Man Wolf sits, too.

"Sit, Rover," Joey repeats.

Reluctantly, I obey. Then Man Wolf extends one of his hairy hands toward Joey who takes it in his left, his right hand hovering over the knife.

Man Wolf hold his other hand to me and says, "Shake, Rover."

Almost by reflex, I obey, resting my boy's hand in his rough-furred grasp.

"Good boy," Joey says, and I hear the words twice, once with my ears and once, somehow, through Man Wolf's hand.

I growl and would fold my ears back, but they do not fold. Man Wolf tightens his grip on my hand and speaks and, though my ears know only a few of the words, what comes through his hand is as clear as the scent of a squirrel run across wet grass or bat song at twilight. I stiffen and listen.

"Good, Rover. You obey Joey wonderfully."

I growl softly and Joey laughs happily.

"I understood that, Rover. Obedience and agreement aren't the same things. Still, I think you need to hear what Mr. Lobo has to say."

Man Wolf—or Mr. Lobo—smiles, his fangs shiny in the moonlight, "Briefly, then, Rover, when the car

hit you you were bleeding inside. The doctors at the
ASPCA emergency clinic needed a source of fresh
blood to keep you alive while you were made well."

"A transfusion," Joey says, nodding.

"Yes, but keep the words simple, Joey. I'm afraid
telepathic translation works best with basic concepts."

"Sorry." Joey sounds shamed and I growl.

"Yes, Rover, I understand. I won't hurt Joey. Now,
as I was saying, because German shepherds (like you
are most of the time) are big dogs, they need lots of
blood. The easiest dog available was a big mix-breed
(or so they thought) who had just been brought in and
was still in a squeeze cage for his routine medical
exam. Unfortunately, the dog was actually my friend,
Clyde, over there—who has a rampant case of
lycanthropy."

"Clyde?" Joey giggles and the wolf growls,
thumping his tail playfully to take the edge off his ire.

Mr. Lobo shakes his head ruefully, the emotion
translated through his hold on my hand, "Yes, Clyde.
Well, as I've already told Joey, the lycanthropy made
you, Rover, into a boy."

"Why not a wolf?" I wonder, wishing that I had the
words, but Mr. Lobo understands.

"Because a dog, especially a German shepherd, is
still awfully close to a wolf, I'd guess. But, honestly,
I don't know. How old are you, Rover?"

I blink, puzzled, but Joey knows the answer.

"He's about eighteen months."

"Then that's why he's a boy, not a man, like Clyde
is when he's not a wolf. I had wondered how the virus
designed the human form. An eighteen-month-old dog
is about equal to an eight- or nine-year-old boy."

"I though it was seven years to one," Joey comments, "Wouldn't that make him closer to ten?"

"That formula is a bit outdated, especially with
modern canine health care. If Rover gets a balanced

diet and his shots regularly, you'll extend this vital period. Still, you're, what, fourteen?"

"In October," Joey agrees.

"Before Rover is three his human form will be older than yours."

"Oh," Joey becomes thoughtful.

I am rapidly discovering that translation doesn't help much, but since Joey doesn't seem scared I mentally thump my tail and wait for them to make sense.

"Well, you know the story now, Joey. Your dog will turn into a human, once, sometimes twice a month. As you may have discovered, his lycanthropy will make him brighter than normal—and as long as you are patient this will be a bonus. But if you're not, he'll have a greater tendency toward boredom. He may even become aggressive because of it."

Joey waits, sensing more is coming. I wait, too, suddenly apprehensive again.

Mr. Lobo sighs, "You've kept Rover's lycanthropy hidden so far, but it will get more difficult. What if he changes on a winter night when the moon may be visible for twelve or more hours? How do you conceal that? What if your parents walk in and find a man sleeping buff naked on the foot of your bed? Or if the neighbors are watching the dog while your family is away?"

His words come as pictures to me and I begin to shiver. Joey pats my leg with his free hand.

"Easy, boy. Good dog." His words are soft, but his blue eyes stay on Mr. Lobo, "What do you want?"

"Give us Rover, Joey. Clyde and I are both respectable businessmen with country houses. I was born with lycanthropy. (That's why I can manage a halfway shape and a couple of other tricks. They come with practice.) We'll understand and protect Rover, even when you can't. And you can visit him, of course."

I stiffen, a whine escaping. Absently, Joey pats me,

but I can feel his thoughts are on Mr. Lobo's promises of safe, green pastures.

"Like I told you before, Mr. Lobo, I sort of guessed what must have happened the first time. I've seen horror films and, I mean, Occam's Razor and all. This kid had to be Rover; he couldn't be anyone else. But to check, I took pictures and showed them around. Nobody had ever seen that kid. I can see what he's going to face, so if he wants to go—I'll let him. Okay, boy?"

He looks at me, "You understand, Rover. These people can keep you safe in a place with lots of squirrels to chase. If you stay here with me, honest, I don't know what Mom and Dad will say if they learn. So, you do what you want and I'll come and see you. Okay, good boy?"

I can see the options, feel Joey's emotions bittersweet, but there is no real choice.

My lips shape their first words, "Rover, stay."

Joey throws his arms around me, sobbing with joy, squashing my tags into my soft boy's chest. Mr. Lobo and Clyde stand.

"I'll get in touch when the moon has waned a bit," Mr. Lobo promises, while Clyde wags his tail, "You're going to need help—but hopefully this'll be a unique situation."

Then the lycanthropes leave by the window, stopping to wave as they open the gate and step out into the shadows.

Joey hugs me again, "Oh, good boy. Such a good dog."

Clumsily, I hug him back and then, dissatisfied, lick him sloppily across one salty cheek.

MISTS

by Kristine Kathryn Rusch
and Dean Wesley Smith

The canoe paddle cut into the velvet water, near-silent on the cold lake. In the distance a bird shrieked, its call echoing off the pine and mountains. Phil shivered and zipped his jacket tighter under his chin. He had never been here alone, never worked the lake by himself in the early morning hours.

Wisps of ground fog traveled from the underbrush to the corner of the lake, curling over the surface like smoke. A fish jumped ahead of him, but Phil kept paddling, his reel untouched in the bottom of the canoe. He wasn't out here early to fish. He was out to think, to be alone. To be away.

Another bird called out, different this time, and hollow, almost human in its ululation. He shivered again, and placed the dripping paddle across his lap. With a silent breath, he let the canoe glide of its own accord. He drifted forward, toward shore opposite the cabin, toward the tendrils of fog.

The trees stood out like white ghosts, flanked by the dark mountains behind them. The fog kept shifting, re-forming. Through it, he saw a woman walking along the rocky beach.

He quickly paddled toward her, keeping his strokes firm and quiet through the water. His cabin was the only one on the lake. There was no access to the beach she walked on—at least from the ground. She had to have come across the water. Half of him wanted to know what she was doing this far into the wilderness. Another half just wanted to leave her alone.

The cold grew stronger, more intense and oppressive the closer to shore he went. His hands were numb, the paddle heavy and rough as he fought to keep it straight. It had never been this cold before—not in July.

She stopped as his canoe came closer. The fog caressed her, giving her an opaque sheen. She turned and looked directly at him, then pressed her hands against her breasts and let out a wail. The bird call he had heard. No bird at all, but a sound of such deep and abiding pain that it barely sounded human. His shoulder shivered uncontrollably as the canoe bottom scraped against rock. He climbed out, wincing as his waders hit the icy water. She watched him as he staggered toward her. He got closer, fighting against the cold that seemed to emanate from everything. Her wail grew louder, ear-splitting. Her blue eyes opened wide, and she took a step back.

And then she vanished, leaving him alone in the cold morning mist, his ears ringing with her pain.

That afternoon, Phil was invaded by civilization. George, his Dodgers cap on backward, kept trying to back the Bronco into the driveway, ignoring the gravel the wheels were scattering in all directions.

Eli put two bags of groceries on the counter and moved around toward the refrigerator, while Ray stood in front of the picture window, hands in his pockets, keeping himself as far away from Phil as possible.

"You say she just disappeared?" Eli asked, wiping his hands on his jeans before opening the fridge.

"Yeah," Phil said. He was leaning against the table,

watching all the activity, wishing he had kept his mouth shut. For a moment, just a moment there, he had been happy for the company.

"She probably took one look at Phil, the soul of sensitivity, and decided she had a better chance in the woods," Ray said without turning around.

"This isn't going to be one of those years where you two fight, is it?" Eli asked.

Ray pushed away from the window, and threaded his way through the room, turning his back to Phil as he passed. He slammed open the screen door, and headed for the roar of the Bronco.

"Why do you let him come?" Eli asked.

"I have no say in it," Phil said. "He owns half the cabin. Besides, we've been doing this for twenty years."

Phil looked down at his fingers, nails ragged. Then he laughed a cold laugh, shaking his head. "We've been doing this for twenty years."

"And he's hated you for eighteen," Eli said. "Makes things a little tense, you know?"

"He doesn't hate me," Phil said. "And we don't always fight."

Eli ignored the comment. He began pulling things out of the bags: catsup, milk, beer, watermelon, orange juice, beer. . . . "What were you doing up here so goddamn early? I called your house yesterday. Nell said you'd been gone for two days."

Phil shrugged. "I had to get out." He moved away from the table, paced. The trapped feeling returned as the words of the fight echoed.

She's your daughter. She wants your support.

She has my support. I'm paying for it, aren't I?

The screen door slammed and Ray leaned in, sunlight reflecting off his balding head. "Truck's stuck."

Neither man looked up. Ray went back outside.

Eli shoved the refrigerator door closed. "What's really going on?"

"That woman. She's got me spooked."

Eli leaned against the counter, folded his arms in front of his chest. "You saw a tree shrouded in mist, heard a bird call. It was nothing."

"It was something." Phil felt the anger he had been suppressing for three days well up inside him. "For an English professor, you don't have a lot of imagination."

"And you have too much."

Phil opened his mouth, but Eli waved him silent. "Look," Eli said. "If it had been George, who spends his entire day giving comp tests to freshmen, I'd believe him. He couldn't even imagine what it's like to have a hard-on every night. But you, you're a mathematician who specializes in chaos theory. You live in your imagination, for God's sake, seeing things no one else can see. And when you're upset, your imagination works overtime."

"Yo!" George's voice echoed from the lawn. "We going to get some help out here?"

"Yeah," Phil shouted. He lowered his voice, then faced Eli. "So you think I'm upset."

Eli laughed. "I know you are."

"You're right," Phil said. "I'm upset because she disappeared." He turned and shoved open the screen door. This was going to be one long fucking week.

Twilight made the mountains dark blue. The edges framed the skyline, shoving the rest of the world far away.

Phil inched closer to the fire. He hadn't been warm since the morning. An untouched beer rested near his hand. Inside he heard laughter. Poker hadn't interested him, and he hadn't said much over the steak dinner Eli had fixed. George said three days alone had made Phil boring.

Depressed would be a better way of putting it, and the dark mood wasn't lifting. It had arrived the morning that Kerri confronted him and had remained until now, coloring everything with a numb sameness he had only felt once before.

Kerri had handled the whole thing right. Nervous, her hands shaking, cheeks flushed, she had come to him at breakfast, his best time. Nell hovered in the door, watching, protective mother afraid of her husband's reaction.

"Daddy," Kerri had said. "Can we talk?"

He had put down his newspaper, knowing from her tone that she had never broached anything this important to him before, not once in her sixteen years. He watched her sit, his pretty daughter with the wide blue eyes and the flowing blonde hair. She looked away from him, tried to pour herself a cup of coffee, but her hands shook too badly. He poured it for her.

"I'm pregnant," she said.

He set the pot down, made himself swallow, made himself breathe. Made himself think calmly.

"It was an accident." Her red flush deepened, hiding beneath the roots of her hair. "The condom— broke."

He felt heat fill his own cheeks. He had never expected to discuss things this delicate with a little girl who once fit in the palm of his hand. "Does Stevie know?"

"He's really mad."

Then he recognized her restraint. She expected him to be mad, too. He could understand Stevie's anger. Varsity football player, scholarship to Notre Dame. A wife and a child would just slow him down, take away his future. His father's words: *She'll ruin your life, boy, sure as shit.* "What do you want to do about it, honey?"

The softness in his voice brought tears to her eyes.

"I don't want it. God, Daddy, I'm sorry." She started crying in earnest then, big hiccuping sobs that shook her entire body. He touched her shoulder, feeling awkward, but she didn't lean into him like she used to do as a child. Finally he folded her into a hug, looking over her perfumed hair to Nell.

"She wants an abortion," Nell said, "but she can't afford it on her own."

Then, without warning, the anger was there. Not anger at Kerri, but at Nell for involving him at all. This was a woman's thing to be taken care of by women. If Kerri had needed the money, Nell should have written the check and told him about it later.

Nell had seen the anger, so fierce that she took a step backward, then he made himself suppress it. He had to remain calm for Kerri's sake, for the sake of his little girl. . . .

Phil leaned back, his hands in the dirt. The fire burned low, crackled in the clean night air. Inside the laughter had died down. He glanced at the beer, decided against it.

The fight had come after Kerri had left the house. Nell wanted him to go with them to the clinic. The appointment was in a week, she told him, and she thought it would be good if they both went along to show their support. He had grabbed his fishing gear, and his clothing, promising to return in two weeks, long after the deed was done.

Two days. His little girl was going to the clinic in two days. He probably should have talked to her before he had gone. He probably should have said his good-byes in person.

He shook off that train of thought. Such memories did him no good. This time he picked up the beer, flipped open the poptop, and guzzled as much as he could.

"Hey, Phil!"

He turned. George's face was mashed against the screen of the kitchen window. "Five card stud, nothing wild, just the way you like it."

He was here to have fun. What the hell. He got up, brushing the dirt off his pants. "I like it better if you've got money on the deal."

"You can buy in for twenty-five dollars."

Another sip of beer. It didn't soothe the ache. Maybe the game would. "Hope you're warmed up," he said. "I'm feeling lucky."

George laughed and disappeared from the screen. Phil took one last look at the outline of the mountains against the night sky, then let himself inside.

Maybe for just an hour he could forget.

Phil watched for her as dawn colored the lake. The mist was thinner, the air warmer, and the fish were biting constantly. The men were silent as they could be while reeling in catch after catch. Phil caught two rainbows without a glimpse of the woman.

By the time the sun hit the tops of the trees, the fish had quit. George pulled the motor to life for the first time that morning, and headed for the middle of the lake. Lunch and beer at 9 a.m.—a fishing week tradition.

"You know, I was thinking," George said as he pulled a sandwich from the cooler. "Maybe yesterday, you saw a ghost."

For a moment, Phil didn't realize George was talking to him. Then he leaned over the cooler himself, checking out the sandwiches and snacks, determined to remain calm. "A ghost?"

"Yeah." George pawed through the cooler until he found a ham on rye. "A see-through woman who disappears. Ghost."

"A crying woman." Eli picked up a beer, popped the top and leaned back. "A banshee."

"Shit." George sat down. "Means someone's going to die."

Phil took a roast beef, a bag of chips, and a lite, then wandered back to his spot, pushed his reel aside, and sat down.

"Depends on the folklore," Eli said. "Sometimes they're harmless."

"A banshee is a woman who died in childbirth." Ray's voice was soft, but his gaze was on Phil, watching for a reaction. "Maybe she's haunting you."

The world stopped. The sunny glare on the aluminum, the rumble of conversation. Only Ray's eyes were alive, staring at him, assessing him. Eyes fifteen years older than the last time he looked in them, still as brown, still as foreboding.

You should have been there. She didn't want me. She wanted you.

"Where the hell'd you learn that?" George asked, and the world returned. Buzz of a dragonfly on water, rustle of wind in the trees.

Ray shrugged, and looked away. "Irish history is full of little side paths you don't walk in other history courses."

"I always thought it meant somebody was going to die," George said.

Phil closed his eyes, saw Kerri being wheeled down a hall, white sheet over her still form. He shook his head and focused on the shimmering surface of the water. These thoughts weren't doing him any good.

"An owl used to hoot in the woods," Eli said between bites, "and my grandmother'd say, 'Someone is going to die in that direction.' And my grandfather wouldn't miss a beat. He'd say, 'Yes, hon. Wait long enough, and someone is going to die in that direction.' "

The laughter echoed across the lake. Phil felt it as a foreign thing, something that made the pictures of

Kerri stronger, not weaker. Stronger, interspersed with—

"Shit!" He opened his eyes and stood in one fluid motion, catching the sun glare on the water, feeling the sweat hold his shirt to his back. He set his beer and sandwich down, and took a dive into the lake.

The ice-cold snap of the water shoved the air from his lungs and cleared his head. He opened his eyes to the blurry vision of a deep blue world, and looked around. It seemed so quiet, so peaceful. He let the trapped air in his clothes bring him to the surface.

"Jesus, Phil, you're scaring the fucking fish," George said.

"You okay?" Eli called.

Phil sprayed water out his nose and mouth, then pushed his wet hair off his forehead. "Fine." He glanced at the shore. Half mile at most. He was in good condition. He ran every day at home.

George leaned over the edge of the boat and reached out a hand. Phil stared at it, then let his clothes drag him under. Rays of sunlight penetrated the surface, and down below he could see the darkness. Buried secrets, underwater treasure. He didn't care. He only cared for the light.

He came up once more for air, then shucked his clothes like his swim coach had taught him in high school gym almost two decades before. He pushed forward in an underwater breast stroke, watching his possessions sink into the unknown depths.

The others followed him in the boat all the way in, hooting and cheering him on, yet not letting him get far from them. He announced, once he was dry, that he was going to take a nap. And when he woke up, he discovered the others in the living room, discussing him in low tones. Not until he volunteered to make the fire at twilight did he get his first real chance to be by himself.

The afternoon had clouded over, and so darkness came a bit early. Ground fog had formed along the edge of the lake, and scattered through the trees. Phil placed dried-out wood on the ashes of the previous night's fire, interspersed kindling and paper, then lit a wood match. The flames took a second to catch, and for a brief moment, the smell of sulfur overcame the damp. He sat with his arms on his legs, shivering. He hadn't really gotten warm since his dive into the lake. Crazy man, Eli had called him. Perhaps he was.

The screen door slammed. Phil sighed. They weren't going to let him alone. Crazy men in the wilderness die young, as George would say. Footsteps approached, then stopped. "Need company?" Eli. He couldn't leave things alone.

"No," Phil said.

"Then you at least need a beer."

Phil reached up, took the can, wincing as the cold aluminum touched his hand. He never understood why they went somewhere cold in July. Wouldn't they be better going to the beach, swimming in the warm California ocean, turning their faces toward the sun?

Eli sat down on the log beside the fire. Phil stared at the flames, jumping now, the base turning blue. "You going to tell me what's going on?"

"No," Phil said. Even if he wanted to, he couldn't. This was Kerri's secret, not his. His reaction was his problem, no one else's.

The mist coalesced in the near-darkness, looking white and opalescent against the deep blue mountains. In the distance, a bird cried.

"Wonder what that was?" Eli said.

"Loon," Phil said as a shiver ran down his back.

The screen door creaked open, remained so for a moment, two voices drifting down to the fire. "We're going to do a wienie roast." Eli said. "Can't bring Phil to the party, bring the party to Phil."

"Thanks," Phil said, unable to keep the sarcasm from his voice. Still, the numbers might protect him, prevent him from seeing that sobbing woman again. "Got marshmallows?"

"Sure as shit do," George said. "And chocolate and graham crackers, if you want. And enough beer to keep us all happy."

Phil doubted it.

They put the cooler down behind the log, and sat. Ray took his place at the edge of the log, near the growing mist. "Creepy night," he said.

The cry again, long and hollow, almost human.

Eli stuck raw hot dogs on dowels and passed them out. Phil shoved his in the fire, making himself watch the meat sweat. Out of the corner of his eye, he saw the mist take a female form.

"You see that?" Ray whispered.

"What is it," George asked, back turned. "Phil's ghost?"

The cold had grown, so deep that it shook Phil to the bone. He took the hot dog out of the fire, saw Ray turn his down. They were both staring in the same direction, at the woman walking toward them, trees and mountains visible through her thin form.

"You see that?" Ray repeated.

George turned. "What?"

Eli shook his head. The woman stopped in front of the fire, hands pressed against her breasts, tears falling off her chin and dripping onto the log. She was wearing an open collar shirt, and blue jeans, and her gaze was on Phil.

"Jesus, Kerri," he murmured.

"Kerri?" Ray said, his voice soft, almost a whisper. "That's Pammy."

At the sound of her name, the woman looked up, saw Ray, reached out for him. He reached back, then stopped as she turned her attention back to Phil. He

stumbled toward her, around the fire, the heat doing
nothing to hold off the growing cold.

"Pam," he said, and the tunnel opened letting in
the blackness. Regret, bitter as bile, filled him, and
he remembered:

*Pam, her face tear-streaked as he held her, promising
he would help.*

*His father's rumbling curses—She'll ruin your life,
boy, sure as shit. You're nineteen years old, and promising. What do you need with a wife and baby?*

*The check, left in her mailbox on a sunny Saturday
morning.*

*And Ray's phone call, a week later—they botched it
up so bad. Her dad's going to sue. She was waiting for
you, man. You should have been there. She didn't want
me. She wanted you.*

"Jesus," he said. "Pammy." He had loved her.
More than any other woman. More than Nell. More
than anyone, except, perhaps, Kerri.

She took his face in her cold, dripping fingers, made
him look into her eyes. He saw, not forgiveness, but
anger, deep and abiding. He had made the choice for
her, and then not come through. Her father had said
she was so depressed it was a wonder she had managed to go through with it. Perhaps, he had said, if
Phil had been there. . . .

"I'm sorry," he whispered. His cheeks were going
numb. The wet splashes on his legs were seeping
through his jeans, sending chills up his thighs. His
arms ached with the effort to hold them still.

But her gaze didn't change. Sorry wasn't enough.
But sorry was all he had to give. Sorry and Kerri.

Kerri. At the thought of her name, Pam disappeared, leaving only the chill remnants of her touch
on his face, Ray's wide-eyed stare, and the confusion
of men behind them.

"Why now?" Ray said. "We've been up here for the last fifteen years. Why now?"

Phil wiped his cheeks with his sleeve. Because, he wanted to say, he had a second chance and he was blowing it. He glanced at his watch. If he started now, he could be back before the clinic opened in the morning. If he started now, he could be there with his little girl.

He got up, staggered a little from the cold and the shock, made his way to the cabin. Eli followed.

"You saw something," he said as Phil opened the door.

Phil grabbed his duffel, shoved his clothes inside.

"What are you doing?

"Going home."

"Now?"

"Yeah," Phil said. "I'll explain later." He slung his duffel over his shoulder, picked up his fishing gear, and walked to his car. Ray was standing there, waiting for him.

"The others didn't see her."

Phil flung everything in the back seat, closed the door. "You and I were the ones who knew her." He leaned his head on the cool metal. He had repeated himself, so many years later. *She has my support. I'm paying for it, aren't I?* No wonder he felt the despair. No wonder he felt the blackness. He had been acting it out, all over again. "I'm sorry, Ray," he said, voice muffled against the door frame. "You were right, all those years ago."

"I was so damn angry at you." Ray's voice sounded small. "She loved you, and you weren't there. And there I was, in love with her, convenient, facing her father when it should have been you."

Phil turned, took Ray's outstetched hand. They remained there, looking at each other for a moment, understanding, two old friends who had been bound by a secret, unwilling even then to let the friendship die. Then Phil pulled away. "I gotta go," he said. "Kerri needs me."

Ray nodded, as if it suddenly made sense.

Phil opened the door, got inside.

Ray leaned in. "She'll be okay, you know. It's legal. The techniques are better. Safer."

Phil made himself breathe, slowly, deeply. Ray had all the information put together. And Ray kept secrets.

"Thanks," Phil said. "See ya." He pulled the door closed, started the car, and headed down the bumpy dirt road. He had never driven out of the cabin in the dark before. The ground fog looked like white ghosts running through the trees, guiding him, showing him the way.

He sighed, and followed them as the tension drained away, one curve at a time, and he headed back, finally, to the place he belonged.

ANOTHER KIND OF ENCHANTED COTTAGE

by Hugh B. Cave

Jennifer awoke in the middle of a disturbing dream and found herself staring at the bedroom's north window. She was alone in the house. Her carpenter husband was on a job in Miami, too far south to be able to drive home except on weekends. What she saw at the window was even more frightening than the dream she had just escaped from.

She swung her feet to the floor and stood up, trying not to shake so much because it might hurt the unborn child inside her. Seconds passed before she could stop shaking long enough to risk a forward step and start for the window.

The window was open, and it shouldn't be. She knew it had been shut when she went to bed, because this was August and the air conditioner was running. But it was open, yes, and a hot, wet breeze drifted in from the yard, smelling of . . .

Smelling of what? Garlic? Cooking oil? Something dead?

Maybe a dead raccoon, she thought. Or a rat. Even an armadillo. Joe and she were pretty far out of town here, with no other houses around yet, though the real estate people had said there would be. But the thing at the window was not dead, and it was not part of the dream. It was an eye, a huge human eye that filled the whole window and was peering in at her.

The colored part of it was dark brown with an even darker center, like Joe's, but the part that should have been white was blotchy red. And though the eye was too big to be real, she knew it was alive because even while she stared back at it, scared half to death, the eyelid came part way down over it in a kind of squint.

Then suddenly it wasn't there any more. Through the open window—which was not supposed to be open—she could see the wax myrtles in the backyard garden standing pale in a wash of moonlight.

Still shaking, she was almost afraid to touch the window, but at last worked up the courage to close and lock it. Then she swung about to look at the clock on her dresser.

Two-twenty. She couldn't call Joe. Down there in Miami he roomed with a buddy who had a wife and kids, and a phone call at this hour would wake up the whole house. What would she say, anyway? *"Joe . . . something was looking in the window at me. Something so big, its eye filled the whole window. . . ?"* He would believe her, of course. After the other things that had happened, he wouldn't think she was crazy. But what could he do?

No way was she going back to bed, though, to lie there staring at the window and waiting for the eye to reappear. Turning her back on the window, she ran into the living room and snatched up the TV remote, not caring what was on, only wanting something to fill the silence.

When daylight came, she was still sitting there, still shaking and afraid.

This house . . . Joe and she had loved it the minute they saw it. Their enchanted cottage. Now the enchantment had turned into a series of nightmares, but they couldn't move out. After putting everything they owned into the down payment, they hadn't the money for another move, even if a good fairy were to come

along and *give* them another house to live in. And
in five months there'd be a baby. Babies, too, cost
money.

The deed to the house was in their safe-deposit box
at the bank, but they kept a copy at home. On his
knees in the bedroom where the face had appeared,
Joe fished it out of the bottom drawer of his dresser
and held it up.

"Here it is, hon. 'The grantor, Desmond Shartz, a
single man . . . conveys and warrants to Joseph A.
Nelson and Jennifer C. Nelson, husband and wife . . .' "
He leaned back on his knees and looked up at her.
"Desmond Shartz. S-h-a-r-t-z."

Seated on the bed, Jennifer opened the phone book
on her knees and began to flip pages. "Okay. He lives
at one-sixteen Greenwood Avenue. Should we call
him first?"

"No!" When her good-looking husband shook his
head that emphatically, his thick blond hair did a kind
of break dance. "He must know what kind of house
he sold us, damn him. He'd think up some excuse not
to talk to us."

"Joe, he never lived in this house." She had to be
patient with him sometimes. He was big and
protective.

"He built it, didn't he?"

Jennifer finished writing the man's address on a
piece of paper. "Not even that. At least, not all of it.
I told you what Mrs. Anson said when I was doing
her hair. Someone else started it and went broke or
something. But, like you say, he might not want to
talk to us." She put the phone book aside and stood
up. "So let's go."

It was Saturday. Joe had worked half the day. He'd
gotten home an hour ago, and his first words had
been, "Did anything else go wrong, hon?"

He'd been away since before daybreak Monday morning, and she had a list of things to tell him. Every time something had gone wrong, she'd written it down. And every day there'd been something. The front door open when she got home from the beauty parlor where she worked. Windows open when she knew she had left them locked. The garage door opening by itself when she was in the kitchen. And, of course, the thing at the window last night. That huge, horrible eye, peering in at her.

"God, I hate working in Miami at a time like this," Joe said as he backed the car out of the garage and got out to pull the door down. "But what can I do?"

"It's all right, Joe."

"It isn't all right!" He was a quiet man who almost never raised his voice. He even hated loud music or having the TV up too loud. But his voice boomed now because he was so uptight. "With the baby coming, I ought to be home with you," he said. "I shouldn't be—"

She silenced him by reaching out and touching his leg. More than touching it—squeezing it. "Joe, I'll be okay. There's an explanation somewhere for what's happening. We just have to find it, is all."

The day was hot again. It was the hottest August she could remember. One of the reasons they'd been so keen on the house was that it had a really good air-conditioning system, she remembered. At least *that* hadn't gone bad yet. But why were so many other bad things happening in a house that was still almost brand new?

"You have the list?" Joe asked.

"Uh-huh." But she didn't want to talk any more about the house until they'd confronted Mr. Shartz. "Tell me about your job in Miami. What are you doing there?" Her Joe was a good man, always doing his best. He needed to know she was proud of him.

"It's no big deal," he said. "Like I told you on the phone, we're rebuilding a dock."

"So how do you rebuild a dock? Tell me."

He told her. Was still telling her when they turned onto Greenwood and she began looking at names and numbers on mailboxes.

All the houses here were bigger than their own. Much bigger. The one Desmond Shartz lived in stood on a double lot and the car in the driveway was a Mercedes.

They had come in her little car because Joe didn't like to use his old pickup when she was with him. He parked it just beyond the extra-wide driveway, and she reached out to touch him again. "Joe, remember. No matter what he says, don't get mad."

He took in a deep breath and looked at her, then let the breath out and nodded. "Okay, okay." Most likely he would have behaved himself anyway, she thought. It was just that what was happening to them was so—so *unreasonable*—that even a sweet guy like him might blow a fuse.

They went up the walk side by side, and Joe put a finger on the bell. The door opened. They were face to face with Mr. Desmond Shartz, whom they had seen only once before. That had been at the office of the Title Guarantee Company, when he'd signed the house over to them.

"Mr. Shartz?" Joe had his voice under control, even if his face did look like a thundercloud. "You remember us, Jenny and Joe Nelson? We'd like to talk to you about the house you sold us."

Desmond Shartz was a short, fat man with a head that looked something like a happy-face sticker with the smile-line upside down. His nose was small and he had hardly any hair or ears. "Which house is that?" he said in a surprisingly raspy voice. "I'm a developer. I sell a lot of houses."

"One-sixteen Cornell Drive."

Mr. Shartz tipped his head as if looking up at the sky would help him think. "Cornell Drive . . . ah, yes I remember. How can I help you?"

"This may take a while," Joe said. "Can we come in?"

"Of course, of course."

They stepped in past him, and Mr. Shartz shut the door. Then he led them into a living room that was twice the size of their own and said, "Have a seat, won't you?" And when he himself was seated, he said again, "How can I help you?"

Joe looked at the list in Jennifer's hand, and Jennifer began to read from it, filling in details. "And that's only the worst of what's been happening," she finished. "If I included all the *little* annoyances, we'd be here a long time, believe me."

Mr. Shartz put a pudgy hand to his chin and said with his smile-mouth upside down again, "In more than twenty years of building houses, I've never heard of anything like this. Are you serious?"

"You'd better believe it," Joe said. "Tell me—who actually built our house? You're a developer. You don't swing a hammer."

"Built it? Well . . . the Anson Home Builders finished it, and they've done more than a dozen homes for me. They're a fine firm with an unblemished reputation."

"What do you mean, *finished* it?"

"Well, they—ah—the house was begun by someone else. By a man named Kelly Burdick."

"Why didn't *he* finish it?" Joe asked.

"There was—ah—there was a problem with the financing." Mr. Shartz tipped his head again, this time apparently trying to read something on the ceiling. "As I recall, I bought the house unfinished and . . ." He rubbed the palms of his hands together and lowered his gaze to Joe's face. "Yes, of course. What happened, Burdick ran out of money, so as a favor to him I took the place off his hands and paid the Anson people to finish it. Then I sold it to you." He smiled, apparently pleased with himself at having remembered all the details so quickly. "But these strange things that you say have been going on . . ." The smile faded and he shook his head. "I'm afraid I don't understand."

"Well, if you can't explain it, maybe the Anson people can," Jennifer said. "Come on, Joe. We'll get to the bottom of this somehow."

Desmond Shartz hurried ahead of them to open the front door, then stood there sort of bowing, but not quite, as they stepped past him. As they went down the walk, his voice caught up with them like an afterthought, saying, "I'm sorry. Perhaps if I were to come over there and look around . . ."

They stopped and looked back at him. "Yeah," Joe said sarcastically. "Why don't you?"

The man was still standing in his doorway when they drove away. Still there when Jennifer looked back, as they turned a corner. He was not a nice man, Jennifer thought. Not honest.

"Hey, why were you in such a hurry to get out of there?" Joe said. "We might have gotten the truth out of him if we'd kept the pressure on."

"You think he was lying?"

"Sure he was."

"I think so, too." she said. "Do you know this Burdick fellow he talked about? The one who started the house but didn't finish it?"

"I've met him. He's a small-time independent, a loner. You want a house built and go to him with plans, he'll give you a bid on it."

"Have you ever worked for him?"

"Uh-uh." Joe shook his head.

"And what about the Anson Home Builders who finished the house? Do you know them?"

"They're big time. I've never worked for them either."

"Well, it so happens I'll be doing Mrs. Anson's hair again Monday morning, and she likes to talk," Jennifer said. "So by the time you phone me Monday night, maybe I'll know something."

They went to bed early that night and made love, Joe being very gentle because of the baby. Then just after three o'clock Jennifer awoke and knew at once that something new was wrong.

At first she thought it was only the bed shaking. Then she realized *all* the furniture in the room was shaking and the windows were rattling.

"Joe!" She leaned over him, gripping his shoulders. "Joe, we're having an earthquake or something! Wake up!"

He was always a deep sleeper. Kidding about it, he liked to say it was one of the rewards a man got for being honest and hard working. He woke up fast enough now, though, and was out of bed even before she was. "Come on!" He grabbed her by the hand and pulled her across the room to the door. "We have to get out of here! Out of the house!"

She stumbled, probably because of the baby. Then before she knew what was happening she was swept off her feet into Joe's arms and he had the front door open and was running down the front walk with her. Not until they were in the road did he put her down.

They looked back and she saw the house really was shaking, yes. It wasn't another dream or her imagination. She could even hear the sounds it was making— like something human groaning in torment. But nothing else was in motion. The wooden lightpole by the side of the driveway was as steady as always. There was no movement of the ground under her bare feet. On the eucalyptus trees in the yard, not a leaf was even fluttering.

"Wait here," Joe said, and strode back up the walk to the front door, which was still open. He put his hand out to touch the frame with his fingertips.

The house was shaking. Yes, it was, and she wasn't crazy. She could see his hand moving. His whole arm moved because his fingers were pressed against the door and *that* was in motion.

Suddenly it stopped.

Joe came back to her and put his arm around her and they stood there staring at the house in silence. A minute must have passed before either of them spoke. Then Joe said, "We weren't just seeing things. It really happened, like something took hold of the house and shook it. Like a kid might shake a dollhouse."

"Like someone is playing games with us," Jennifer whispered. "To drive us out of our minds."

"Come on." With his arm still around her waist, he led her up the walk. Then at the door, "Wait here," he said, and went in alone. She could hear him going through the house, the whole house, even into the garage, to make sure it was safe. *My Joe,* she thought, *who loves me and won't let anything bad happen to me. Or to our baby.*

Returning to her, he reached for her hand. "Whatever it was, it's stopped," he said. "But what if it happens again? Maybe we should go to the Seadrift." That was a motel in town. Expensive.

They talked it over and decided to save the money. Went back to bed. For an hour or more she lay awake in Joe's arms, knowing he was also awake even though he had stopped talking. The house was quiet, as if ashamed of what it had done. Finally she went to sleep.

* * *

It was Tuesday. Tuesday morning. Joe was at work in Miami again. Hearing a car pull into the driveway, Jennifer went from the kitchen to a front window to look out. Then, eagerly, she hurried to the front door and opened it.

"Mrs. Anson." The lady she had talked to the day before at the hairdresser's.

"I thought I'd come by instead of just phoning you, Jenny." The wife of the head of the Anson Home Builders Corporation was overweight but pretty, with a friendly smile and a warm handclasp. "As I promised, I asked Arnold about this house and I think I have the whole story for you."

They sat in the living room, and Mildred Anson took a folded sheet of paper from her soft-leather handbag. "My notes. I always take notes. I was sixty-three on my last birthday, and you know what happens to one's memory as one gets older." Without waiting for a reply, perhaps expecting none, she unfolded the paper, put on glasses, and peered at it.

"Now then, yes, this house was begun in May of last year by a builder named Kelly Burdick, just as Mr. Shartz told you. He was building it for a man named Emile Migaud, who lives in Ft. Pierce. From his name, Mr. Migaud must be French or of French ancestry, wouldn't you say? Anyway, I have his address here if you and your Joe feel it might help to go there and talk to him." She looked up and fluttered the sheet of paper. "But that can wait, can't it? Let me go on.

"What happened," Mrs. Anson continued, "was that Kelly Burdick was building this house for Mr. Migaud, and the house was almost finished—I mean really almost completely *finished*—when Mr. Migaud told him to stop. Just like that, out of a blue sky, without any explanation. Stop, period. Can you imagine? But, of course, Kelly had to do as he was told, and then, two or three weeks later, Desmond Shartz came to Anson Home Builders, my husband's firm, and hired *them* to finish it. Arnold says Mr. Shartz is not the most honest man in the state—in fact, he has a most unsavory reputation—but the home-building business has been slow of late, and, after all, one man's money is as good as another's."

Jennifer leaned toward her. "And does your husband have any explanation for all the weird things that keep happening in this house?"

"No, dear, he doesn't." The woman shook her head, obviously unhappy at being unable to help with that part of the problem. "He says he inspected the house thoroughly before allowing any work to be done on it—under the circumstances he felt he had to—and as a matter of fact it was so well constructed it surprised him. He hadn't been aware that Mr. Burdick did such good work." She sighed, shaking her head. "Perhaps you should talk to Mr. Burdick, dear. I have his phone number here. And, as I said, I have the name and address of the man in Ft. Pierce for whom he was actually building this house." Rising from her chair, she offered the piece of paper.

"Thank you," Jennifer said.

Mrs. Anson departed. Before her car was out of the driveway, Jennifer was on the phone.

Kelly Burdick himself answered the call.

"Problems?" He had a deep, booming voice that Jennifer pictured as coming from someone big and brawny. "Sure, sure, we can talk, Mrs. Nelson. Hey, look. As it happens, I got to be in your neighborhood this afternoon, so why don't I just stop by? Say around four?"

He came at four-twenty and was not big and brawny at all, but short and wiry, red-haired, with quick, jerky movements that made her think of cartoon characters on television. While seated in the same chair Mrs. Anson had occupied, listening to Jennifer's recital of all that had happened, he never once interrupted. In fact, his gaze never left her face and his bright blue eyes didn't blink once.

"I never heard of such things happenin'," he said when she had finished. "Jeeze. 'Scuse me, ma'am, but I just dunno what to say."

"Well, they're happening, Mr. Burdick. And something new seems to happen every day or so."

Burdick gazed at her with his face in motion, constantly changing shape as though it were made of rubber. "Here's what I know," he said then. "This feller Emile Migaud called me up, then come to see me. Said he'd bought this lot here on Cornell Drive and wanted a house built on it. Knew exactly what he wanted. Even had plans he'd sent away to some magazine for. So I said, 'Okay, leave me make a copy of the plans and I'll get back to you with a bid.' And when I give him my bid, he accepted it."

Burdick leaned toward her now with his hands gripping his knees—rough, carpenter's hands like her Joe's. "So I hired some helpers and went to work on the job, and everything went along just fine. He'd come out every couple of days to look things over. Always told me he liked what we was doin'. Never once made a complaint."

"And then, out of the blue, he told you to stop work on it," Jennifer said.

"Right. Never give me a reason. Never said I was doin' a bad job. Just, 'I have to stop you, Mr. Burdick. I'm sorry, but I can't let you finish it.' "

"Didn't you *ask* for an explanation?"

"Course I did! Because I knew I'd done a good job. But all he'd say was he was sorry. Next thing I knew, I come by here one day and seen Anson Home Builders finishin' the house."

"But it wasn't Mr. Migaud who hired Anson Home Builders to do that," Jennifer said. "It was Desmond Shartz, the man who sold the house to Joe and me. How do you explain that?"

"You got me there, lady. Maybe you oughta talk to Mr. Migaud."

"I suppose I'll have to."

"All I can say is, good luck. He seemed like a nice enough guy, I'll give him that, but he sure wouldn't tell *me* nothin'."

This time she did not wake up from a dream; she was already wide awake. After a lot of talking, Joe and she had decided he ought to return to his job in Miami and he had left that morning. After all, the baby was going to cost money, and jobs didn't grow on trees. "But if anything happens, you call me, y'hear?" he'd said when he kissed her good-bye. "You get on the phone and call me right away, fast! To hell with the job!"

She would be all right, she'd told him. But when she came home from *her* job to an empty house, she was lonely and scared. What would the house do next?

She'd fixed herself something to eat and looked in the paper to see if there was a good movie on TV. There was, but it was a horror thing, just the kind she didn't dare watch when she was so jumpy. So she lay on the sofa and watched a couple of other things for a while, and then at ten o'clock went to bed.

Sleep wouldn't come, though. Being scared with Joe at her side was one thing; being that way without him was a hundred times worse. Everything inside her felt so tense and tight, she even worried that it might be hurting the baby. Then she heard the window open. It was shut like before because the night was hot again and the air conditioner was on, and she was nowhere near it, but it opened. Not slow and quiet, the way a person trying to break in would have opened it, but with a loud *thud* that had her sitting up in bed with her mouth and eyes wide open even while the sound was still booming around the room.

The window was open and there was a light behind it, a yellowish kind of light, and then what looked like a big glass tube full of milky liquid came sliding through the opening into the room. The tube had a point on it, or anyway the end was smaller than the rest of it, and it slid straight at her like it was meant to stab her, and she heard herself shriek as she clawed her way off the bed to get away from it.

Everything went crazy after that. In trying to get off the bed too fast, she fell on the floor. Then the thing sliding through the window spat out the milky liquid like water from a hose, and while she was scrambling to her feet, scared to death she might have hurt the baby, the room filled with a smell of rotten eggs. The bed was wet, and globs of the milky liquid clung to her hair and face and pajamas, and the smell was so strong she felt she couldn't breathe.

"Joe! Joe!" she yelled, running out of the room. She knew he wasn't there, but she yelled anyway. "Joe! Joe! Help me!"

She ran out of the house, out onto the front lawn, and didn't stop until she reached one of the eucalyptus trees near the road. There, with her heart still pounding like it would leap clean out of her body, she clung to the tree and looked back at the house to see what it would do next. For what must have been at least half an hour she stayed there, wanting to go back in and call Joe, but afraid to.

Nothing more happened.

Not quite so scared then, she dared to walk around the house, in the dark, to the window that had been opened. To find out, if she could, what had opened it and what the thing was that had slid in through the opening to spit the stinking milky liquid all over her and the bedroom.

The window was shut, just like it had been when she went to bed. There was nothing on the ground outside it, not even footprints. If there had been footprints she'd have seen them, because the night wasn't all that dark.

So what had happened?

She couldn't even guess. But after a while, when she had stopped being so scared, she went back into the house and telephoned Joe.

"Hon, get out of there," he said. "Get out now, this minute. Get in your car and go to the Seadrift. I'll be there as quick as I can."

"Joe," she moaned, "I can't go to any motel smelling like this. I have to clean up first!"

"Well . . ." She could almost hear him thinking. "No, don't. Don't do that. It's only one-thirty. You're in your pajamas, huh?"

"Pajamas. Yes."

"Just throw on some clothes, then, and take some others, some clean ones for after you've had a shower at the motel. Tell them—tell them you were alone in the house and the septic system backed up somehow, you don't know how, and you have to stay with them till I get there. You got that?"

"I—I think so."

"So go! Get out of there!" he shouted. Then in a softer voice, "Look, I didn't mean to yell at you, hon. I'm sorry. You know I love you. But go."

Braver now because she knew the window was shut again, she went back into the bedroom and switched on a light. The room smelled like vomit and almost made her throw up. But in the bathroom, as she took off her stinking pajamas and stepped into the shower, she was even more afraid. Because, no matter what Joe had said, she couldn't go to the motel smelling like a sewer. She just couldn't. And what if the house played some other trick on her now, like making the hot water so hot it would boil her alive?

It didn't. Nothing like that happened. Back in the bedroom she hurriedly put on clean clothes. Then she drove to the motel.

"For two," she said to the man at the desk. "My husband's on his way up from Miami." And she told him about the septic system backing up, like Joe had said.

All he said was, "It can happen. Mine went bad once the same way. But not in the middle of the night, thank heaven."

With so much on her mind she didn't even try to sleep. When Joe arrived, she was sitting in a chair by the window, waiting for him.

"You're tired," Joe said. "Let's talk in bed."

They went to bed and she lay in his arms and felt safe again at last. She always felt safe when they were together. He stroked her while she told him what had happened. Told him everything, from the minute she had heard the window open and seen the yellow light outside.

"All right, that does it," Joe said. "What we'll do is call on this French guy who hired Burdick and then fired him. There's no point in going back to the house till we get some answers. You say you have his address?"

Yes, she said, she had Mr. Migaud's address.

At 8:25 that morning they were in Ft. Pierce, at the Frenchman's door, and Joe was ringing the bell.

It wasn't much of a house. She was surprised, really, that a man living in such a shack, on such a poor street, would have had the money to build the house Joe and she were living in. She was even more surprised when the door opened and she saw the man himself.

The first thing she noticed was his eyes. They were dark brown, like Joe's, but the whites of them were streaked with red. Then when she could stop staring at his eyes, she saw that he was a small, skinny black man of middle age, wearing dark pants and a yellowed undershirt, and he was barefoot.

"Good morning," he said, peering at them as if he was surprised to have callers. "Is it that you are looking for Emile Migaud?"

"Yes, we are," Joe said. "And if you're him, we'd like to talk to you. I'm Joe Nelson and this is my wife, Jennifer. We live in Sebastian in the house you built. Or started to."

Emile Migaud rose up on his toes, there in the doorway, and leaned forward to look at them more closely. As if Joe had said something crazy like, *We are from the planet Vulcan.* "You live where?" he said, and his mouth stayed open showing his pink tongue and gums.

"In the house you built. The one you started, anyway, and the Anson people finished. On Cornell Drive in Sebastian."

The man stepped back and motioned them to enter. "Come in, come in," he said, and led them into a sad little room that had only a broken-down sofa and two seedy-looking chairs for furniture. "Please to sit down," he said, motioning them toward the sofa. He himself perched on the edge of a chair and leaned toward them again. The room stank of garlic.

"*You* are living in my house?" he said then.

"That's right," Joe said.

"But I thought—I was given to understand that Mr. Shartz would live in it."

"No, no," Jennifer said. "He never lived in it. He sold it to us."

Mr. Migaud whispered something in a foreign language. French, Jennifer guessed it was, because part of what he said sounded like "*Mon Dieu!*" and she

knew those were French words. Then in English he
said, "Oh, dear. What have I done to you? What have
I done?"

"What's that supposed to mean?" Joe said with one
of his rare big scowls.

The little man stood up, his face looking like licorice
that had all at once begun to melt. "Come," he said,
and waited for them to stand up, then led them into
another room, a bedroom so small and dark he had
to light a lamp. The lamplight was a peculiar yellow,
Jennifer noticed. The room itself smelled of garlic
even worse than the front room had. And of rotten
eggs, too.

Against the wall stood a table with a sheet draped
over it, a clean white sheet, and on it were some
things that looked like earthenware jars painted in
different colors. The bed was only a cot, but close to
it were a second table and a chair, and on that table
was a model of their house, like a dollhouse, about
three feet high. A really good model, with every door
and window in the right place. When Joe saw it, he
stopped in mid-stride and said, "I'll be damned."

"I made it myself," Emile Migaud said. "In Haiti I
was a wood carver. You have been in that country,
perhaps?"

Haiti, Jennifer thought. Of course. There were
quite a few Haitians in Ft. Pierce now, just like in
Miami. And she knew a little about their homeland.
Had even read a book about that West Indian country
once, from the library, after seeing a movie about
Haitian voodoo. They spoke French there, and a kind
of French called Creole.

She stepped closer to the table and saw, next to the
house, a mayonnaise jar half full of milky liquid. That
was where the rotten-egg smell was coming from, she
realized, and alongside the jar lay one of those plastic
tubes with a rubber bulb on one end, for basting meat.

Mr. Migaud reached out to the house and opened one of its tiny kitchen windows. "At your house this very moment," he said, "this same window is opening."

He closed it. "Now it is shut," he said. "But if you live there, you know what has been happening. One night I put both hands on the house and shook it. I am so sorry. I must have frightened you terribly."

Joe clenched a fist and stepped toward the man, but Emile Migaud stopped him by holding up both hands and saying, "Wait, wait. Please hear me first."

Joe stood still and slowly let his breath out. Like he was lowering a loaded gun, Jennifer thought.

"Let me tell you why I did these terrible things to you," the little man said. "But first I must close your garage door. I opened it just before you arrived."

The garage door on the model *was* open, Jennifer saw. Mr. Migaud reached out and pulled it down, then sank onto his cot and sadly shook his head at them.

"You see how I live," he said. "In my country I was poor, too—wood carving is not a way to become rich—but I was a respected houngan in my village. Do you know what a houngan is? No, of course you don't, not even if you think you do. You would know only what you have seen in bad American movies, about sticking pins in dolls. But never mind. I came here because life in Haiti under the Duvaliers was not good, not good at all.

"Here I was still a poor man," he went on. "Perhaps even poorer than in Haiti. But I worked hard and saved every penny, as you can see by the way I live, and at last I had enough money to buy a small piece of land and have a decent house built. There is a woman I am fond of, you see—a woman I would ask to come and live with me but not here, not in this miserable house, only in something better. This far do you understand?"

"Yes," Jennifer said. "Go on."

"So, having bought the piece of land, I hired Mr. Kelly Burdick to build the house I wanted," the Haitian continued. "And it was a good house, it was fine, I loved it, until one day when it was almost finished, a Mr. Desmond Shartz came to me and said my house was on the wrong lot. We had built it not on my lot but on the one next to mine, which belonged to Mr. Shartz." He spread his hands, palms up, and looked at them with a wetness in his eyes, one of which Jennifer now realized she had seen at home, peering through the bedroom window at her.

"I think I can guess the rest," Joe said quietly.

"You have met Mr. Shartz? But, of course, if he sold you the house. He is a wicked man, that one. Both lots were exactly alike and we could simply have exchanged deeds, you understand. But he would not. The house belonged to him because he owned the land it was built on, he said. I thought—I swear to you, I thought he meant to live in it."

"Instead, he sold it to us," Jennifer said. "And all these things that you've been doing to get even with him were done to us."

"All I wanted was to make him afraid to live there," Emile Migaud said. "To make him move out of the house because it was rightfully my house. But now, of course, I will stop." He peered at Jennifer. "You are expecting a child, madame? You are pregnant?"

"Yes, I am."

"Then you must take this as a gift from me." He reached for the house on the table.

Joe's yell shook the whole room as he grabbed the man's hand in midair, *"Don't do that!"* he boomed. "You'll lift our house off its slab! Take the curse off first, for God's sake!"

Emile Migaud smiled. "There is no curse on my little toy here, mon ami. It has no power of its own. The power is here." He freed his hand from Joe's grip and tapped his forehead, then lifted the model house from the table and offered it to Jennifer. "Take it as my atonement, madame. For your child to play with."

Joe stared at him. "The power is in your head?"

"In my mind, m'sieu. But you would not understand. Here in America you only think you know about such things. Take the house. Do not be afraid. It will not harm you again."

"Well, thank you," Jennifer said.

"Wait," Joe said. "What about Shartz? I don't like that bastard. I knew from the start there was something shady about him. So will you still keep after him?"

The man from Haiti sighed and shook his head. "I think not. But perhaps someday he will be punished as he deserves."

They said good-bye to Mr. Migaud and Joe carried the little house out to the car, where he placed it carefully on the rear seat. Jennifer was already calling it "the baby's dollhouse." On the way home they talked a lot about little Emile Migaud and his attempt to even the score with Desmond Shartz.

At one point on the journey, Joe said with a frown, "You know, I hope he really did close our garage door. If he didn't, some prowler could have got into the house."

He needn't have worried. The garage door was closed.

It must have come down hard, too. Because Desmond Shartz, who had promised to come and look around, lay under it in a pool of drying blood, with his head crushed.

ON HARPER'S ROAD

by William F. Nolan

Joanna Morland was a cynic. Her cynicism had been born when she was very young, amplified by unloving parents and nurtured by a town that didn't seem to give a damn about her. She had never believed in Santa Claus. Or the Easter Bunny. To her, fairy tales were nonsense and the classic Disney films saccharine and ridiculous. In *Bambi,* when the young deer's mother was shot to death by the hunters, and the other children in the theater were all sobbing around her, Joanna was tearless; the death of her own mother, some years later, left her equally unmoved.

Her parents were, in fact, totally alien to her. She had never been given proper care or attention. Her father was a ruthless, poorly educated man who had financially destroyed his longtime partner in order to gain control of a small local hardware store. Her mother, cut of the same amoral cloth, always agreed with her father; he totally dominated her life. Joanna harbored a cold contempt for them both. In the family, she loved only her "Gramps," Joanna's grandfather on her mother's side. (Her father's parents were both deceased.) He, too, felt alone in the world, his wife having died in 1961, the same year in which Joanna was born. When things got too bad at home, Joanna would run over to Gramps' house and he would soothe and comfort her.

She had only one school friend, Linda Whittaker,

and in no way were they like other teenagers. Both of them hated popular music and had no interest in going to movies. They refused to "run around" with the local boys (whom they considered to be "terminally stupid"). Instead, they spent their time together playing classical music (Linda was crazy for Bach; Joanna favored the Hungarian rhapsodies of Franz Liszt). And they would read the short stories of Ernest Hemingway aloud to one another. They liked Hemingway because his stories had the ring of hard truth about them, at least the early ones did, the stories he wrote in Paris.

Joanna had grown up in Oakvale, a small town east of Kansas City in the Missouri heartland, and for the first eighteen years of her life had seldom ventured beyond the town limits. (She'd been to Kansas City just twice, on trips with her father.) When both of her parents were killed in a highway car crash in 1975, and her grandfather expired of a heart attack shortly after the accident, Joanna found herself suddenly alone in the ugly, drafty house on Flora Avenue. She had inherited no money, only the house and her father's debts at the store.

By then, she had come to detest the stifling, mean-spirited atmosphere of Oakvale and (in desperation) had married Jack Bryson, a big-boned, gawky boy she'd known since grade school. There was no love involved, at least not on Joanna's part. Jack had been promised a foreman's job in his father's Chicago refrigeration plant, and shortly after high school graduation he took his new bride with him to Illinois.

Life in the big city was exciting for Joanna, but Jack wasn't. He was a bully, and he drank too much. They got a divorce two years after their arrival in Chicago. Joanna had worked, during the marriage, as a low-paid ad writer for a very small city newspaper, the kind you pick up free in all night coffee shops. She

went to New York to join an agency that specialized
in auto accounts, starting as a secretary. But her abil-
ity to write outstanding copy was quickly recognized
and, on her thirty-first birthday (in early October of
1992), she was promoted to the position of senior vice
president.

That was the same day Joanna saw the Gypsy fortune teller in Greenwich Village. She was visiting the
old woman as part of a research project, her "crystal
ball ad campaign" for the Ford Motor Company
("You are destined to own a new Ford!"). Madame
Olga startled Joanna by telling her that, within the
month, she'd be "going home."

"Me? Go back to Oakvale? That's ridiculous. I
haven't gone back once since I left thirteen years ago.
There's nothing for me in Oakvale."

The old woman raised her shadowed eyes, scanning
Joanna's face. "Yet I *see* you there . . . on Harper's
Road . . . trapped in a storm."

Joanna smiled. Impossible. Harper's Road had been
permanently closed when she was still in high school.
Although it led from the main highway directly into
town, the road was impassable in heavy rains; the surface quickly turned to sticky gumbo and cars would
mire down, buried to the bumpers in thick yellow
mud. Faced with the expense of paving Harper's
Road, the City Council had voted to close it, and
heavy wooden gates had been placed at each end,
sealing it off to traffic. Some of the local kids would
come in from the open fields flanking the road and
race their bicycles over the dirt. More often than not,
they were caught by the police and taken home to
angry parents. By now, thought Joanna, the old road
would be so overgrown that driving on it would be out
of the question. (It had taken on a legendary status in
Oakvale. "Odd" things were said to have happened
there. Kids and animals were rumored to have disap-

peared during storms in the area—but Joanna had never believed any of these fanciful tales.)

Naturally, she dismissed the Gypsy's prediction. Joanna was far too cynical to believe in fortune telling. But she did get some good photos of the old crone gazing into a crystal ball. She'd turn these over to a sketch artist at the agency with her ideas for rough copy.

It would all work out fine.

That night she had the dream again. About her mother's red necklace. The dream was always the same. . . .

She was running. In darkness. In a fierce thunder storm. Rain slashed down at her like a thousand tiny knives, sharp enough to cut her flesh. Lightning forked the sky, sizzling silver bolts of electricity, reminding her of Frankenstein's castle—the one in the late night movie she'd seen on TV. Wet grass whipped at her legs and the ground was soft and spongy beneath her running feet, like the body of an immense animal.

Then, suddenly, the way things happen in dreams, she was inside some vast structure with the rain fisting the roof, trying to reach her, to cut her with its sharp, daggered drops. She was trapped here, in this dim, openfloored structure (a garage, perhaps?), totally vulnerable, quaking with fear.

A figure advanced toward her—her mother—unclipping a heavy red-bead necklace, the one she usually wore when they went out. Someone behind Joanna grabbed her, pinning her arms. She screamed as her mother looped the necklace around Joanna's neck. Then, relentlessly, her mother began to tighten the loop, eyes fired with fierce determination. Joanna felt the beads of the necklace bite deeply into her flesh.

At this point in the dream she would abruptly

awaken, hands to her throat, gasping and choking, tears running down her face. And it was like that now. She sat up in bed, shaking from the horrible intensity of the nightmare.

She got up. It was two a.m. A clear night, with the stars out. Joanna walked into the bathroom to wash her tear-streaked face, then returned to bed. But she couldn't sleep for the remainder of the night.

At the agency the next morning she received a phone call. From Jason Whittaker, Linda's father. His voice was low and strained. "Linda's in the hospital," he told her, "dying of cancer. The doctor says she won't last out the week. She's been asking for you." He hesitated. "You're the only one she wants to see."

Joanna didn't hesitate. She booked the next flight to Kansas City. Oakvale didn't have an airport, and trains no longer stopped there. She planned to rent a car in K.C. and drive out.

It was only when she was on the plane, airborne, that she thought of Madame Olga.

Just as the old Gypsy had predicted, Joanna Morland was "going home."

The sky above Kansas City was gray and somber with the threat of an oncoming storm when Joanna drove away from the airport in her rented Ford Probe.

She headed due east, driving fast, her mind tracking memories of Linda . . . of the long sunlit afternoons when they played chess in Joanna's small bedroom on Flora . . . of the school production when Joanna had been in charge of the ketchup for Shakespeare's bloody *Macbeth* and Linda had played Macbeth's treacherous wife ("Out, out, damned spot!") . . . of Linda's rapturous smile as they listened to one of Bach's Brandenburg concertos . . . of the Sunday picnic when a line of ants had climbed under Linda's

skirt when she was dozing in the sun. (Oh, how she'd
hopped and danced around slapping at those ants!)

And now she was dying at thirty-one in a bed at
Oakvale Hospital. My God, why hadn't they at least
sent her to a modern facility in K.C. for treatment?

It was late afternoon when Joanna encountered the
paint-flaked metal sign on the outskirts of town:

HOWDY, NEIGHBOR!
WELCOME TO OAKVALE!
HEART OF THE GREAT MIDWEST
A FRIENDLY TOWN OF FRIENDLY FOLKS

Joanna had always found the sign ironic, with its
bright words of good cheer in sharp contrast to the
meanness of spirit lurking beneath Oakvale's placid
surface.

Then, instead of turning left onto the two-lane access highway leading into town, she found herself ac-
celerating, heading toward the old route. . . .

Toward Harper's Road.

This is crazy, Joanna told herself. Why are you
doing this when Linda is dying at the hospital and
might not last out the day? Joanna couldn't justify her
action; there was no rational way to explain this sudden, overwhelming impulse.

I have to see it again. Have to.

At the gate blocking the entrance to Harper's Road
(WARNING! THIS ROAD IS CLOSED! NO TRES-
PASSING!), Joanna got out of her car, opened the
trunk, and removed the tire iron. With this, she
smashed at the large metal padlock securing the gate.
Three blows did the job and the rusted lock snapped
open. Struggling against the heavy brush which had
grown around it, she strained at the wooden gate.
Pushed it wide. There! Done!

But why? Why are you doing this?

Without attempting to give herself an answer, Joanna got back into the Probe and drove onto Harper's Road.

Trees lined it to either side, next to a sagging split-rail wooden fence—solid black oaks and heavy maples, their fat limbs scraping the top of the Ford as Joanna drove deeper into the storm-threatened afternoon. The day had turned dark and ominous, with swollen rainclouds now cloaking the sky.

She had been right about the years of unchecked growth. The road was wildly overgrown and full of deep ruts. Navigating it, the Ford wallowed and pitched like a ship in choppy seas.

Then the October storm which had been hovering over the area since she'd left Kansas City broke with a tigerish roar of thunder and savage, down-rushing sheets of steel-colored rain. A ragged spear of lightning split the stretched fabric of sky, like the flashbulb on a giant's camera.

Another few minutes of this and the packed dirt under her tires would turn to clinging sludge, as treacherous as a bed of quicksand.

Joanna still had time to put the car into reverse and back out to the paved highway. But she didn't. It was as if she were compelled to fulfill the old Gypsy woman's prediction ". . . on Harper's Road . . . trapped in a storm."

The wheels of the Probe were rapidly losing traction, the tires beginning their whining spin in the mud. Soon she'd be completely mired down; it was now too late to reverse direction.

Then she remembered the old Hennessey place. An abandoned farm, with the main house fallen to ruin, but with the feed barn intact. At least, it would serve to shelter her until the storm passed.

Within moments, she saw it ahead of her—a tall,

age-slanted wooden structure a few hundred feet left of the road.

Joanna pulled to a stop, cut the engine, and eased out into the mud. Immediately, she sank to her ankles, with the cold rain pelting her skin. The wild grass was waist high, clinging and slapping at her as she cleared the fence and ran awkwardly for the barn.

Forcing open the wide door, she ducked inside. Countless gaps in the badly-weathered roof admitted chilled gusts of rain; a damp odor of mold permeated the barn's interior.

Maybe I should have stayed in the car, she told herself. This place is—

Her thoughts were abruptly shattered by a cannon blast of thunder, followed by an impossibly bright radiance; the crackling explosion from above told Joanna that a bolt of lightning had struck the barn, deflected and absorbed by the rooster-shaped lightning rod mounted on the roof.

Instinctively, she had closed her eyes against the fierce assault, and when she opened them again . . .

The storm had gone.

No rain.

No thunder.

Nothing but silence.

No! This was beyond logical reason. A major rainstorm doesn't blow over in an instant.

Yet when Joanna stepped into the outside yard a full moon rode the clear evening sky and a net of silver stars shimmered above her.

Stunned, she walked back to the rail fence, slipped through it, and climbed behind the wheel of the Ford. Joanna started the engine, engaged gear, and the car began rolling forward.

Harper's Road was now passable. The surface on this end stretch was stable, providing ample traction for the tires. And the road was oddly free of overgrowth.

She didn't question this. It seemed right somehow. Then she rememberedthat Linda was waiting for her at Oakvale Hospital.

She had to hurry.

The road took her straight into town. (No gate at the other end; perhaps it had been vandalized.) Oakvale's only hospital was a three-story building of smoked red brick topping the hill at Wornell and Prospect. Joanna had been born there.

Crossing the lobby, she approached a dour-faced nurse at the reception desk.

The nurse didn't look up. She kept writing in a small white pad, her head down as she spoke to Joanna. "May I help you?"

"I've come to see Linda Whittaker. It's urgent."

"Does she work here at the hospital?" Head still lowered over the pad. Scribbling.

"No, no. She's a cancer patient. In critical condition. You've probably got her in Intensive Care. She's been asking to see me."

The nurse finally looked up, sighed, pushed aside the pad, and began leafing through the admissions book. "We have no patient here named Whittaker."

"You must have. There's some mistake."

The nurse stared at her. "There's no Whittaker here," she repeated.

Had they taken Linda to Kansas City after all? But not now. Not with her *dying!*

Joanna decided the best thing to do at this point was to go see Linda's father. After all, Jason Whittaker was the one who'd phoned her.

The house was just seven blocks from the hospital, on Harrison, a big Southern-style mansion, set well back from the street, with a white wooden veranda built around its exterior. The yard was beautifully kept, the bushes neatly trimmed—the work of a full-time gardener. Mr. Whittaker was President of the Oakvale Bank, and the family had always been well off.

When the door opened, Jason Whittaker was there behind the screen, looking not a day older than the last time she'd seen him. Well, some people don't age as fast as others.

He scowled at her over his reading glasses. "If you're selling anything, we don't—"

"I'm Joanna," she said. (After all, it *had* been thirteen years.) "I came as soon as I could get a flight to Kansas City—right after your call. But Linda wasn't at the hospital. Did you have her moved?"

Whittaker looked confused. "Call? Hospital? I don't know what the devil you're talking about, young lady. And I sure don't know *you*."

"But you phoned me in New York about Linda—about her cancer—and that she was asking for me."

Whittaker stared at her. "My daughter is in perfect health—and I've no time for this nonsense." He stepped back from the screen, firmly shutting the heavy oak door.

Joanna hesitated, then stumbled down the veranda steps. Dazedly, she returned to the Ford, wondering if this was another of her nightmares. Am I just *dreaming* I've come back to Oakvale?

No, damnit! This is all real. The street, house, the car—*all real.*

But the ultimate reality lay ahead . . . .

Keying the ignition, Joanna put the Probe in gear and drove toward Flora Avenue. Toward the shoddy, one-story frame house she had abandoned thirteen years ago. She'd never tried to sell it after the death of her parents; even when they were all living there together it had needed major restoration. Joanna hadn't cared to spend the money to have it fixed properly. Cheaper to have the house torn down and put

the lot up for sale. Someday she intended to do that.
But, for now, it was a boarded-over time-weathered
relic of her past.

Except it *wasn't*.

She parked directly in front of the house, staring at
it. No boards on the windows. A trimmed yard. Lights
glowing warmly from the living room in the late evening's darkness.

Suddenly chilled, Joanna crossed the yard and
mounted the wooden porch steps. She stood there,
feeling lost and helpless. Somehow, she couldn't bring
herself to knock at her own door.

She'd been heard. The porch light bloomed to life
and the inner door opened. A heavyset woman peered
at her from behind the locked screen. "Who's *out*
there?"

Her mother. Alive! Exactly as Joanna remembered
her.

She didn't know how this could be, how such an
impossible situation could exist—but she *accepted* it.
And, in that instant of acceptance, she felt that in
order to survive, to keep from losing her mind, she
must establish her own individual identity, her own
subjective reality.

"I'm your daughter," she told the woman behind
the screen. "I'm Joanna." She paused, searching for
words of explanation. "I—I came here from . . . your
future . . . from 1992 . . . through some kind of . . .
I don't know . . . a kind of 'time gate,' I guess . . .
out on Harper's Road." She drew in a nervous breath.
"Mama, I swear I'm telling you the truth. I swear it!
I *am* your daughter."

"You're crazy, is what you are," snapped Doris
Morland. "I got me just one kid, an' she's eleven
years old. Up to her room right this minute, doin' her
studies. Now, you get the hell off this porch or I'll
call the law!"

"Shut up and let her in!" Joanna recognized the harsh voice from the dimness of the hallway. A dark figure was silhouetted against the wash of yellow light from the living room.

"Daddy . . . is that *you?*"

"Yeah, it's me all right." He stepped forward to unlatch the screen. "C'mon in, girl."

He was precisely as she remembered him: tall and angular, with hard eyes and a tight, cruel mouth. "—Well, don't just *stand* there. C'mon inside."

Joanna stepped into the house, into her past, into a world she had always hated and feared.

She was baffled at her father's casual acceptance of this incredibly bizarre situation. It was almost impossible for *her* to accept, despite all the tangible evidence.But her *father.* . . .

Ned Morland smiled, showing the gold tooth in his upper jaw. There was no warmth in the smile, only a cool irony. "You're wonderin' how come I believe you so quick an' easy. That right, girl?"

"Why *do* you?" she asked. "I wouldn't—in your place."

"I been expectin' ya, *knew* you'd show up." He nodded, sitting down on the overstuffed living room sofa (it still needed upholstering) while she remained standing near the hallway door. Her mother hovered at Ned's shoulder, pale and quiet. "Last summer, at the county fair," Ned Morland continued, "I went into this little tent they had set up, with an old Gypsy woman inside who told fortunes. Called herself Madame Olga."

Joanna felt a sharp chill sweep through her. The *same* woman! How could it be?

"She had me sit down at a fancy table in front of this big shiny crystal ball an' she told me all about you . . . how you'd be comin' home from the future, to Oakvale. In the fall, in October, she said. You'd take old Harper's Road an' it would send you right home. Way she said it, the way her eyes locked inta me, I knew it would happen. Yessir, just damn well knew it. Some things ya just don't question."

"You and Mama . . ." Joanna spoke slowly. "You both died—"

"—in a car crash." He nodded again. "In 1975, three years from now. That's when the old Gypsy said it was gonna happen." He rubbed a fist thoughtfully along one side of his stubbled cheek. "Unless, that is . . ."

"Unless what?"

"Unless I stop it. Keep it from happenin'."

Joanna stared at him. "What are you saying?"

"I'm sayin' you got to die, girl. To save us, me and your Mama here." He reached up to squeeze his wife's hand. "It's real plain, how the Gypsy spelled it all out. We kill you now an' that car crash don't happen. What we do here in your past changes *our* future. You die an' we go on livin'. Just like the Gypsy said."

"That's *insane!*" gasped Joanna, backing away. "My death won't save you."

"How do you know that?" asked Ned Morland. He stood up, his hands fisted, walked over to her. "If everthin' else that old Gypsy bitch said come true, an' it *has,* then why not this, too? Makes sense ta me." He swung his head back toward his wife. "What about you, Dorry?"

Doris Morland nodded slowly, eyes bright as a bird of prey. "I don't claim to understand none a' this, not a whit, but . . ." She peered closely at Joanna. "You know best, Ned. You always know best. I'll do what you think we ought." And she fingered the red-bead necklace at her fleshy throat.

"Me an' your Mama here was about to go out," he said. "Figgered to look around the new shopping center some, then get us a bite to eat. But all that can wait." He put a big-knuckled hand on Joanna's shoulder. "Right now, let's just us all take a little ride in that fancy car a' yours." And, once again, he smiled. "Out to Harper's Road."

They forced Joanna to drive. Her father sat next to her, with her mother in the back seat.

Joanna was rigid with fear. She had always been afraid of her parents. They were violent, cruel people who had never shown tenderness or compassion. For her, or for anyone else. But the idea that they were willing to commit *murder*—to kill their own daughter—was beyond comprehension.

Yet it was happening.

The Probe bumped its way onto Harper's Road, tires digging into the packed dirt.

"Head for the old Hennessey place," her father told her. "It's got to be done there in the barn. Just like the Gypsy said." He nodded. "Gotta do this proper."

Despite her fear, Joanna was taut with anger. "You're just as I remembered you, Daddy," she said. "You're a miserable bastard! Never wanted me, never loved me or did anything to make me love you. And Mama always siding with you against me—just the way she's doing tonight."

"Wife's gotta stand by her husband," nodded Doris Morland. Her voice was soft, placid. "Ned's the man a' the house—an' I was taught a woman stands by her man."

Joanna glared at her. "Even when it comes to murder?"

"Well, my goodness, honey," declared her mother, "it's not really murder. You don't *exist*—not here in 1972 you don't. So how can we be killin' a person who don't exist?"

"Your mama's right," agreed Ned Morland. "Way I figger things, the Gypsy sent you back to us so's we could stay alive." He grinned in the darkness. "Shoot, maybe we'll end up bein' immortal! Never *been* a case like this—chance to change the future an' all. No sir. Never been."

The car jolted to a stop. Just beyond the fence, the tall bulk of the Hennessey barn loomed against the sky.

They got out. The night air was cold. A wind was rising. Another storm was due to break.

"You first under the fence," said Joanna's father, directing her with a flashlight. "Your Mama an' me, we'll be right behind ya."

Joanna decided to run. But where? To Gramps! Impossible. To him, she was an eleven-year-old child. He'd never believe her story about coming here from the future. But she *had* to try.

Had to.

And she ran.

Her father caught her easily, just beyond the rail fence. Ned Morland gripped her arm hard, digging into her flesh. He hurried her toward the barn. Joanna moved mechanically, fear numbing her. The door was opened and she was pushed inside.

With the door closed behind them, Ned gestured to his wife. "This is where you do it, Dorry."

"Me?" Doris Morland looked uneasy. "I thought you was gonna do it."

"The Gypsy said you was to be the one to strangle her. With that." And he pointed to her heavy red-bead necklace.

Now, finally, Joanna understood her dream. *This* was the killing place! Dark, with open flooring all around. Not a garage . . . a barn.

"Well," sighed her mother, unclipping the necklace, "if this is the proper way. . . ."

Frantically, Joanna looked around for a weapon, something with which to defend herself. A pitchfork stood in one corner, near the hayrack, its tines glimmering faintly in the illumination from Ned Morland's flash. If she could just reach the pitchfork. . .

But her father's rough-fingered hands closed on her arms, pinning them, holding her vise-tight. "All right, Dorry. Let's get to it."

As she had always done in her nightmare, when the bead necklace was looped around her, Joanna screamed.

Her mother said, "Hold her, Ned. She's squirmin' like a fish!"

The beads of the necklace bit deeply into Joanna's neck as her mother tightened the loop.

Then the storm hit.

Thunder like a collision of freight trains. Rain assaulting the roof in blowing, savage gusts.

And lightning.

It was the lightning that did it. To Doris and Ned. Stabbing down from the sky in jagged fury, blasting them to the barn floor in mounds of writhing, sizzling flesh. The interior of the barn danced with electrical energies, bright as day.

Joanna reeled back, squeezing her eyes shut against the dazzling illumination.

Then darkness again.

And silence.

Joanna opened her eyes.

The barn floor was empty.

The rain had stopped.

The storm was gone.

She ran wildly for the road, thrashing her way through the high grass, slipped under the rail fence, pulled herself, sobbing, gasping, almost breathless, into the Ford, fired the engine, began roaring forward . . . stopped. . . .

She knew that there would now be a locked gate at the town end of Harper's Road.

She put the Probe into reverse and backed out. The dirt was solid beneath her tires, just as she knew it would be, and the highway gate, with its broken padlock, stood open for her.

It was over. She had returned from her nightmare.

No . . .

Joanna looked down at the red-bead necklace still clutched in her right hand.

. . . not a nightmare.

Reality.

OUTSIDE THE WINDOWS

by Pamela Sargent

A diner next to a gas station was the small town's only bus stop. John gazed out of his window as the driver paced near the bus. No passengers had boarded here. The driver stomped out his cigarette, then climbed back inside.

Three boys raced across the two-lane road, followed by an unleashed collie. There was little traffic here; John had seen only three cars and a panel truck moving along the street. People, he thought, should be more careful anyway. Letting dogs off their leashes was risky, and lots of children had never been taught to cross roads safely.

A white Victorian house marked the edge of the town. The bus rolled on, then passed a sign marking the way back to the interstate. John was sure the driver usually took that turn, but instead the bus continued along the narrow road. He had not taken this particular bus in over a year, but couldn't see why the company would change the route. The interstate would get the bus to its final destination in two hours; this old road would add at least one more hour to the trip.

"Don't know the way," a stocky gray-haired man sitting across the aisle muttered. His companion, an old bald man in a plaid shirt, nodded glumly. The stocky man leaned toward John. "That driver don't know the way," he continued. "Missed his turn."

"Are you sure?" John asked. "Maybe they changed the route."

"Make no sense to change the route." The man leaned back in his seat and folded his arms; the bald man next to him scowled. Apparently neither of them was going to alert the driver to his error, however annoyed they might be. This road would get them to where they were going, and they did not look like men with pressing engagements. John peered up the aisle. A big auburn-haired woman was the passenger nearest the driver, but from the way her head was lopsidedly resting against her seat, he guessed that she was asleep.

The driver probably was lost. It wouldn't surprise him; the company had been bringing in drivers from other parts of the country to take the places of those still on strike. John was fairly certain that they would soon come to another sign directing them to the interstate, and that the driver would realize his mistake then.

The sun was dropping toward the western hills; the trees were beginning to show red and orange foliage. A wooded slope suddenly blocked his view. On the interstate, the countryside had seemed spacious, the towns only distant clusters of buildings nestled in hollows. Along this winding road, the hills were barriers hiding what lay ahead.

Air travel was bad enough, John thought, but buses were much worse, and that damned strike hadn't helped. This trip was too short to justify a plane ticket, and the train had been discontinued some time back. He hadn't expected much comfort, but this rattling bus with its lousy shocks should have been retired long ago. People were forced into driving cars, with so few other ways to get to where they were going. Sometimes it seemed to him that vehicles operated the people behind their wheels, rather than the other way around, that the metallic beasts had claimed the world.

The bus suddenly swerved; its horn blared. John clutched at his armrest as the trees to his left swelled; their leafy limbs reached toward him as an invisible hand threw him back. He heard a loud, wet smack against the front of the bus before the horn sounded again.

"For crying out loud," the gray-haired man across from John shouted. The bus hurtled on for several yards, then slowed as the driver pulled over and parked along the shoulder of the narrow road. John looked down at his hands, surprised to find that they were shaking.

The driver opened the door, got up, and left the bus. The other passengers were silent. The big woman near the front of the bus was awake now, leaning across the aisle to say something to the boy in the next seat. John recalled the wet, splattering sound and closed his eyes for a moment.

"What happened?" a voice said behind him. John moved to the seat on the aisle and looked back. A young woman in a down vest and jeans was getting up from her seat; she shook back her long blonde hair. "What's going on?"

The big auburn-haired woman rose slowly to her feet. "He hit a dog," she announced in a hoarse voice as she turned toward the back of the bus. "A big black dog—looked like a Lab to me. Run right into him."

"Is he hurt?" A young black woman wearing a Cornell University sweatshirt was speaking; she was sitting next to the blonde. "Is he dead?"

"I don't know," the big woman replied. "The way we hit him—I don't know. He just run right out in front—didn't look like he even saw us coming. I'll go see."

"I wanna see, too," the boy near her shouted.

"Then come along."

The boy followed the woman off the bus. The child, who looked about nine years old, was traveling by himself; John had seen a wan, brown-haired woman hug him, then press a luggage claim ticket into his hand. The big woman had been keeping an eye on him since then.

"Gross," the blonde college student murmured. John assumed that she and her sweat-shirted companion were students, with their duffels, jeans, and thick economics textbooks. "Why would he want to see something like that?"

"Good thing the driver stopped," the stocky gray-haired man said. "I thought he was just going to barrel ahead." The bald man next to him nodded. "If he had, the state troopers would have radioed ahead and pulled him off at the next stop and we'd be sitting around for God knows how long. Guess he thought better of that. This way, we might lose an hour, maybe."

A young man in a leather jacket came down the aisle and left the bus. "We're going to lose more than an hour," John said, "if that driver doesn't get back to the highway."

"Could be. I meant we might lose an hour on top of whatever other time we lose."

John stood up, stretched, then decided to go outside. At this rate, he wouldn't have time to do more than call the district manager before he went to bed. John's supervisor sometimes kidded him about his eccentricity, as did the others in the home office. Luckily, he did not have to take that many business trips, and usually went by air when he did. It gave his co-workers something else to gossip about, his insistence on cabs rather than rented cars, the apartment he had moved into so that he would no longer have to drive to work.

John stepped down to the ground, then took a deep breath of the cool autumn air. The three passengers who had already left the bus were standing by the rear of the vehicle. Farther down the road, the bus driver stood near a fence talking to another man. A long driveway wound up a hill toward a large gray house; John glimpsed a woman and child on the porch.

He walked toward the other passengers. "I don't see the dog," he said.

"He got drug off the road." The big woman pointed. "That must be the owner. He came and drug the dog off the road—he was a Lab, sure enough." She pulled her long brown coat more tightly around herself. "That dog's dead."

A gray car with emblems on its doors passed the bus, then pulled up next to the two men in the distance; a uniformed man got out. "There's the cops," the boy said as he tugged at his baseball cap. "What'll they do?"

"Probably not much," the young man in the leather jacket replied. "Ask questions, maybe write out a report." His mouth hung open after he stopped talking, as if he had simply forgotten to close it.

"It weren't the driver's fault," the woman said. "I woke up just before he hit. That dog was standing by the road, and then he run right out in front like he didn't even see us coming. The driver tried to miss him, but he run right out in front. Must of killed him right away, the way we hit, but it really weren't his fault."

"He was going kind of fast." The young man brushed back a strand of his long brown hair, then thrust his hands into his pockets.

"He weren't going over the speed limit."

"He was going the wrong way, though. Why didn't he head back to the highway?"

"I would of told him to, if I'd been awake. Why didn't somebody else pipe up?"

John wandered away from the others and their pointless discussion. The policeman was writing in a notebook; the bus driver shifted from one foot to the other as he spoke to the dog's owner. The trees near the house swayed as the wind picked up; the woman and child who had been standing on the porch had gone inside. The child would be crying, his mother trying to console him.

He turned and walked back to the bus, then climbed inside. "Anything going on?" the stocky gray-haired man asked.

"A policeman's there," John said as he sat down. "The owner seems to be talking to the driver calmly enough, so we should be on our way soon." He looked back at the college students. "I couldn't see the dog. That redheaded woman said the owner dragged him off the road."

"This is all we needed," the blonde student said. "Some poor dog going about his business, then getting hit by a bus."

"Chill out, Sloane," the black student said.

John settled back in his seat. He had brought some work in his briefcase, but felt too distracted to pull it out. The incident had unnerved him. He wouldn't have been on the damned bus in the first place if those penny-pinchers in Accounting had been willing to cough up enough for a plane ticket.

The leather-jacketed man came back aboard the bus, followed by the big woman and the boy. "Don't you worry none, Ted," the woman said.

"Tad," the boy said. "My name's Tad."

"Well, don't you worry none, Tad. I'm sure your father'll wait till the bus gets there."

The boy took one of the seats in front of John, then leaned over the armrest to peer back at the other

passengers. The big woman sat across from the boy.
The passengers were all grouped in the middle of the
bus now, as if hoping for reassurance from one another. John opened his briefcase and rummaged
among his papers, hoping the others wouldn't try to
drag him into conversation.

The driver soon came back. He stood in the front,
rubbing at his face. "Er, we had a little accident," he
said, telling them what they already knew. "I tried to
avoid that dog, but if I'd gone any farther left, we'd
have gone off the road and into a ditch. I just thought
you ought to know. My responsibility's to my passengers." He looked around thirty years old, and had a
southern accent. John wondered if he was an experienced driver or a strikebreaker the company was still
training. "We'll be running about half an hour late.
Sorry for the delay." He wiped his brow, then turned
to sit down. John pitied him a little. Obviously shaken
by the accident, he would still have to drive the bus
to its destination.

The bus rolled back onto the road. The sky was
growing darker; dusk shadowed the trees and made
the distant hills look black. John turned on the light
above him, then pulled out his newspaper.

"They shouldn't let dogs run around near roads like
this," the young man in the leather jacket said from
the seat just behind John's.

"Well, there isn't that much traffic." John recognized the black student's voice. "If it had been my
dog, I would have assumed—"

"He might have been old, maybe going deaf," the
blonde student said. "Dogs can't see very well, and
maybe this one couldn't hear well, either. Poor thing."

The big woman leaned out from her seat. "Look at
it this way." Her voice was loud enough to be heard
above the bus's engine. "Thank the good Lord it

weren't a human being." John's hands tightened on
his newspaper.

He looked toward his window, unable to concen-
trate on reading. The unfortunate incident had apparently given his fellow travelers a sense of camaraderie;
they would probably review the matter during the rest
of the ride. The bus was slowing. An intersection lay
ahead, and another large sign marked "I-88" with an
arrow pointing east, but the driver continued along
the old road.

"Missed another way back," the stocky gray-haired
man said. "Somebody better tell that young fella what
to do."

"Don't look at me," the big woman replied. "I ain't
about to go up there and tell that man where to go.
He's probably jumpy enough already."

John stared at his paper. He could not get up and
move to another seat without seeming downright hostile; the only way to avoid getting drawn into the conversation was to pretend to be reading. He was about
to shift to the seat nearer the window when he saw
the dog.

The animal was standing at the side of the road near
a field. It was a large dog, a Labrador retriever, and
before John could wonder what it was doing in that
empty, overgrown stretch of land, the dog vanished.

"Whoa," somebody shouted. The boy named Tad
peered around his seat at John. "Did you see that,
mister? That dog—did you—"

"Lordy," the big woman cried. The dog was in the
aisle. It turned and trotted toward the front of the
bus, then disappeared.

John's mouth was dry. The driver, intent on his
driving, had apparently not seen the dog. John
glanced at the men across from him. The gray-haired
man gaped; the bald man was leaning over him and
staring into the aisle.

"What was that?" the young man behind John said. "What the hell—"

"A Lab." The big woman's hands tightened on her armrest. "A Lab, just like the one we hit."

"Jesus Christ."

"What's going on?" the blonde student called out. "Are we all going crazy?"

"Chill out, Sloane," her companion said.

"Holy shit, Liz, didn't you see it?"

"I saw it. Don't know what it was, but I saw it."

"It's a ghost," Tad said. "It's a ghost."

"Hush your mouth," the big woman said. "Whatever it is, won't do no good to start hollering about it." She looked back. "The driver didn't see it, and maybe we're just all kind of batty from what happened and all. We can sit here nice and quiet, or we can start acting up and get thrown off. Besides, it won't do the driver's nerves no good to have us all carrying on."

"You're talking sense, lady," the bald man said. "All we need is to get that driver even more upset."

All of the passengers had their seat lights on now. John wanted to turn his off, to slip into the illusory safety of darkness. The sun was still above the western hills, and there seemed to be nothing along this stretch of road except untilled fields and, in the distance, forested slopes. The bus had slowed; he wondered if the driver was worrying that he might hit something else. *The guy can't get back to the interstate,* he thought, *and now we're seeing ghost dogs.* Better if he had been the only one to see it; he could have explained it away as a delusion. To have everyone else see the dog was impossible. He was asleep, dreaming. That was the only explanation, but he didn't believe it.

"I am really freaked out," the student named Sloane murmured.

"It's all right, son," the big woman was saying to Tad.

A gray kitten had curled up near a shrub by the road. The bus was moving so slowly that John could see the small animal clearly, and then it was gone. No, he thought, not again.

The kitten winked into existence in the aisle; John heard a muffled moan behind him. The creature scurried past him; he followed it with his eyes. It stopped next to the leather-jacketed young man, then slowly faded away.

"Oh, my God." The young man ran a hand through his long brown hair. "That cat. It's like—" He glanced from the students to John. "I hit a cat once. Killed the poor little thing right off. This girl came out of her house—she was crying like she'd never stop. I'd been drinking, so I knew it was my fault. I said I'd buy her a new kitty cat, but it didn't do any good."

"This is totally weird," Sloane said.

John did not want to look out of his window, but found his head turning in that direction. A deer was out there, standing at the edge of a field, and then it was gone.

The deer took shape in the aisle. It was a small one, not much larger than a fawn. The deer's head turned toward the stocky gray-haired man; its soft dark eyes gazed at him steadily.

"That's ours," the man said calmly, "mine and Ralph's here." He gestured at his bald companion. "We were driving along, and this deer jumps out. Now, we should have been able to miss it, but the thing is, I was driving a little fast, and jawing with Ralph, and by the time I saw . . ."

"There were signs," Ralph said. "We noticed that later, when the car was towed. Deer crossing. Signs like that all over the place, but we weren't paying much attention."

John thought of going up to the driver and asking him to stop the bus. Let me off at the next town. Hell, let me off now, even if it's in the middle of nowhere. He felt bound to his seat, unable to move. Something else would be waiting outside, and he did not want to see what it might be.

The sun was setting; deep blue clouds were growing darker against the reddish sky. Up ahead, near a billboard advertising a motel, sat a Siberian husky. As the dog vanished, John heard a cry.

"Bessie!" Tad lunged from his seat as the husky appeared near him. "Bessie!" The dog became translucent as the boy stumbled into the aisle. The big woman caught Tad as the husky disappeared. "Bessie!"

"There, there," the woman said.

"She was my dog." Tad climbed into her lap. "A truck hit her." The boy was crying now. "Mom told me to keep her on the leash, and I didn't."

"Hush, son." The woman glanced toward the driver, who apparently had noticed nothing. "Don't cry. Bessie only came to tell you it's okay, that she's in dog heaven now." Tad wiped at his face, then straightened his cap. "It's all right. Can you go back to your seat?"

Tad got off her lap. "Jesus," Sloane said. "This is totally insane." Her voice rose. "Road kill spirits appearing in a bus. I can't take any more."

"Pipe down, young lady," the gray-haired man said. "You want to get us all thrown off?"

"I wouldn't mind." The blonde student crept forward, then squatted in the aisle. "We have to do something."

"Like what?" he asked.

"You're college girls, aren't you?" Ralph leaned across his companion. "You and your friend. You ought to know something. Maybe you can explain it."

"I don't know." Sloane frowned. "A mass delusion. Somehow, we're all seeing a mass delusion, but why? And why isn't the driver affected?"

"Be glad he ain't," Ralph said.

"They're outside," the young man behind John said, "and then they come in here. You can see 'em outside from this side, and then they come in here. It doesn't make sense."

"An optical illusion," Sloane said. "Maybe that's it. A trick of the light that makes something outside seem to disappear and then reflects it inside the bus."

"I don't believe it," Sloane's friend murmured. "Those animals looked too real for that. And why would they be ones all these folks recognize?" The young black woman bit her lip. "I'm scared."

John said, "We have to get back to the highway."

Sloane turned toward him; Ralph scowled. "The highway?" The bald man lifted his brows. "Think we'll stop seeing these critters if we get back on I-88?"

"It makes as much sense as anything else."

"You gonna tell the driver?"

They were all looking at him; the big woman narrowed her eyes. Sloane rose and went back to her seat; at last John stood up. "I'll tell him."

He moved toward the front and sat down in the seat nearest the door. "Uh, excuse me."

"What's the problem?" the driver asked.

"You're going the wrong way."

"What do you mean, the wrong way?" The bus was still moving slowly, probably doing no more than thirty-five.

John said, "You're on Route 7. You should be on I-88."

"Think I don't know where I am? Look." The driver paused. "I mean, look, they've got a crew on a big long stretch of I-88. That's what the dispatcher said. If we'd gone that way, we would have been moving about as slow, maybe slower. Now, my feeling is we'll probably make better time this way, which is what the dispatcher told me, and we'll be back on 88 as soon as we pass Sidney. You won't lose much time."

"Okay. Thanks for letting me know."

"Look, I know I had an accident, but that doesn't mean I don't know my business."

"Sorry."

"And tell your friends back there that there's no alcoholic beverages allowed on this bus, and no illegal substances, and no standing around or walking unless you have to use the can."

"What?"

"From the way you're all clumped together, looks like you're having a party or something."

"We're just talking. I'll tell them." John got to his feet. He should have known the driver would try to cover up his mistakes. It was easier to make up a story than to admit the truth. No wonder the man hadn't seen the ghost of the dog he had killed. He had repressed his guilt, putting it behind him, keeping his back turned to the evidence of his deed. John understood that kind of failing.

He was nearly to his seat when the next apparition appeared, a Siamese cat this time. It leaped gracefully to the big woman's armrest and faded away.

"That's mine." The woman clutched at John's sleeve. "Only thing I ever hit—gooshed the poor thing. I was in a hurry, and my mind weren't on my driving. Going along this street with houses and little kids playing and all—I knew I should have been more careful."

John freed himself. "I spoke to the driver," he said. "He's going to get back on the highway after we reach Sidney. Apparently there's some work going on along this stretch of I-88." He straightened his tie; his hands were shaking again. "We'd better settle down. He thinks we're all up to something back here."

"He see them animals?" the big woman asked.

"I'm sure he didn't. He would have mentioned it. I don't think he'd still be driving if he had."

"I've got a theory," the black student in the Cornell sweatshirt said. "I think—" She was silent for a while.

"Go on, Liz," her friend murmured.

"The driver had this accident, okay? Seems like the rest of us folks were responsible in some way for accidents recently, and this one's reminding us of them, and because we all feel guilty, we're seeing the victims. We're blaming ourselves unconsciously—that's why we're seeing them. And the driver isn't seeing what we are because his accident really wasn't his fault."

"But why are we all seeing them?" Sloane asked. "Why aren't we just seeing the ones we hit? Why are we seeing animals someone else hit?"

"I can't explain it," Liz replied, "but it's got to stop pretty soon, because there're only three of us left that haven't seen something we remember. Unless the rest of you hit a lot of animals."

"Never hit anything," the young man said, "except that kitty cat."

"Me neither," the big woman said.

"You college girls." The stocky man turned in his seat. "You ever hit anything?"

"Yes." Liz leaned across her friend. "And I think I see it now."

A white duck was waddling down the aisle, followed by three ducklings. Liz closed her eyes as the birds disappeared. "They were trying to cross the road, and I was going way over the speed limit. Suddenly, there they were, and I was going too fast to stop. It was horrible." She settled back against her seat. "If I'd only been going more slowly, I could have avoided them."

John gritted his teeth. "What about you, dearie?" the big woman asked Sloane. "Did you—"

A cocker spaniel scurried down the aisle, panted as it looked up at Sloane, then gradually faded away. "That dog," the blonde student said in a low voice. "I was arguing with my boyfriend, and then I hit that dog—I didn't even see him. I should have pulled over until we settled it. I can't even remember what we were fighting about."

John's mouth was dry. The world outside the window was black now. He thought of another night, hands clutching a wheel, the shriek of brakes, the thud, pebbles pinging against metal as a car raced away.

"I guess that leaves the fella over there," Ralph said.

John struggled to clear his throat. "I don't drive."

"What?" the big woman said.

"Says he don't drive."

"I don't drive," John repeated, remembering how slippery the wheel had been under his sweaty palms. He had kept his secret. His neck prickled; his face was hot.

He jumped to his feet, then staggered toward the driver. "Stop the bus," he shouted. The driver hit the brakes; John braced himself against a seat as the bus rolled to a stop.

"What's wrong with you people?" The driver got up and turned toward them. "Do I have to—"

John stumbled toward the door, thinking only that he had to get off the bus. The Labrador retriever appeared in the aisle, blocking his way, forcing him to take a seat. The driver stared at the dog, then covered his face as the animal disappeared.

"I guess he felt guilty after all," Liz whispered.

The bus was parked along the side of the road. John saw the little girl then, on the other side of a ditch. A knife seemed to twist inside him.

He wrenched himself away from the window. She was moving toward him along the aisle; her short black hair framed her face and her hands held a doll. She stopped by his seat and gazed at him for a long time. He felt the others watching him, and thought he heard someone curse at him.

The ghostly child drew her doll to her chest, then vanished.

THE EXTRA

by Jack Dann

The smoke-machine was blowing noxious vapors that smelled like automobile exhaust toward the tables of the makeshift 50s diner; and although it was a cloudy day, kleig lights poured midafternoon sunlight through the plate glass window. Michael Nye had been sitting in a booth for what seemed like hours while a scene was being shot at the table beside him. The actor and actress were being paid three thousand dollars a day.

He was being paid fifty dollars a day to be an extra.

But he was only doing this to see what it was like. He was an advertising executive who specialized in political campaigns. He was very well paid, and a family man.

Of course, he had once wanted to be an actor.

And this movie was about an actor coming back to his hometown. The director was German. Now what the hell would a German director know about coming home to a small town in upstate New York?

Michael stared fixedly ahead, past the old man sitting directly in front of him: another extra. The old man looked like the sort of lean, determined character Grant Wood would have painted, which was probably why he had been picked for the scene. Michael was dressed as a construction worker. His tee-shirt was stained, and he was sweating, which was in character. It must have been ninety degrees in this room.

As Michael fingered his red hard hat on the table,

he glimpsed something familiar out of the corner of his eye. He turned, ever so slightly.

And saw his dead father watching him from the sidewalk.

The man was standing outside the window of the diner, between two spotlights. He wore a gray suit and a wide, striped tie. He carried his worn briefcase and looked very young.

Michael pulled himself awkwardly out of the booth and rushed outside.

It was drizzling: typical Binghamton weather. A small crowd of spectators stood in and around the doorway of the Security Mutual Building, which was across the street from the diner that had been constructed for the film. Two policemen stood beside sawhorses that formed a police line, and a few businessmen looked in Michael's direction as they walked beneath some scaffolds. It seemed that the movie company was doing construction work on every building in the town.

Of course, Michael could not find his father.

Michael was called back to work the next day, for the scene was not finished. Ordinarily, he would have turned them down flat, but now he felt compelled to be on the set. He had not told anyone of his "hallucination."

He had simply seen a man who looked like his father.

As they shot the scene over and over, Michael kept glancing out the window. The man across from him just stared down at his bowl of soup and would mechanically begin to eat whenever the assistant director ordered him to do so. And Michael would do his part by sipping coffee and smoking unfiltered Chesterfields.

It was noon when Michael saw his best friend Greg

Chambers stop on the sidewalk in front of the plate glass window. But it couldn't be Greg.

Greg was forty-five and overweight.

This young man could not have been older than twenty-two or twenty-three, and he was thin as a reed. His beard was reddish, and his wispy blond hair was long, held in place with a headband.

Nevertheless it *was* Greg.

There was a woman with him, who looked about nineteen. She wore an embroidered cotton dress and was very pretty: freckled, with unkempt curly hair. Yet there was a certain poise about her, as if she were used to having things her own way. Framing her face with her hands, she looked directly at Michael through the window. But she didn't appear to see him. After a beat, she stepped back and grimaced at Greg. Then they both laughed and walked on.

And Michael remembered. How could he have ever forgotten? She was Sandra Delaney. He had been in love with her twenty years ago.

Michael ran outside after them. "Greg, Sandra, wait," he shouted.

The afternoon shower had passed . . . vanished; it was a hot August day with only a few cirrus streamers in the clear sky. Somehow the air smelled different.

"We were wondering where the hell you went off to," Greg said, stopping and smoothing his beard back toward his throat. Sandra linked her arm through Michael's and kissed him. She smelled earthy and slightly sweaty; he remembered that she never wore perfume, nor did she shave her legs.

Michael wanted to ask questions, but couldn't form the words. He stopped, looked around, and imagined that he was in some sort of shock because it took all his strength of will to pull away from Sandra and Greg and walk back to the diner.

"Where are you going?" Sandra asked.

"I've got to check out something," he heard himself say; yet, somehow, his voice was not his own. "I'll be back in a second."

The diner, of course, wasn't there.

He peered through the tinted window into a large, unfinished room: the new addition to the First City Bank. And in the dark glass, he could see the reflection of himself. A gangly boy with thick brown hair, aviator glasses, and pimples. He was wearing jeans, a black tee shirt, and a faded, jean jacket. The middle-aged man with the shock of gray hair had melted into the darkness behind the glass. He was trapped, yet free; and he knew, he knew, that it was 1972 and he was twenty-two years old.

He was in love with Sandra, and so was Greg. She was in love with both of them, which suited everyone fine.

He had somehow walked into a distant summer.

Just like that.

Gone were wife and family.

Gone were the stale, dreamless years.

He had left them all behind, walked out, as it were. He looked around, feeling a dead weight slide away from him; yet out of habit he felt in his pocket for money. A few crisp bills collapsed reassuringly inside his fist.

Across the street was the Security Mutual Building. Unchanged. Cars passed, all twenty years out of date. The *Strand* and *Riviera* theaters were still in business; in fact, two matinees were playing: *The Godfather* and *The Poseidon Adventure*. And there ahead of him were Greg and Sandra, waiting.

He caught up with them; and they took his car, which was parked nearby in the lot of the Treadway Inn, and drove into the country. It was a new '72 Toyota Corona, with a four-speed stick shift, and black bucket seats. Sandra sat beside him and Greg

sat in the back seat behind her. She rested her hand
between the seats, and Greg leaned forward to hold
it. She turned around, smiled at him, kissed him, then
turned to Michael. "Let's go fast," she said. All the
windows were open, and the breeze blew through her
hair.

"It's only a four cylinder," Michael heard himself
say. Even now, he had begun to understand it. He
was, quite literally, only along for the ride. Although
he could exert his will—the will of the mature man
from a faraway present—he could not remove his
young self, his host, from the deeply set runnels that
were his life.

"Well, gun it, anyway," Sandra said, turning up the
volume of the radio to a roar of static, then twisting
the station knob, resting on a song here or there, then
moving along the band: "Where Is the Love," "Rock
Me On the Water," "Summer Breeze." She finally
settled on "Doctor My Eyes."

Michael brought the needle up to eighty, and ninety
on the downhill. There wasn't another car on the
road, which dipped and curved. He decelerated to sev-
enty-five. The wind smelled like new-mown hay. The
world suddenly seemed larger, tastier, filled with clarity and color. He embraced it even as he drove, as if
he were awash with it, as if his best friend in the back
seat and their mutual girlfriend in the front seat were
simply manifestations of the leafy world in which he
was the hunter supreme. He was Adam and Paul Bun-
yan; he wanted to eat the trees and squeeze the Cats-
kill mountains together; he wanted to press the rocks
of palisade road walls against his face and swim in the
heat mirages that looked like pale pools of water in
the highway pavement.

And he could not help but confess his love for Sandra, right there with Greg in the back seat.

It was an exercise in humiliation, this eavesdropping

on the past, which could not quite merge into the present.

Michael heard himself go on about wishing to make babies together, getting married, the strength she gave to him; but he could not stop himself. Greg interrupted, tried to change the subject, but nothing could stop Michael.

Michael could feel the power of these emotions; but the man, the visitor who was old and tired and heavy with it all, could not stop the boy.

There seemed to be a change in the atmosphere. Sandra leaned against the door, putting distance between them. When they stopped for ice cream, she left them alone for a few moments, and Greg said, "Man, was *that* fucking embarrassing."

Michael smiled and said, "I couldn't help it."

They laughed until Sandra returned; then they mooned all the customers at the Carvel's ice cream stand.

That Toyota might be only a four cylinder, but it could certainly lay rubber.

They spent the rest of the day driving in the country, walking through Recreation Park and the zoo, talking about writing and the politics of liberation, and shopping in the antique stores and pawnshops on Clinton Street. Sandra bought some old postcards and a silk blouse. She held hands with Greg and Michael, and played to every passerby.

Here was a real menage-a-trois.

Here was a living example of the sexual and political revolution, of men's and women's liberation.

But Michael, the older Michael who was little more than a ghost in this palpable world of radiant color and emotion, began to experience an odd fatigue, a forgetfulness. The joys and powerful endocrinological pleasures of youth were slowly and subtly overwhelming him.

While Greg discussed *new criticism* with Sandra, Michael desperately tried to remember everything he could about his wife, Helen. He had to remember, lest he lose himself in this bright but empty place.

Helen came sharply and suddenly into focus, resolving in his mind, as if she were standing before him; and Michael memorized every feature of her face, which was almost Oriental in its delicacy: almond eyes; small upturned nose; fair, smooth skin; full mouth; and even teeth. Her hair was auburn, straight and long. And in his mind's eye, she was young, as young as Sandra.

If she could see him now. . . .

She would laugh at him. She would think that he was affected and silly. Now that she was lost to him, he missed her. He was free of her, yet he desired her. He wanted to press himself into her familiar and comfortable body. . . .

And he realized that he did, indeed, love her.

But even now it was becoming difficult to visualize her.

Sandra smiled at him and put her arm around his waist. "I want you," she whispered.

Michael became himself once again.

"I want you, too," he said, feeling suddenly empty, as if he had forgotten something very important.

When they returned to Michael's apartment, Greg became quiet, sullen. He talked of returning home to New York to "take care of business." But the only business he had there was a notice of eviction that had been nailed to his door. Sandra flitted about the small, shabby apartment and talked about her work. She was an art major, and Michael had framed one of her charcoal drawings: a nude. It was a self-portrait.

They made a stir-fry and watched TV until Greg said, "I'm going to bed."

For the last few days he had been sleeping on the couch in the living room.

Michael and Sandra had become a couple.

Although Greg had lost Sandra to Michael, he pretended that nothing had changed. But he could not stand being alone on the couch at night while Michael and Sandra made love in the bedroom. Neither could he leave, for Sandra teased him with the hope that she would soon be ready to bestow her sexual favors upon him.

"Are you sure you don't want to come to bed with us?" Sandra asked.

"You know you're more than welcome," Michael said, although he didn't mean it.

"Nah, it's all right," Greg said, and then he turned away.

Michael quickly closed the door, and Sandra undressed.

Overcome with emotion and desire, he watched her. She was attractive, but certainly not beautiful. Her face was wide, tan, and freckled; and her body was soft and fleshy, although certainly not voluptuous. Her breasts were small, her hips wide.

He was lost in a frothing ocean of adrenaline, lost in all the juices and chemical connections of passion. It was as if he needed to wear her flesh, to get so close to her that they would become each other. And Michael, the Michael who had slipped through time to find his youth, was as overwhelmed as his host.

Sandra allowed Michael to mount her; and as they made love, she watched him. She did not try to feign passion, nor was she cold. Her face expressed only curiosity. He looked down at her, staring into her steady, green eyes, trembling as he moved inside her. Michael worshiped her.

And she rewarded him.

She studied him and answered his questions. "Yes, I love you, yes, I can feel you."

But she would not give herself to him, for she was a god, an icon; and he was . . .

Spent.

He could not catch his breath for a moment. He let her take his weight, but she subtly shifted beneath him. He took her cue and lay down beside her. She took his hand and guided his fingers to the place that gave her pleasure. She moaned and thrashed about, her eyes closed tight, thinking thoughts that Michael would never know. Then she slept, her chest moving slightly as she breathed, her curly hair damp upon her forehead, her mouth open to reveal widely-spaced teeth, her arms outstretched, as if she were dreaming of flying.

As Michael watched her, in the lull of fatigue and satisfaction, he remembered. He remembered all the years that had not yet passed, he remembered his wife and children, he remembered his work, his friends, his associates; and he remembered the boy sleeping in the next room as a man. Greg would become a New York publisher. He would gain weight and cut his hair. He would wear suits and carry a briefcase and ride the train and go to conventions. He would laugh at himself and pine for the good old days. He would wish to be back here, in love, in pain, alive again.

Michael carefully got out of bed, pulling the sheet over Sandra, who was a distant stranger now. He dressed and slipped quietly out of the apartment, but Greg called to him before he could close the door. "Where are you going?" Greg's voice was hoarse, thick from sleep.

"Just out for a walk." Michael looked at his friend, as if this would be the last time he would see him.

Greg switched on the light. He had covered himself

with an army blanket. His long, blond hair was tangled and his frizzly beard was flattened along the right side of his face where it had pressed against his arm. His eyes were blue and piercing; the years might change everything else, but not those eyes. They would burn with the same excited interest in the world, and reflect the same sad soul of the outsider, the observer. "You want company?"

"No, I just need to take a walk."

"Everything okay with you and Sandra?"

"Yeah, everything's fine. And you? Are you okay in here?"

"I'll survive," Greg said. "But I do think I'll go back to New York tomorrow."

"Give things a chance," Michael said, feeling guilty even as he spoke, for he could read the future, which was nothing more than recent memory.

"Yeah, maybe. You sure you don't want company?"

"I'm sure," Michael said; and he closed the door behind him. Down three flights of stairs, the banister worn and the walls stained and greasy. Everything familiar, yet ghostly. The night was clear and warm. The street empty. The branches of evenly spaced trees shifted slightly in the wind, eclipsing stars. He walked past the neighborhood grocery store and cemetery, until he found himself on the well-lit streets of the prosperous West Side. The lawns and leaves seemed almost phosphorescent in the artificial light. His young host daydreamed as he walked; he dreamed of living with Sandra. He would marry her, and she would bear his children.

And he dreamed of writing.

Intricate plots for short stories waved and tangled in his mind like brightly colored pennons. He would become famous. He would be another Salinger, another Fowles, another Hemingway. . . .

Michael found himself on Ackley Avenue, the street where his parents lived. He stopped before the square, white stucco house. Its windows glowed with buttery light. Upstairs a television flickered, and Michael knew he must not go inside. His father was there. He could visualize him lying on the bed and watching television. His mother would be in the bed beside him.

As he stood there, Michael yearned to see his father once again. And he remembered the funeral ceremony, remembered looking into his father's deep, open grave . . . remembered shoveling dirt over the top of the plain pine casket. He could hear the sounds of stones and dirt hitting its surface, smell the loamy soil as he mechanically dug and pitched the darkness over the remains of his father. Then he passed the shovel to his brother. Their white-haired mother stood beside them and stared into the grave in disbelief.

Michael remembered; indeed, he remembered.

Family and friends stood in line behind the dumpster load of soil, which would soon cover his father. Everyone would have a chance to drop a few stones and clots of earth over Michael's father.

But in *this* here and now, his father was alive. He was right inside that house, and all Michael had to do was take a few steps and knock on the door.

Instead, he turned and walked away.

It would be too dangerous to knock on that door. If he did, he would certainly be lost. He would disappear into this loop of time and cheat the future.

He would forget.

Helen. . . .

The beautiful Colonial and Victorian homes along the river seemed faded now. The air was sweet and heavy. Michael hurried, racing against the amnesia that was overtaking him. He walked back to the business district.

Back to Chenango Street, which was deserted, except for a bag lady who pushed her grocery cart as if it were a pram.

Back to the *Strand* and *Riviera*.

The movie houses were dark, as were the office buildings. A cab slowed down, but Michael waved him on. He stopped before the new addition to the First City Bank, where in a different time he had sat in a film set. He peered into the window, but it showed him only his own reflection: a young man wearing a tee shirt. He leaned his forehead against the thick pane, pressing his weight against it, as if it was the only thing holding him back from his future. The glass felt cold and lifeless against his forehead. But he was determined to pass through it, to fling himself back into his life.

He stepped back from the building, and then threw himself into the glass.

Mercifully, it accepted him.

He passed through it.

Into blinding light.

Into sunlight.

Into kleig lights.

INSIDE OUT

by Karen Haber

"Isn't he perfect?" Gayle said. Her gray eyes shone with the incandescent pleasure of new motherhood. "Beautiful and perfect." She held up the red-faced newborn in his yellow hospital wrapper with the S-B logo, displaying him for Wayne as though he had never seen a baby before.

Privately, Wayne Madison thought his firstborn looked like a tiny, wrinkled version of his grandfather in diapers. But he knew Gayle wouldn't appreciate that opinion, so he nodded gamely.

"Perfect," Wayne said, and his face crinkled into an affectionate smile. He was proud, giddy, relieved, a bit light-headed with exhaustion. Eighteen hours of labor were hard on the father, too, he thought, and rubbed his neck under his brown leather jacket. Especially hard after ten hours of SONY-BRAUN NET work. Weren't first babies supposed to be tough? Gayle had screamed and cursed and sobbed until that final nerve block, administered at the last minute: so much for the carefully rehearsed huffing and puffing. A touch of the electrodes and whammo—sorry, Gayle can't come to the phone right now and suddenly I'm the star catcher in rubber mitts, clutching six pounds of squirming, slimy infant. Hi, Dad.

Wayne glanced at his reflection in the glossy monitors that lined Gayle's headboard. The face he saw didn't look much like that of a father. Wavy brown

hair, barely receding along the hairline. Straight nose
with the bump in the middle. It looked like Wayne
Madison with dark circles under his eyes. No magic
transformation there. Not yet. But the SONY-
BRAUN counselor had said a baby would help. So be
patient, he told himself. For me, for Gayle, for David,
for that promotion. A deep breath, now. And another
one.

"His toes. Look at his toes, his nails," Gayle said.

Obediently, Wayne admired them. "Wonderful,"
he said, reaching for the appropriate awe-filled tone,
fearful of overshooting into detectable irony. "At the
very least, David has the toenails of a future high-
tension gymnast. He'll be a champion at the intercom-
pany games."

That seemed to satisfy her. But more was required.

"Aren't his knees wonderful?"

"Delectable. He can use them to climb toward middle management in SONY-BRAUN purchasing, just
like his old man and mother."

A small frown formed between Gayle's blond eyebrows. Delicate eyebrows, and fair, like the rest of
her.

"Can you get over his nose?" she said. Her eyes
dared him to come back with another sardonic quip.

He knew better. "He's great. Really." Wayne said.
His patience held, held, held, then failed. "Jesus,
Gayle, haven't I told you he's wonderful at least a
hundred times since he was born? I've had even longer
to marvel at him than you—I saw him first while you
were still zonked. What do you want, a medal from
the hospital that says 'Best baby ever born here'?"

Gayle's eyes were cloudy. Storms brewed in their
gray depths and threatened to boil over.

"Sorry. Honey, listen. I'm sorry." He squeezed her
hand.

The storm clouds dispersed. "I know you're tired, Wayne. You work so hard."

"We both work hard." He sank down on the pink love seat by the bed in the private room paid for by SONY-BRAUN. Just another employee perk for the company family. Hell, the entire hospital was an employee perk, and the compound that surrounded it: the SONY-BRAUN mini-city lined by high walls with shock fields that kept out the street gangs. A mini-city filled with company stores, schools, skating rinks, housing units, and athletic fields. Better living with S-B than without, employees said.

And if he was a good boy and worked a whole lot more overtime and managed to stay married and fertile, SONY-BRAUN might just let him and Gayle grow another baby someday and have it in the nice, shiny company hospital. He might even get an extra week of vacation at the S-B family camp. His parents had done it. He was a son of S-B, just as his boy would be.

Jesus, he was tired. Wayne rubbed his eyes, then looked at the glowing red and yellow readouts on the headboard. Red meant good luck in Chinese, didn't it? And blood everywhere else. "Why aren't you exhausted?" he said.

"Adrenaline high." Gayle fluffed her pale hair. She looked almost cute in her blue inflated bed coat. "Besides, I had that nice little zonk-nap. You've been up almost twenty-four hours."

"Okay, then. Guess I win the tired award." He tried and failed to conceal a yawn.

"Go get some sleep before you fall over," his wife said.

He knew she knew that he relied on her resilience and that she worked hard to furnish it whenever she could. Even right after childbirth. The thought shamed him. "Thanks. You're good," he said, and leaned over to give her a kiss. "See you in a couple of hours, honey."

The office of S-B Child Development Counselor Letitia Farrell was cool green and white. Dr. Farrell sat behind a broad desk-screen, nodding at glowing amber letters. She was neat, precise, her black hair cropped efficiently, her dark face well-scrubbed without a trace of makeup. Wayne sat in a not-well-padded chair on the other side of Dr. Farrell's desk. He felt like squirming, trying to find some comfortable position. If only Gayle were here. She might actually warm up to this ice-cold clinician. But a last-minute meeting in Gayle's department meant that Wayne got to fly solo.

"I see your son did very well on the Klein-Skinner tests," said the doctor. "He scored in the highest percentile."

"Really? That's good news."

"We'd like to start him in accelerated mode next month at preschool. He should be reading on a third grade level in two months."

"But that means an implant," Wayne said. "He's only two years old."

"We can start them as early as eighteen months," Dr. Farrell said. "The sooner, the better. As you know, the accelerator, used in concert with the implant, boosts development of verbal and social skills. His math will improve as well."

"Math? He can hardly count to ten—"

"Don't worry, Mr. Madison. Our implant will take care of that. And, by the way, congratulations on your promotion. I saw it on the company news burst this morning."

"Thanks." Wayne sat up a bit straighter in his chair. As new chief of purchasing data support, he had taken to his responsibilities eagerly. He liked to think that he gave it all he had.

"I understand that Mrs. Madison is being considered for promotion as well."

"Yeah. Gayle could make division head."

"Wonderful." Dr. Farrell's face warmed with the briefest of smiles. "It's a pleasure to see company-minded families succeed. We're proud of you and Gayle. And I know we'll be proud of David as well."

"You can count on that, Doctor."

"I know SONY-BRAUN can count on *you*, Mr. Madison. Now if you'll see the receptionist on the way out, she'll make an appointment for your son's implant session."

As Wayne left Dr. Farrell's office, he felt nine feet tall. SONY-BRAUN could rely on him, all right. But as he walked down the med corridor he began to feel less buoyant, especially as he thought about the implant. Was David really ready? Wayne himself had been nine before he had received his first implant, and that had been put in specifically to boost his math skills. He remembered how his head had ached for a week after they had slipped in the chip. After that came the dizziness, the nausea. Of course David was smart, but wasn't he too young and a bit too tender for this? Or was Dad here just overreacting? Dr. Farrell wouldn't have recommended the procedure if there was any risk. By now they had probably perfected the procedure. There was nothing to worry about.

He waited to tell Gayle about it until after the hour-long ritual of putting david to bed had been completed.

"Implant?" Gayle said. "But they don't usually implant them so young, do they?"

"I don't think so. But if Dr. Farrell thinks it's okay—"

Gayle's eyes began to sparkle. "It's a good sign, Wayne. David must have special potential. I told you we should have had a child years ago. It was the right move."

"Yeah."

"When does he go in?" she asked.

"Tomorrow."

"Tomorrow?" Gayle frowned at him. "That's not much time."

"To prepare David? I know."

"Not that. I'm sure he'll be fine. No, I meant not enough time to plan a reception."

"For what?"

"Division managers and associates. To celebrate the event. I want everybody to know. But how can I get it catered on such short notice?"

"I thought you had some pull," he said. "Aren't there any cooks on your short list?" She didn't seem to notice the edge to his voice.

"Wayne, you're a genius. Stan Brawley owes me a favor—I'll bet his kitchen staff could whip something up for me overnight. I'll call him right now."

"Will there be enough time to send out engraved invitations?"

But Gayle wasn't listening. She was on the room-screen, dialing.

She's right, Wayne told himself. She knows what it takes to get ahead. I have a bad attitude. Maybe I'm tired. He peered in at his son, balled into sleep in his floatercrib. Poor little guy. After tomorrow, he would be just another part of the machine.

* * *

Bright/noise/Mommy/Daddy/hardnoise/pain/
stopohstopstopstop/ccccccccccccccccccccccccccccccccccccc
cccccccccccccccccccccccccccccccccccccccccccccccccccccccc
ccccccccccccccccccccccccccccccccccccccccccccccccccccccc

ccccccccccccccccccccccccccccccccccccccccccccccccccccccc
ccccccccccccccccccccccccccccccccccccccccccccccccccccccc
ccccccccc Oh. I see. See Mommy, Daddy, Snowy
Bear. Dark and light, and no color in between. And
outside, soft softnoise.

*   *   *

Occasionally somebody from S-B married somebody
from a different company. Officially there was no policy on this. Unofficially, corporate intermarriage
meant lateral movement on the corporate chart.
Marry "outside" and you were dead in the corporate
waters—everybody knew that, Wayne thought. He
hadn't made that mistake. One glimpse of Gayle in
his entry-level NET class and Wayne was smitten.
Later, much later, Gayle told him that a friend had
helped her purloin his files from personnel.

"My files? Why did you want to see them?"

"Just to compare our goals, to see if there was any
real compatibility."

"Why didn't you just ask?"

"Don't look so hurt," she had said, laughing. "You
passed with the greatest of ease." That had been back
when she had laughed with almost every other breath.
He couldn't remember the last time he had heard
Gayle really let loose and laugh, at least not since
David was born.

Wayne listened enviously to her deep, even breathing as she lay beside him in bed. Gayle was a good
sleeper, always had been. He was the one who
ghosted around half the night, plagued by insomnia.

Aren't women supposed to be the light sleepers? he
thought, with a twinge of resentment. Tonight, especially, you'd think Gayle might have been a bit less
somnolent. David's surgery had gone flawlessly, in

and out in half an hour. But he was just a little boy. Shouldn't a little boy's mother be awake, checking on him instead of snoring next to Dad?

Well, I'll do it, Wayne thought. I can't seem to sleep anyway.

David's room was lit by pink and amber night lights disguised as sea shells. The undersea murals rippled along the walls with simulated life. Against the far wall of the room, in the quietest corner, sat a floatbed designed to resemble a laser diver. David was on his stomach, his head turned toward the big stuffed polar bear that Wayne's coworkers had given him.

Wayne admired his son's soft pale hair and the innocent curve of his rosy cheek. How he envied the confident, untroubled sleep of children. He moved closer.

David's eyes were open. Fixed.

Wayne snatched him up out of the crib. David was cool to the touch and his eyes, wide and staring, had an odd silvery blue sheen. He was a dead weight in Wayne's arms.

"David." Wayne shook him and his plump little legs swung back and forth like a rag doll's. His head lolled to one side. The silvery gaze was fixed elsewhere.

He didn't seem to be breathing. Wayne put him down on his back on the bed and pressed his ear to his chest, trying to find a heartbeat. His own pulse pounded in his head, drowning out all other sound.

"Gayle?" he yelled. "Gayle, wake up. Something's wrong with David!" Did she hear him? He didn't have time to wait. Breathlessly, arms full of unresponsive child, he reached for the hallcom and punched the blue emergency button to summon the section medic.

"Med-3," a male voice responded. "Situation?"

"My son's not breathing."

"On my way."

Gayle was standing in the doorway, half into a pink robe. "What's happening?"

"David isn't breathing. I can't find a pulse."

"What? Let me try—"

The front door buzzed.

"Go let them in," Wayne said. He bent over David, squeezed the nose shut, puffed air into the small, perfect mouth.

The medic was young, with dark hair, brown skin, and a day's growth of beard above the collar of his white coveralls. His bloodshot eyes testified to too many all-night shifts, too many calls made too late. He opened his blue med sack, pulled out a respirator, and pushed past Wayne. In a second, David was hooked up and the pump was humming.

The medic peered over his shoulder at Wayne and Gayle. "Any unusual symptoms?"

"He had an implant this morning," Gayle said.

"Looks like shock," the medic said. He held up a pressure syringe filled with red liquid. "It's fairly common with the new implants. A shot of adrenaline fixes them right up."

David coughed, coughed again, and began a thin, persistent wail.

"Guess he didn't need this after all." The medic put the syringe back in its packet and tossed it into his sack. "He seems fine now. I'll leave the respirator here—keep him on it for another half hour. And in the morning you should probably have him checked out. G'night."

When he was gone, Wayne and Gayle tucked David back into bed. For a moment they stood together silently, watching him. Then Gayle yawned and turned away. "Will you sit with him?"

Wayne knew it wasn't really a question. He nodded and settled into the old-fashioned wooden rocking chair by the bed. It was the only anachronism in this undersea room: he had inherited it from his mother. He sat rigidly against its hard walnut slats, watchful by his son's bed until sleep finally came and found him.

* * *

Sing with Mommy. Sing with Daddy. Bright song, softnoise song. Find Snowy Bear and rock. Rock, rock, rock. In and out, rock.

* * *

Wayne surfaced from oblivion like a diver fighting his way up from great depths, gasping for thought.

Gail stood next to the bed. Her old pink robe was pulled tightly around her and her face was lit by the red light of the bedside clock.

Wayne sat up. "What time is it? Two o'clock? Jesus, Gayle, you know how hard it is for me to sleep. What's wrong?"

"I heard him."

"Heard who?"

"David. Rocking the floaterbed across the room. He gets down on all fours and rocks the thing across the room. It's his new game. He usually does it in the morning, after you leave. This is the first time he's done it at night."

"Maybe he's just trying to escape."

She glared at him. "Very funny."

"Then tell him his teddy doesn't like it. Maybe he'll stop." Wayne rolled over and pulled the covers up toward his head.

"Don't be silly." Gayle yanked the yellow blanket away from him. "I don't want to mention that toy. You know that Dr. Farrell told me to put it away in the closet where David can't reach it."

"You locked up his teddy? Why? How can a teddy bear be bad for a kid?"

"I don't understand it either. But she said that David is developing an unhealthy dependency on it and that his attention must be drawn away from inanimate objects. He can't bring his teddy to class any more."

"Poor David. They're teaching life's hard truths awfully early these days. When did he start this rocking?"

"When I put Snowy Bear away."

"I see." Reluctantly Wayne swung himself out from under the mound of covers. Duty called. "Okay, let me talk to him." The air was cool and he grabbed up his robe before padding into his son's room.

The undersea mural glowed with subdued greens and blues. No, of course David wasn't asleep. He sat in bed, staring across the room with bright eyes that looked silvery in the moonlight. In his arms was a frayed toy polar bear with black button eyes. But hadn't Gayle told him that she had locked Snowy Bear up? Wayne hesitated, confused. Well, he would ask her about it in the morning.

David beamed at Wayne. "Daddy!"

"Son, what are you doing up?"

"Rock, David rocks."

"I see that. But this is a bad time for rocking, don't you think?"

"No. Good. Good time. Farther. Helps David hear. See." He pointed urgently toward a green lily pad painted on his closet door.

Despite himself, Wayne smiled. Nice ambitious spirit, this one. David would do well. He just needed to get his time frame—and grammar—nailed down.

"You can go farther tomorrow," Wayne said. He hugged David briefly and lowered him into a sleeping position. "Night-night now. See? Snowy Bear is already sleeping." He nodded at the recumbent teddy. "He wants to sleep too."

"No. Snowy listens. With me."

"Tomorrow," Wayne said sharply. He thought his son's attempts at self-assertion were kind of cute, but not at two in the morning. "Now I don't want to have to come back in here again. Understand?"

David's lower lip quivered. "Yes."

"Good boy. Sleep tight." He patted him on the rump.

"Snowy, too."

"Yes, yes, good night to Snowy Bear, too." Wayne patted the fuzzy white toy for a moment. He had to talk to Gayle about this. Raising a child just wasn't the same as running an S-B department. You had to be flexible sometimes. As for Dr. Farrell, well, she was just being a hardass. Why couldn't his kid have his teddy? What harm could it do? But how had David liberated Snowy Bear from the closet? Wayne yawned, pushed aside all thoughts of stuffed animals and child behaviorists, and went back to bed.

In the morning, Wayne peeked into his son's room on his way to work. The floatbed had been moved across the room to its usual place. Snowy Bear sat in the corner on a purple pillow, staring out with bright button eyes. On a whim, Wayne tried the closet latch. It was locked tight.

*   *   *

"Gayle," Wayne said. "I'm worried."

She was curled on the wall seat scanning quarterly reports. The reading lamp gave her a deceptively soft, golden look. But her eyes were a cold gray as she looked at him. "What's up?"

"Something peculiar is going on."

"What do you mean?"

"I thought you said you locked up David's teddy."

"I did."

"Then how did he get hold of it last night?"

"You must be dreaming."

"I saw it."

"You were half asleep."

"And I saw it on his bed this morning."

Gayle took a deep breath. "I was in his room half an hour ago. No sign of his teddy."

"None?"

"Nothing." She looked down at her portascreen again.

"Don't you think that David seems, well, kind of odd?"

She kept her eyes on the screen. "Odd? How do you mean?"

"He seems withdrawn. When I try to cuddle him, he pulls away or doesn't respond."

"Maybe it's just a phase in his development," Gayle said. "Boys have to separate from their parents and all that. They have to learn to channel all those aggressive hormonal drives."

"At three and a half?"

"Well—"

"It's too soon. And it's not right. That accelerator has changed him."

"Of course it has," Gayle said evenly. She had a maddeningly patient air as though he were an assistant to whom she was explaining a not-very-complicated procedure. "I remember how it felt when I first got mine: like a motor was revving up my thoughts. He's probably so busy taking in and processing information that he doesn't have time to be as involved with us." Her tone of voice said that she hoped Wayne wasn't going to become one of those always-worried fathers. "You know it jumped him at least a year, maybe more, in development. And that's just the beginning. We're lucky he was selected." It was one of Gayle's favorite refrains.

"I know, I know."

"Then what's the problem?" She looked up now, frowning.

"I wish he didn't seem so distant. He was such a happy little boy, singing and playing. Now he sits in his room—if I walk in, he grabs up a toy and sort of pretends to play. But as soon as I walk out, he puts it down and just stares at the walls. I know. I've seen him do it when I watched on the wallscreen."

"Has Dr. Farrell said anything about this?"

"You and your precious Dr. Farrell," Wayne said. "I don't like that woman. Or trust her. When she looks at David, she doesn't see a little boy, our son. She sees future profits for SONY-BRAUN."

Gayle stared at him coldly and did not reply. Obviously, she agreed with the doctor. "Are you sure this isn't your problem, not his?"

"How do you mean?"

"Wayne, you know you haven't been spending as much time in the office as you used to. You never put David in night care when it's your turn to watch him. Maybe you can't bear to see your little boy grow up."

"Don't be ridiculous." Wayne said.

But Gayle wasn't listening. She was staring at the gym bag at his feet, frowning.

"Where are you going?"

"To work out. After all, you're home."

"But I told you I've got work to do."

"It wouldn't hurt you to spend a little more time with your son—remember him?"

"Now don't give me a lecture about motherhood, Wayne. You know how busy I am. This new job is eating up my life."

"Tell me about it. You've worked over the last three weekends."

"I can't help it. In S-B, either you take on more, or you're left standing still. I *have* to work tonight."

And without another word she went back to her quarterly reports.

Dr. Farrell sat in her green, high-backed chair and gazed coolly at Wayne. He thought she looked like the perfect ice queen.

"Mr. Madison, we must insist," she said. "For David's own good. We feel that that stuffed teddy bear is obstructing his socialization process. None of our accelerated children are encouraged to keep toys in the classroom. And for obvious reasons. That teddy bear has become David's companion. Instead of interacting with the children, he plays alone. Your son scored high, very high, on developmental tests. But we've noticed a certain lack of eye contact, a dislike of physical contact—although he does seem to enjoy pulling the little girls' hair." She paused and her lips quirked in sudden, unexpected amusement.

Wayne relaxed a bit. Nevertheless, he knew this was a warning. A serious one. He couldn't tell Dr. Farrell about what he had noticed, that would only reinforce her conviction that David was antisocial. And then she might hold him back, put him in a lower class. No, he mustn't hinder his son's development by blurting out foolish fears, as his mother had done. He had sworn to himself that he wouldn't be one of those kind of parents. Was Gayle right? Could he be spending too much time on David and too little on business? But where was Gayle? Had she forgotten this appointment?

"Your wife had told me that she locked that teddy away, Mr. Madison. But David brings it to class every day."

"He's just a little boy."

"Which is the ideal age to begin discarding bad habits."

"Can't he at least sleep with it?"

"We recommend complete separation. He'll adjust more quickly that way."

"My wife says she never sees it around the house." Careful, Wayne thought. Play it safe.

"Perhaps he conceals it. Have you noticed any other unusual behavior? Found him hiding? Refusing to respond to direct statements?" Dr. Farrell's dark eyes glittered.

"No, nothing." Wayne said quickly, "In fact, he's developing exceptional skills. You said so yourself, Doctor."

Gayle burst into the room, her portascreen under her arm. Wayne thought that she looked like a stranger in her charcoal stretchsuit: just another professional SONY-BRAUN cog. "Sorry I'm late," she said. "Got caught in a meeting."

"Mrs. Madison," Dr. Farrell said. "We were just discussing David's development. In isolated areas, such as numbers and memorization drills, he seems to do very well. But there's a lack of systematic exploratory activity that we're beginning to question."

"I don't know what you're talking about—" Wayne began.

Gayle cut him off impatiently. "Honey, you told me yourself that David seems distracted lately—that he doesn't seem to want to cuddle the way he used to."

So she *had* been listening to him. Wayne flashed her a furious look, but she seemed not to notice, so intent was she on betrayal.

"We've seen David rocking back and forth on all fours for hours," Gayle said. "When we call him, he doesn't seem to hear us. And if we interrupt him, he throws tantrums."

Dr. Farrell leaned forward in her padded chair. "Why haven't you reported this before?"

"I just thought it was a phase," Wayne said. "Something he would outgrow."

"Mr. Madison, what you're describing is atypical behavior with autistic components." Dr. Farrell's voice rose. She seemed genuinely frightened. "We'll have to do a brain scan to be sure. I wish you had come to us sooner. There are steps we can take if we catch this in time. But for the boy's sake, we've got to move quickly."

As if to illustrate her words, the doctor jumped to her feet. She punched the intercom panel. "Bring the boy."

Briskly, she led the Madisons into a room filled with shining machines, masked technicians, and David. Then she closed the door.

*   *   *

Bright/pain/stop/Daddy/hardnoise/painstopstopstop/
ccccccccccccccccccccccccccccccccccccccccccccccccccccc
ccccccccccccccccccccccccccccccccccccccccccccccccccccc
ccccccccccccccccccccccccccccccccccccccccccccccccccccc
Bright machines. Cold machines. Don't talk. Bear says. Listen. I can hear them talking inside, Mommy, Daddy, Dr. Farrell. They can't hear me. Doctor Farrell thinks like the machines, and Mommy a little bit, too. Machines that want things. Daddy doesn't. He thinks he's a machine, but Daddy loves.

Talk, so much talk. Don't talk, listen.

*   *   *

Wayne had watched, wincing, as the technicians probed and poked, hooked David up to this shiny machine and that, ran their tests, scratched their heads, and ran more tests.

Autistic. The word sent chills along his spine. Was David autistic? It couldn't be. He was fine. He had to be fine.

Please, make him be fine.

Throughout the tests, David sat, impassive, almost limp, obviously distracted. Once he turned and flashed Wayne a reassuring grin, as though he sensed his concern. Could he? No, that was ridiculous. Three-year-old boys don't reassure their fathers.

"The results are inconclusive," Dr. Farrell said. "We'll have to keep an eye on him."

"Don't worry," Gayle said. "We will."

Wayne reached for his son and lifted him down from the diagnostic table. David smiled brightly. "Daddy." He put his thin little arms around Wayne's neck.

"Interesting," Dr. Farrell said. "He seems to respond well to the father. Mr. Madison, you must spend as much time with your son as possible. It's absolutely crucial to his development. Do you understand?"

"Yes, of course." He fingered David's small hand. Such perfect little nails.

"O' course," David parroted, nodding his head vigorously. "O' course."

*   *   *

Fat, fat, too fat. Can't hear, can't get in or out. Bear says come in, come in, but I can't can't can't. Fat talk. Fat thought. Machine thought. Listen. Only listen.

*   *   *

Wayne was coming to dread his monthly meetings with Doctor Farrell. Somehow he felt they had become his responsibility, just as had David, while Gayle took on more and more and more at work. He knew he should feel grateful that Gayle had deigned to attend this appointment at all although she had said, three times, that she couldn't stay long. Thanks, Gayle.

"Your son is losing weight at an alarming rate," Dr. Farrell said. "And just as we began to make real progress dealing with his withdrawal over these past months. I see he lost five pounds in the last month." Her eyes probed Wayne, then Gayle. "Are you certain that he's eating all his food?"

"Of course he is," Wayne said. "In fact, he's eating as though there were two of him. Maybe he's just growing too fast."

Dr. Farrell shook her head. "Could he be faking it? Hiding the food and disposing of it elsewhere later?"

"David?" Gayle's tone was almost contemptuous. She was growing braver with the doctor, more impatient. "He's barely four years old. Where would he hide food without one of us noticing? And why would he even bother?"

"Children can be secretive, Mrs. Madison." Dr. Farrell tapped an immaculate white enameled fingernail against the laminated green desktop. "I needn't remind you we have high hopes for your boy. And he has been doing very well, aside from that incident a couple of years ago with the teddy bear. But if this weight loss process isn't reversed, we may have to use intravenous methods to help him gain weight. I'd hate to do that. David doesn't like needles."

Wayne smiled sympathetically. "I don't blame him. Isn't there any other way?"

"Force feeding. Even worse."

"But, Doctor, he eats everything we give him, and more."

Dr. Farrell shook her head, obviously stumped. "I suppose we could use the accelerator to try and boost his appetite."

"Is that wise?" Wayne said. "He didn't have a wonderful reaction to the implant in the first place."

"It might help," Dr. Farrell said. "Certainly, his interaction with others improved after the last treatment. If he has developed some aversion to eating which he's managed to conceal from you, as I believe is likely, this should cure him."

Gayle glared at him. Her eyes were like gray ice. He knew that look meant play along, play through, be good.

Yes, dear, Wayne thought. Be a good man, good worker, good husband, good father. Yesyesyes. He was beginning to see parenthood as a constant series of betrayals—of the child, first off, then of the parents.

All right," said the good father. "All right. Use the accelerator if you think it will do any good."

* * *

cccccccccccccccccccccccccccccccccccccccccccccccccccccc
cccccccccccccccccccccccccccccccccccccccccccccccccccccc
cccccccccccccccccccccccccccccccccccccccccccccccccccccc
cccccccccccccccccccccccccccccccccccccccccccccccccccccc
cccccccccccccccccccccccccccccccccccccccccccccccccccccc
cccccccccccccccccccccccccccc I am teeth I am teeth I am teeth.

* * *

Dr. Farrell welcomed Wayne with a smile. "Mr.

Madison. I'm so pleased to see how well David is doing."

"Glad to hear it, Doctor." Wayne had to admit that his son was looking good and he seemed to have regained his playful spirit. "He's full of beans, singing and talking up to the minute his head hits the pillow. I envy his energy."

"Wonderful. Any sign of problems with his eating?"

"He's gained back all he lost. Seems to be growing fast, too. All his clothing is too small."

"That's natural." Again, Dr. Farrell smiled. "Just the sign of a healthy, growing little boy. Just what S-B wants. Congratulations. And I'll see you again next month." She stood up and held the door open for Wayne. As he left, he thought that maybe she wasn't such an ice queen after all.

* * *

I like school. I sing with the helmet like they taught me. Tomorrow we all sing. Su-lyn and Raina are my girlfriends like Daddy has Mommy. I'll sing with them tomorrow and . . . Bear! Bear talks to me again. Good, oh, good. But hardnoise between us. He says the helmet will help me hear him and cccccccccc cccccccccccccccccccccccccccccccccccccccccccccccccccccccccc cccccccccccccccccccccccccccccccccccccccccccccccccccccccccc cccccccccccccccccccccccccccccccccccccccccccccccccccccccccc cccccccccccccccccccccccccccccccccccccccccccccccccccccccccc ccccccccccccccccccccccc so I will tell them about the good warm cccccccccccccccccccccccccccccccccccccccccccccccccccc cccccccccccccccc but never talk to machines. Daddy and Mommy talk and don't talk but cccccccccccccccccccccccc cccccccccccccccc hardnoise all night cccccccccccccccccccccccc cccccccccccccccccccccccccccccccccccccccccccccccccccccccccc cccccccccccccccccccccccccccccccccccccccccccccccccccccccccc

ccccccc don't talk to machines don't talk to machines
don't talk cccccccccccccccccccccccccccccccccccccccccccccc
cccccccccccccccccccccc

*   *   *

"Just how long is this assignment?" Wayne
demanded.

"At least two months. Maybe three." Gayle was
packing her underwear into a travel sack, avoiding his
determined gaze. She looked uncomfortable, even a
bit sorry. "But it'll be great for us. Really. I might
even get a vice presidency out of it."

"I don't see why you can't do the work here and
fax it to Denmark."

Now she was intent upon her cosmetics. "They need
me on site. I told you that." Her tone was a mixture
of entreaty and impatience.

"Yeah, so you said." When had he stopped being
pleased by Gayle's ambition? It was as if he didn't
care any more. But that wasn't true, was it? "You
know that leaves me with total responsibility for
David. And, need I remind you, I work, too."

"Of course you do, honey. As I've said before, the
company has day care and night care facilities. You
should use them more often. I know I've encouraged
you to use them in the past."

"Yeah, yeah, yeah. When you weren't telling me to
spend more time with David."

Finally, she looked him in the eye. Hers were dark
gray, almost black. "Don't double-bind me,
Wayne."

"Fine. Have a nice trip. Don't forget to fax us once
in a while."

"You're being childish."

"Go ahead," Wayne said. "Just go."

He didn't wait to see her pick up her screencase,

her travel sack. But he knew when she was gone. He felt abandoned, angry, and completely alone.

* * *

Gogogogogogo. Mommy goes. Outside. Bear said ccccccccccccccccc but Daddy misses her. Hardnoise. I want her to come back. Bear says no. Says stop. ccccccccc too soon. Tomorrow is helmet. Bear says don't be afraid. I'm not. Not really.

* * *

Wayne was at his desk and deep in the midst of magnetic rivet shipments when his private line buzzed and Dr. Farrell appeared onscreen.

"Mr. Madison? Can you come down here?" The normally unflappable doctor seemed pale and shaken.

Wayne's heart thudded painfully. "What's happened? Is something wrong with David?"

"I—you'll have to come down here. It's too complicated to tell you over the phone."

A terrible fear began to push the air out of his lungs. "I'm on my way."

He hurried down to the children's level. David had to be all right. He just had to be.

Dr. Farrell met him at the door and ushered him into the test area. David sat on a wall seat, playing with a set of neon holocubes. Beyond him, the remains of an acceleration unit could be seen, charred and melted almost into slag.

"What happened here?" Wayne said.

"We're not sure. There seems to have been a short circuit. A small fire."

"Small—"

"And the accelerator stopped working. It's ruined."

"Was David in it at the time?"

Dr. Farrell nodded. "Don't worry, he's fine. I checked him myself. Not a bruise. Not even a scorch mark."

"Thank God."

"I was told these machines were perfectly safe," she said. "We may want to file a lawsuit against the company that makes them. This has never happened before. Never."

"Did you tape the session?" Wayne said.

"Of course."

"May I watch it."

"All right."

Reluctantly, as though she were revealing the secrets of her profession, Dr. Farrell cued up the record of David's session in the accelerator.

Onscreen, David was seated in what appeared to be the control pit of a fighter jet. As he played with various toggle switches and buttons, a bright golden helmet slowly descended along a railway and onto his head. David looked up for a moment as the helmet locked into position. Bathed in amber light cast by pin spots in the ceiling, he seemed absorbed in his play, oblivious to the helmet and apparatus around him.

Dr. Farrell's voice could be heard offscreen. "Now, David, we're concerned that you're not listening to us all the time."

"I listen," the small boy replied. With remarkable self-possession he sat beneath the accelerator helmet His voice was oddly flat and lifeless. "I listen all the time. The helmet makes me listen." The peculiar tone in his son's voice bothered Wayne.

"And what does the helmet have you listen to?" Dr. Farrell prompted.

"Math and spelling mostly." His voice began to warm up. "I really like spatial dynamics."

"Spatial dynamics?" Wayne said. "For four-year-old children?"

Dr. Farrell turned away from the screen and nodded crisply. There was an eager, hungry look to her face now. "The accelerator brings them along very quickly. I'd speculate that he is learning on the sixth level already."

"Is that such a good idea?" Wayne was glad that Gayle was still in Denmark. She would have kicked his ankle for daring to raise any question about the company's plans for David.

Dr. Farrell drew back, obviously insulted. "Our results speak for themselves," she said coolly. "On average, SONY-BRAUN children read and write long before TOSHIBA-GE or QUADROPHONIQUE children. They take to the screens by age five."

"Of course." Wayne wanted to sink into the chair. David was receiving special attention. Why didn't he just shut up?

Onscreen, Dr. Farrell was speaking again. "David, what do you like most in school?"

"Playing with the teacher helmet." He laughed in a high crescendo of notes that caused Wayne to catch his breath.

David looked so strange, he thought. Almost robotic, with a strange, silvery sheen to his eyes. And as Wayne watched, the acceleration helmet grew brighter, more golden, as though lit by inner fires. Now it was burning, burning while, inside it, David laughed.

The tape grew blurred, unclear, while many things happened: Dr. Farrell pulled David from the acceleration unit, her assistants sprayed foam upon the machine, David laughed and laughed and laughed.

The screen went dark as the tape ended.

David gazed up at them from his cushions and smiled impishly. His eyes had the same steely appearance that had bothered Wayne before. Then he glanced at his father, alone, and a light came into his face, a softness that showed . . . what? Compassion? Sympathy? Pity? But he was just a little boy, Wayne thought.

"That was a fine joke," Dr. Farrell said with a forced smile. "Perhaps someday soon you really will play with the accelerator, and show us how to do it a better way. I'd like that, and I'm sure your Mommy and Daddy would like that."

"Bring Mommy back," David said suddenly.

"But David, you know that your mommy is doing *very* special, extra special work for the company. Aren't you proud of her? We all are."

"Daddy misses her."

Dr. Farrell flashed a sharp look at Wayne. "Of course he does. But she'll be home soon. Right now the company needs her. And we know how important that is, don't we?"

David stared at the doctor impassively, as though he had not heard her.

"Why don't you go play over there? I'd like to talk to your Daddy alone."

"Okay." He slipped down from his seat and walked over to a small green couch which held a skeletal keyboard. In a moment he had clambered up onto its broad tufted seat and began to place red buttons in white sockets.

"Well, Mr. Madison, I think you can relax. He's showing progress. It will take more work, but I think he just had a bad experience with the accelerator at first and was a bit slow to shake that off. This unfortunate incident doesn't seem to have set him back at all. In fact, he's remarkably resilient. We see that only with our brightest ones."

Wayne nodded proudly and glanced back at David. He seemed completely absorbed in the toy keyboard.

He was going to be all right. Dr. Farrell said he was going to be fine. One of their brightest.

"However, I must ask you if you have been talking about your wife: Are you moping around the house?"

"No. Don't be ridiculous. I'm too busy. I work at least fifty hours a week. That barely allows time for David."

"Mr. Madison, are you neglecting your son?"

Anger made him reckless. "What is this, twenty questions?" Wayne stood up. "I don't have time for this, Dr. Farrell. I thought we were here to discuss David. Not me."

"Everything in your life affects your son."

"I hope not, Dr. Farrell. I truly hope not. I'd like to take my boy home now. Please excuse us."

Wayne hustled David along the corridor toward their apartment. Poor little guy, he thought. What a day. "Ice cream," he promised, and was rewarded with joyful squeals. "We'll have ice cream and cake."

"Bear, too."

So he was still hung up on that toy, even after they had locked it away. Hell, might as well play along. "Absolutely. Cake and ice cream for all your pals. A round for the entire house."

They were through the door and halfway to the kitchen before it registered that something was wrong.

Wayne gasped, then tried to smother it for the child's sake.

The place was a shambles. Chairs lay overturned, papers spilled onto the floor, paintings hung askew. A real mess, as though a giant hand had picked up the place and shaken it.

David clapped his hands and giggled.

"No, son, this isn't a game."

David smiled beatifically at his father. "Game."

"Well, okay, maybe later we can make a game of cleanup then. First I've got to call security."

He hesitated. Nothing seemed to be missing. If someone had broken in and just vandalized the place, there was nothing security could do about it. Nevertheless, he called them just to have it on tape. They might as well spend the next hour or so reviewing their records.

He turned back from the machine and saw that somehow, magically, the place had been transformed. Then he looked closer. Chairs had been righted, but they were in the wrong position. Papers now piled to the ceiling from the top of one desk. It was as though someone had tried to fix the place without understanding anything about the function of furniture and order.

The sound of childish laughter came from the rear of the apartment.

"David? David, get in here."

His son toddled in. "Better," said David.

When the implication hit Wayne he wanted to laugh aloud in disbelief. "Are you trying to tell me that you did this, son?"

David nodded with his entire body.

"How?"

David smiled shyly. "Secret."

"Please, show Daddy."

"No. Bear says no."

"David—"

"Nooooo!" David's voice rose toward a wail. Wayne knew that meant back off. Besides, he didn't really want to pursue this. He didn't really believe that his son had somehow devastated the apartment, and then tried to put things right. No, there had to be some other, better explanation. There had to be. David was just being playful, trying to act like a grown-up. He heard constantly about everybody's great expectations for him. Maybe he was afraid to contradict his father. Wayne decided not to ride him.

"Ice cream," David said. "Cake."

"Right away," Wayne said. "Coming right up."

The next morning, Wayne sat at his desk trying to digest a pile of statistics, but the amber letters danced on the screen, dizzying him. His back knotted and he stood, attempting to loosen up.

What felt like an electric shock shot up his spine. He stiffened, almost fell. Then he caught his balance, leaning with both hands against his desk.

"Wayne?" Mario, his assistant, stood in the doorway. "You okay?"

"Yeah. A back spasm, that's all." He felt sweat soaking his hair, dripping down his neck.

Mario smiled wryly. "It's an occupational hazard around here."

Wayne tried to smile back, but he felt a terrible anxiety seize him and twist the smile into a grimace. Something was wrong, he thought. Something was terribly wrong. With David. He had to get to his son. Right away.

"Where are you going? Hey, Wayne, what's wrong?"

"I'm sorry." He pushed past Mario and, with an anguished groan, hurried out of the office.

David was not in class.

"Where is he?" Wayne said.

"Just a moment," the frightened teacher's aide said. "I'll call Dr. Farrell."

"I don't want to see her. I want to know where my son is."

"Mr. Madison, you're causing a disturbance here. Stop frightening the children."

"I'm not frightening anyone, Dr. Farrell. Not one

of your little wunderkinder has even looked up from under a helmet. Where is my boy?"

"Why, I thought you knew."

"Knew what?"

"Your wife. She picked him up half an hour ago."

Gayle? Back from Denmark without telling him?

"But she's not supposed to come back for another month."

"I'm not involved in company schedules, Mr. Madison. Perhaps you should check at home."

"And if he's not there?"

"Are you suggesting that your wife took him someplace else without telling you?"

"I don't know where he is, do I?"

"I see." Dr. Farrell turned away and made a note on her portascreen. "Well, if David *is* missing, which I doubt, we'll want to begin a search immediately. The company has invested a great deal in that child."

"Thanks for your concern," Wayne said.

"And Mr. Madison," said Dr. Farrell. "Once this matter is settled, I wonder if you would have your wife call me?"

Wayne spun to face her. "About what?"

"I think we should talk about your increasing tendency toward hostility and paranoia. Counseling may be advisable."

"I thought you specialized in child development."

"Please ask her to call, Mr. Madison."

Wayne turned his back to her and strode out of the room.

The front door to the apartment was unlocked. Wayne raced in.

"David? David, are you here?"

From the nursery came laughter. It started out low, an arpeggio of gleeful childish notes, but it quickly left childhood behind, left love, family, humanity, too, in its climb toward something new and strange and metallic and other. The laughter went on and on, rising toward the inaudible, cutting through Wayne like a cold wind.

The nursery was brightly lit, and Gayle was there, frozen, a pale statue, eyes closed. As David watched, she twitched and capered, puppetlike, limbs stiff.

"Mommy dances." David sat in his child-size chair as though it were a throne.

"What have you done?" Wayne cried.

"Mommy's here," David said. "Daddy's happy."

A strange mewling sound came from Gayle, an awful muffled cry that guttered, trapped in her throat.

"Let her go."

David pouted. "Won't."

"David—" Wayne loomed over his son.

A flicker of fear changed David's eyes from silvery blue to cornflower. He glanced away from his mother toward the stuffed polar bear sitting on the floor.

There was the sound of a wire snapping. Gayle tumbled to the carpet, a broken, blonde puppet in a business suit. She didn't move.

Wayne knelt beside her. She wasn't moving. Was she breathing? "Gayle. Gayle, honey!"

She opened her eyes slowly. Her expression was soft, confused. "Wayne, what are you doing here?"

He touched her cheek gently with his hand. "I'm not. You're here."

"That's impossible. I was in a productivity meeting in the Copenhagen facility. I don't understand—"

"I think your son missed you. I know I did."

She covered his hand with hers. For moment she said nothing. Then she stood. "I should call in and tell them where I am."

She reached for the screen at the same moment as the phone rang. Wayne started to tell her not to respond, but she had already answered. The screen lit and Dr. Farrell appeared.

"Mrs. Madison." She nodded grimly. "I hope this satisfies your husband."

"I'm sorry, Doctor. I don't understand."

"I'll be happy to explain it all to you. Could you come see me in, say, a half-hour?"

"But you just got back," Wayne said.

"It's very important," Dr. Farrell said. "It concerns your family."

"Why, of course, if you insist—"

"Say no, Gayle."

"Hush, Wayne."

"Is there some problem, Mrs. Madison?" Dr. Farrell seemed to look beyond Gayle, directly at Wayne.

"No," Gayle said quickly. "No problem."

Wayne cut in. "Yes, there is, Doctor."

"I beg your pardon?"

"I haven't seen my wife in months. The first moment she's back you want to drag her away to meetings to discuss me, to discuss David. I haven't had five minutes alone with her."

"Mr. Madison, you're severely agitated. If you don't calm down, I'll be forced to call a medic."

"I will not calm down," Wayne said. "I want you to butt out of our lives. Do you understand me? Leave us alone, Dr. Farrell."

"Wayne, have you gone crazy?" Gayle tried to push him aside. "Don't pay any attention to him, Doctor. He doesn't know what he's saying."

David began to cry and Wayne picked him up. "Now you've upset the boy."

Onscreen, Dr. Farrell glared at Wayne. "Mrs. Madison, perhaps you had better bring your son in as well. I'm becoming concerned about the kind of example your husband is setting."

"Bad," David sobbed. "Bad lady."

"Put him down," Gayle snapped. She grabbed David's shoulder, pulling him halfway out of Wayne's arms.

"Nooo—" David wailed.

"Gayle, let go, you're hurting him!"

A vibration moved up from the floor along Wayne's legs, his spine, and right on up through the top of his head. He was dizzy, nauseated. Was it an earthquake? Had the S-B armory blown? There was a blinding flash of light and a cold high shrieking which combined metal and, perhaps, human voices.

His vision cleared. He was alone with David in the apartment.

Panic gripped Wayne. "Where's Mommy?"

David giggled. "Bear likes you. But not Mommy. She was mean to him."

Wayne turned to the roomscreen. There was nothing on it, nothing at all. He went to the door of the apartment, swung it open. The hinges groaned.

The hallway had vanished. Instead of tan carpet and recessed lighting, Wayne saw an odd deserted landscape. A flat glaring light gave a metallic cast to his skin and that of his son. Swirling greenish mists blew past them, occasionally forming shapes, staring, hollow-eyed faces and writhing bodies. Just as Wayne thought that the phantasms were becoming familiar, the mist shifted and the images became something else entirely, something he didn't want to look at.

He shut the door quickly.

David stood behind him, smiling. In his arms was his ragged old stuffed polar bear.

Wayne stared at his son, desperately trying to stay rational. "Where are we?"

"Outside." David's tone implied that this was the simplest, most self-evident truth, one that even a thick-headed adult like his father could see for himself.

"Outside where?"

David shrugged, an amazingly good facsimile of an adult shrug. "Just outside."

Wayne felt light-headed. A sound began to build in

the back of his throat—a scream? Hysterical laughter? He clamped his teeth down on it. Was he hallucinating? "And the company? The entire SONY-BRAUN complex?"

"Someplace else."

"Dr. Farrell?"

"Her, too. She was cold. And she smelled like a machine." David wrinkled his nose.

"But I'm here with you?" Not a hallucination. Somehow, Wayne knew this was real.

"Bear likes you."

Wayne took a deep breath. "David, Daddy wants you to make things be the way they were before."

"No. Bear says no."

"Can't or won't?"

David's voice grew shrill. "Bear says no."

Fear gripped Wayne with icy force. "Son, I thought Mommy threw Snowy Bear out long ago."

David stopped smiling. "Mommy was mean to Bear." He hugged the toy tighter. "Bear wants his ice cream now."

"Take us back and then we'll have a treat."

Wayne's son frowned. His eyes were a steely blue, like ice, cold and glowing. "Wants ice cream *now*."

David stared at him until Wayne began to feel cold, nauseated. His toes and fingers tingled and went dead. He looked down to get away from the arctic glow in his son's eyes.

And numbly, Wayne realized that he would have to be careful, very very careful, to make sure that Bear continued to get what he wanted. Perhaps someday, when David was older, he could convince his son to prevail on Bear, and bring the world back. But right now, Bear wanted ice cream.

"Okay," Wayne said, and his voice sounded as though it had nearly frozen solid in his throat. "Coming right up."

SOUL TO TAKE

by Vanessa Crouther

. . . My head is splitting . . .

"Damn this shit."

He dreamed again last night.

. . . What a little fool . . .

"It's a good thing no one can see you, crying like a baby."

. . . Remember, it's not real. Think clearly, boy, it's just a dream.

A roar exploded in his head.

"NO! It's not real!" he screamed and covered his ears, "No! Stop this now. . . . ya hear me? It's not happening!"

Gino fumbled through his jacket for a cigarette. When he didn't find one, he started rummaging through the pile of rags that he used for a bed. He found an old, half crumbled menthol. He stuck the cigarette in his mouth and pulled out his gold-plated lighter from his right jeans pocket.

He then performed the ritual: tossing the lighter in the air twice, he caught it in his left hand. He flicked his thumb up to open it and down to light it. A spectacular display that took less than 30 seconds, something he used to do all the time. But of late, he only performed his liturgy to nicotine when he knew he was alone and safe. His habits—at the very least— could get him killed these days. With a slow drag of nicotine Gino took a look around at his hovel and smiled. "There's no place like home."

He tucked his lighter back into the pocket of his jeans. He took two drags off his cigarette and extinguished it between his fingers. He put the butt in his jacket and headed into the Zone.

The Zone (once known as the Gold Coast) was just another marketplace. It was a place where things were bought and sold, stolen and then bought and sold again. Not just possessions changed hands; a lot of people could be procured in the circular emporium. For a price, hookers, C.P.A.s, drivers, pilots, couriers, babies, arsonists, killers, and politicians could be had. The motto on the streets was "if you don't see it, you haven't set the right price."

Four short months ago Gino had been like so many others, when he paraded down the street to sell whatever he could. He still looked young enough to have a few options; with his long black hair and full beard he was attractive enough to appeal to both sexes. The ladies loved his dangerous charm—they saw him as the kind of man who would probably break a collarbone at the moment of climax.

The emporium offered him quite a selection of opportunities: hired gun, driver, muscle, con artist, whore. If a valid figure was offered, Gino was willing to do almost anything; money was the key.

In the Zone and in the City, money was survival; it was god for many. Each creature worshiped it his own way. Those blessed with the "spirit" endured. Those without sought salvation on the hard, stony path of the Zone that they might endure also. The cycle never ceased. In the City there was the quiet, respectful exchange of resources, but in the Zone the fundamentalist approach (of cold, hard cash) flourished.

Flash to cash to trash: a proper package and sleek

display brought out the bucks and bucks brought all levels of life out for the ride. Last spring, Gino was the king of this playground. He'd owned the Zone; and any time day or night he could be found indulging his passion: to be seen. These days it was important to see—to be aware and protected.

Gino toured the Zone; he discreetly promoted his wares. Sporting a conservative haircut and a neatly trimmed mustache, his distant manner only hinted at the rest of the package. It was on his third trip around, Gino noticed a gentleman leaning against the entrance to the Good Moves Saloon. The man (somewhere in his late 40s) motioned for Gino to follow him into the bar. Gino shook his head and mouthed the word, here.

The man objected and Gino shrugged. The man gritted his teeth and walked over to Gino.

Gino smiled, "What can I do for you?"

"I really don't want to discuss this out on the street."

"Well, your loss," he turned away.

The man cut in front of him, "Please . . . sorry; I have money." He pulled a few bills from his pocket.

"Whatcha want?"

"It's kinda complicated. Can't we talk somewhere? . . . like there. I could use a drink."

"Well, if you're buying, how can I say no."

The man smiled nervously and entered the bar. Gino followed. In the dark, crowded recess of the bar, the gentleman sat down at an empty table. He signaled to the bartender for two drinks. A waitress in a snug-fitting jumpsuit brought over two beers. The man paid her and asked for two more.

As the man drank the beer, he gave Gino a once over. "Much better."

"Uh-huh."

"Well, uh, let's get down to business. Okay?"

Gino nodded.

The waitress returned with the beer; the man settled up. He gulped down his first draft and said, "I've gotta proposition."

"Gotta cigarette?"

"Yeah," he pulled a new pack out of his shirt pocket. He handed them to Gino. Gino took one and started to give them back.

The man refused, "No, keep 'em. This job . . . pays, uh, ya know it pays well—if you do well. Aren't afraid of a little work, are ya?"

"Uh-uh," Gino muttered as he toyed with his glass. "Light?"

"Sure," he tossed Gino some matches. "I could tell right off you're the man for the job."

Gino pocketed the matches after lighting up.

"What's your name, son?"

"Gino."

"Well, Gino, my name's Parks . . . Jim Parks. We could be doing quite a bit of business together. I don't forget anyone who knows how to do a job right. We'll be good friends . . . I take care of my friends. Know what I'm saying?"

"Uh-huh, but what do you want?"

"It's not really what I want—"

"Uh-huh."

"I work for some people. They need someone like you."

Gino took a sip from his beer.

"I get them things, ya know, sometimes I get them people. Right now, they could use you. This guy needs some protection. But not your run-o-the-mill slug off the street . . . someone discreet . . . someone who knows his business. Someone who can take care of himself . . . and don't look like muscle . . . someone like you."

"How much?"

"A thousand a day . . . for three days max."

"A thousand?"

"Well, that's after my commission. These folks don't want to step down and dirty their hands, they pay me for that. And you pay me for hooking ya up."

"How much do you get?"

"A small percentage. Do ya want the job?"

"Maybe. How much?"

"A couple hundred from them, a couple hundred off your fee."

"In dollars?" Gino leaned forward.

"Uh, all together . . . uh, about . . . three g's"

"Hardly fair."

The man paled, "Uh, maybe you're right . . . we could negotiate."

"Uh-huh."

The man swigged his last beer and signaled for another one.

They completed the preliminaries of their arrangement and left the bar around eight p.m. Parks was feeling no pain. Gino watched him stagger into the night toward the cool, clean side of the city. He waited until the man disappeared before starting home.

Gino was very much sober; he rarely drank anymore. Drugs and drink were in the past. Once he would have found solace in the old feeling. He used to allow himself the openness that feeling created. He'd become wary of people: would-be friends, unwanted buddies, acquaintances, family, and enemies (seen and unseen.)

Four short months ago, he could've afforded such luxuries. Gino didn't risk such frivolous diversion. The price for pleasure was too much . . . it would've probably cost his mind (which he wasn't ready to forfeit yet).

*   *   *

His hands shook as he tried to light a cigarette. "Shit!" shouted Gino as the wind blew out another match. He crushed the empty matchbook in his fist, then pulled his lighter out of his jeans pocket.

He pressed the cool metal lighter to his forehead and took two deep breaths. A sudden wave of pain engulfed him; he doubled over, dropping the lighter and cigarette.

"No! God, no."

Gino felt a rumbling deep within—it was as if he were in the middle of an earthquake. The ground was shaking; his stomach roared; his head pounded. He screamed, but the sound was lost as the world reverberated in his ears. His eyes rolled up in his head and he fell forward.

Even in this unconscious state the sound persisted and amplified. Gino no longer struggled. He was lost in a vision of someone else's making:

A brilliant light encircled him. He turned this way and that as he tried to find the sound's source. He could see nothing, but a whiteness on the horizon.

The roar lessened to a soft rumble. Suddenly, he knew what plagued him. It was the whirling blades of a helicopter. He turned toward the sound, and still could see nothing. But once he identified it in his mind, the noise reverted back to a thunderous din.

The intensity of that sound shook the ground beneath his feet. Gino fell to his knees. He couldn't see the copter, but he knew that if he couldn't escape its invisible blades he would die.

He ran.

The earth lurched beneath his feet. Gino tumbled once more. He tried to steady himself with outstretched hands. He got up quickly and raised his hands up to find them scraped and bloody. He couldn't feel them;

or anything else. There was only the pounding of the copter at his back.

He had to get away or die.

As he ran, but found himself no further away from the sound, he knew there was no escaping—no refuge to be found.

Thought eluded him. He was lost. The excruciating sound had killed some small part of him with deafening precision. But he still ran—until his legs and lungs failed him. He sank to the ground and curled up into a ball.

He waited an eternity for death to overtake him. He wanted to cry, but couldn't. He wanted to pray, but had long forgotten how.

The roar was overhead.

He closed his eyes and sighed one last breath.

The blades erupted through his back. He felt each stroke slice flesh from his body.

Misery drowned what was left of his sanity. Finally, all that remained was a bloody pile of severed limbs and muscle. But he wasn't dead. He could still hear— still feel. Sound and pain fused; the torment continued. He knew it was just beginning. He felt it creeping through his disjointed flesh like a rushing river.

Blood trickled down from a deep gash above his left eye. His lighter had broken his fall to the concrete floor.

He lifted his (undamaged) hands up to wipe the blood away. His breathing was ragged as he pulled out another smoke. Gino placed it in his mouth, but didn't light it. He picked up the lighter and put it in his pocket.

"Fuck you, Dryden, right back to hell!"

Parks was waiting on the corner of Rush and Cedar.

Gino was late; he couldn't shake the nightmare. He was tense, but not noticeably so.

"Glad to see ya made it."

"Uh-huh"

Parks coughed, "Deal's been set. Ya can start tomorrow."

"The price?"

"Just what you asked for."

"Details?"

"All in good time. Let's have a drink and discuss it."

"Let's not."

"Ah, well . . ."

"Let's walk."

"Right, keep movin' . . . good idea."

They walked north for twenty minutes. "Where we headed?"

"The zoo."

"Zoo? . . . why?" The man stopped.

Gino didn't slow his pace, "Why not?"

"Uh . . . I dunno. Uh, why not?" he trotted to keep up.

They continued along, with Parks muttering to himself. Gino took a cigarette out of his pocket and put it in his mouth. He lit it with the matches Parks had given him earlier.

At the Lincoln Park Zoo, Gino paid a fee and entered the gate. Parks fished up some money and followed him.

Parks muttered, "What I wouldn't give for a cold, wet one."

"Details."

"Mind if I sit?" he pointed to an empty bench. Gino nodded his head. Parks sat down quickly. "Too much exercise. Okay, from now on, you're Mr. Smith. Got it . . . Smith. Tomorrow you go to the Byrne Building, 93rd floor . . . you ask for Mr. Taylor's secretary . . .

right? She'll give you an envelope with your money.
Then you go to that new hotel . . . the uh . . . the
Excelsior . . . remember, get there before two, okay?
. . . in the lobby . . . Mr. Taylor'll meetcha there . . .
follow his instructions . . . that's all you've gotta do
. . . three days . . . over and done. Real sweet.

"Do a good job . . . and I'll have another one real
soon."

"How much?"

"My, my . . . you've gotta one track mind."

"Cut the crap" Gino towered over him.

"Sorry . . . didn't mean any—" Parks got up
quickly. "A good price . . . a grand or two. Gotta
run."

Gino watched Parks depart. He sat down and lit
another cigarette. He stared ahead into a cage. In the
tiny cage, a lone black leopard prowled rapidly back
and forth. It growled deeply and continually rubbed
its dark fur against the bars, seemingly trying to force
itself through them.

As he waited, he tried to will the cat to freedom.
And the animal, sensing his presence, stopped and
stared back. All Gino heard was the cat's shallow
breathing. His whole world was in that cage. Gino
remained so absorbed that sunset approached and settled without his notice. The security patrol roused him
and sent him on his way.

He woke suddenly at five a.m. He hadn't dreamed
it again, but he felt it resting like a lead weight on his
chest. It was waiting just ahead. If he wasn't careful,
it'd seize him.

Downtown Chicago was bright and shiny; steel and
plastic. The streets were clean (and plated with gold).
Citizens marched in the pecuniary procession; they
strode from banks and offices with their heads held

high. They bore offerings to the financial gods and goddesses in ceremonial envelopes, briefcases, and folders. They trod the paths of righteous in formal footwear of Gucci, NeoPaulo, Louis V, and Kikeo.

The mecca of money had but one true temple, the Byrne Building. At 178 stories, it dwarfed all competition. Those chosen to penetrate its sanctum were honored and feared.

Dressed in a fashionable dark suit, Gino noticed a few worshipers turn and nod. He nodded back. After entering the black and gray marble lobby, he asked for directions at the information center. A young lady clad in lavender ushered him to a security checkpoint.

"Name."

"Mr. Smith." said Gino.

The uniformed guard checked his list and issued him a level 4 passcard. The passcard was a ByrneCorp patent for a micro-encoded access card. Anyone wearing a passcard could be tracked and monitored in any building, zone, or city; if the location was properly outfitted with Y-sensors (another ByrneCorp patent).

Gino fastened the access card to his lapel as he listened to the guard's instructions. He rode an elevator to the 50th floor. He was met by another guard in plainclothes, who escorted him to the corporate access elevators. Gino took a second elevator to the 93rd floor.

The 93rd floor was a scene of highly polished silver fixtures and black furnishings. Four receptionists sat at a large black desk, answering phones and welcoming new arrivals.

Gino was greeted by a young blonde girl, who smiled and said, "Mr. Smith, Ms. Mailing's expecting you. Down the corridor and third door on the right."

"Thank you."

When he reached the third door, Gino knocked, "Ms. Mailing?"

"Come in."

Ms. Mailing was finishing a phone conversation. She covered the mouthpiece and said, "Mr. Smith. Please be seated."

Gino sat in a gray leather chair.

"That's right . . . no later than Friday. By then Mr. Taylor'll have the feedback on this project." She paused, "Right, Friday. Thanks, bye," she hung up. "Sorry, business—"

"No problem."

She took a manila envelope from the center drawer of her desk. "Mr. Taylor feels that this should be everything you need."

Gino took the sealed envelope and said, "This should do it. Thanks."

"You're welcome," she stood and offered him her hand; Gino rose and shook it. He retraced his steps to the first floor. At the security desk, he turned in the passcard and left.

Gino disappeared quickly into the flow of people. He found a quiet secluded spot to check the envelope: all the money was there. He glanced at his watch; noting that it was only 10:30 he left the downtown area. He headed to the Zone to stash the money.

At 1:30 Gino arrived at the posh Excelsior Hotel. Dressed in black, he immediately headed for the bar just off the main lobby. Seated by the windows of the Sir Raleigh Pub, he waited for Mr. Taylor.

Precisely at two p.m., a young man carrying a brief-case strolled in. Gino watched as the man glanced at his platinum watch and crossed the lobby. The man found a chair directly across from the entrance and sat down.

Gino paid for his untouched beer and left the bar. He approached the young man and asked, "Mr. Taylor?"

"Mr. Smith?" he stood up and offered his hand. "You're prompt."

"I try to be."

"Please, sit down. Just a few things . . . I'll be brief."

"Fine."

"Was the payment satisfactory?"

Gino nodded.

"We always want to be fair."

"We?" His head was aching.

"Well, yes. We. A certain anonymity must be maintained . . . for your protection as well as our own. Nothing to be worried about."

"Certainly."

"Good," he opened the briefcase. He took out a small leather pouch and small envelope. "It's pretty straightforward. First, deliver this package to the address you'll find in this envelope. There you will get another item and another set of instructions."

"This is gonna take three days?"

"Well . . . for three days you'll be our courier. All materials you receive are very important . . . very expensive. Handle them with the utmost care. You'll have a precise timetable to follow. Deliveries can't be late. All in all, three days—a number of transfers— and give or take a few about a dozen locations.

"If we like your work . . . we might be able to swing a bonus. Something really substantial," he smiled.

"I'll do my best."

"That's all we can hope for."

Gino pocketed the items and nodded. They both stood up.

"Good luck, Mr. Smith. First dispatch at nine a.m. tomorrow."

"Thanks and good-bye."

Walking swiftly, Gino made it back to the safety of

the Zone in thirty minutes. He massaged his temples and inhaled deeply the sweet scents of poverty. He felt a bit safer in these familiar surroundings. At least in the Zone, he knew which side of the bread was buttered with arsenic.

Early the next morning, Gino hauled himself out of bed and started the day with a nicotine breakfast. Since his trek was arranged to take many turns through the city, he outfitted himself in blue jeans, leather jacket and silk shirt.

He checked the instructions, "Cullerton and Indiana. Soho District." He opened the package once more. It contained two ounces of the federal controlled substance, cocaine.

"Wouldn't ya know it? Running drugs."

As he placed a switchblade in his back pocket, "Remember, Mr. Taylor, in all things moderation . . . even your vices. Just careful enough . . . one ounce more and I'd go to jail for this."

He walked through Uptown, the zoo, the Zone and past the outskirts of Downtown. He arrived in the SoHo district at 8:50 a.m. He wandered by the artist lofts and museums, killing time. At 9:00 Gino entered the appointed building. He was met in the foyer by a janitor. Gino exchanged parcel for envelope.

A quick trade that was typical of most of his stint for Mr. Taylor. It was drugs to money; money to circuits; and money to drugs. Easy as long as he remained wary of the cops.

On the second day of traipsing over the city, Gino sat once more in front of the leopard's cage. Absorbing himself in the instinctive movements of the cat, he relaxed between trips. His mind drifted far from the last few days, away from his throbbing headache. The cat's pacing became his focus. He could see nothing beyond. Only pacing. . . .

*   *   *

She was pacing still. When he left the night before, she'd been walking back and forth in their tiny studio apartment. Jeska hadn't changed her clothes. He knew from the dark circles under her eyes that she hadn't slept either.

"So I guess you didn't get caught," she said as she sat down.

"Jes—"

"Don't start."

"Jes, please. . . ."

"I don't believe this shit. You stay in the streets . . . hustlin' for that last buck."

"Jes, it's what I have to do. We need the money."

"There's easier ways. You could go to Dryden—"

"That's just what he wants . . . just give him another chance to add a few refinements into his program—"

"But they can help us . . . we can go back to the center."

"The center . . . so they can shoot you full of dope . . . and carve you up . . ."

"You're fulla shit."

"And they're not? Get this straight, babe, no one is messin' with my head again. They're not sending me through their brass hoop in the name of science . . . in the name of whatever piece of crap they call it . . . not even you."

"Me! You fuckin'—" She threw a book at him.

Gino caught it easily, "That's right and proud of it."

Jeska stood up and started pacing again. Tears welled up in her eyes as she whispered, "You're so strange."

"What?"

"I don't matter to you. You don't listen to me . . . you don't care about anybody."

"Jes, you're wrong. You're all I care about. I wanna make you happy."

"Make me happy . . . right, night after night you're out there . . ." she started crying, ". . . lying . . . stealing . . . out there selling yourself. You think this makes me happy . . . not knowing where you are or who you're with . . . happy, are you that stupid?"

"Look, babe, this isn't paradise for me either, but as soon as we get enough cash, we'll walk away."

"Walk away now, please."

"Where to? Dryden?"

"Why not?"

" 'Cause . . . what he wants costs too much. Look, Jes, when he gets finished with his little experiments . . . we'll be lucky if we can breathe."

"Gino, you're wrong. He wouldn't hurt us . . . he promised—"

"And you believe him . . ."

"Yes, I do . . . why shouldn't I?"

"He's lying . . . can't you see that?"

"If you really believe that . . . then let's just walk away."

"Not yet . . . we need money."

"Shit, I'm so sick of hearing that—every damn thing boils down to cash."

"And it doesn't for you?" he said sarcastically. "Always wanting to run back to Daddy for a new dress just 'cause the fashions have changed in the last twenty-four hours."

"No, don't be so stupid . . . you've no right to bring my father into this—"

"Right," Gino overemphasized the "t."

"I'm serious."

"Daddy's poor little rich girl—slumming with the trash . . . I've got news for you babe, Daddy is right here in the middle of this mess . . . 'cause every day you stand him up in the corner like some damn measuring stick. And every day . . . I fall short.

"And you're saying to yourself, 'Look at Gino, he's too stupid; Gino's trash; he's got no money and he never will.' "

"Money—"

"That's the problem in a nutshell, money!"

"Only because you've made it your personal god." Gino laughed.

"I'm just wondering what you'd do if you had money? Not just enough to get you through next week, but all the money you'd ever need?"

Gino looked and then turned away.

"Stop! I want to know."

"Do you?"

"Yeah."

"I don't think you'd understand even if . . ."

"Even if what?"

"If I could . . . tell you. If I really understood it myself."

She shook her head and laughed, "Tell me."

"Money . . . money isn't God. It's a way . . . a way to get out. And even if it was a god; it isn't mine."

"Then why do you do this? Why sell yourself to the highest bidder?"

"Why not? Someone's always buying."

"You little—" She tried to slap him, but he caught her hand and she jerked away.

"I'm whatever the doctor ordered."

"Whatever money can make of you."

"Jes, I learned something a long time ago. I don't know who taught me . . . I don't know if it was my mother . . . a cop . . . it doesn't matter. But someplace way back inside I know just how important cash is. I know what it can do and I know what it can't. It's genuine. Without it . . . you know . . . without it you ain't gonna get shit. Without it you've got no one.

Just look at you . . . look at what money does for
your father . . . and what it does for you."

"Me? I don't care about it. I'm not obsessed—"

He cuts her off. "That's not what I'm saying. It's
not an obsession . . . it's an exception. I don't have
it, so I have to do things . . . a lotta things to get it.
You have it and because you've got it you don't see
. . . you don't see its importance. It's become a part
of you . . . it's an appendage . . . an extra arm . . .
that you no longer have to see . . . you no longer have
to think how about to use it . . . it's, uh, it's second
nature. *It's you.* It's all of you . . . but for me . . . for
most of us out there . . . we don't have that arm. We
can't reach out and get anything we want. It's not
there and we're all waiting like those guys who come
back from a war—missing legs and arms. We're waiting to be fitted with the proper equipment so we can
fit in . . . so we can be like you. But we can't be. You
won't let us, 'cause you know what we had to go
through to get that arm . . . and you question us, you
chastise us for being different . . . for struggling . . .
you make us dirty . . . and obscene. And you . . . all
of you . . . make money a god! And you wanna know
why you do it?"

"No!"

" 'Cause it makes you God. You want us to fall
down on our knees and adore you."

As she started to turn away, Gino reached out to
stop her, but she rushed past him. She grabbed her
shoulder bag and slammed the door behind her.

He muttered, "But it won't make you perfect. It
won't even take away the pain."

A long time passed before he went after her, but
he knew that she'd be waiting. He pulled his leather
jacket out of the closet and left.

He spotted her kneeling in the middle of the
sidewalk.

She was rocking back and forth as she read aloud from a tiny, blue leather book. Her words were barely audible, but he knew that they held some kind of energy. She set the book down in front of her and reached into her huge canvas bag. Still reciting, she withdrew a clear plastic-lidded tumbler. She placed it next to the book. A deep brown liquid covered the bottom of the glass; and a rose-colored substance rested on the top. As her voice grew louder, the street seemed to fall back away from him. She removed the lid.

Gino watched in silence as a thick smoke escaped from the tumbler. The brown and pink fluids mixed and mingled into a twirling pattern. Slowly she raised her arms. Her hands seemed to draw the smoke up above her head. It floated up, veiling her within its depths. She stood up and picked up the book.

She held it as though it were a crying babe to be soothed and placated. And like a mother caring for a child, she kissed it and gently closed its pages with the words, "To the wind I send you, to the sky I let you fly."

Jeska shut her eyes and whispered, "It's in the hands of the wind. I set you free."

When he tried to wrap his arms around her, she pulled away.

She opened her eyes and whispered, "Go, while you can."

"Stop this nonsense."

"Go . . . run now . . . soon it'll be too late—we'll destroy you."

"Jes, stop this now." He shook her.

"Please go . . . please."

"Hallelujah! After all this, I'll be ready for the Olympics."

Gino read his latest instructions. He skirted the

downtown area and headed to the 11th Street police station.

"Well, well . . . deliver a box to the chief of detectives . . . and pray like hell this ain't a trap."

His only thought was to stay cool as he walked into the lion's den.

He took a lunch break at 3 p.m. He walked back to the zoo and stood at the leopard's cage. Gino lit up his fifteenth cigarette of the day. He rubbed his temples and leaned against the cage. The cat stopped pacing, but didn't back away.

The cat roared loudly to warn him away, but Gino stood firm. He inhaled the smoke deeply. They stared at each other for a long time, neither giving ground. Finally, the cat sat down on its haunches and Gino sank down beside the cage.

For a time all was peaceful. He only heard the cat: the animal's rapid breathing and its occasional bellow.

He woke up to Jeska's screaming.

Her skin was on fire. He felt the heat radiating from her as he touched her arm. He tried to wake her up, but she couldn't hear him. She was lost in another world. She was still screaming when he turned on the light.

Her color wasn't good. She was turning red. It was as though she'd been out in the sun too long. As her skin grew brighter, her fever elevated. Gino knew that if she didn't wake up soon she would die. He brushed her cheek.

"Don't touch me, please. It hurts."

"I'm sorry, but you need the alcohol. It will bring your temperature down."

"No! I can't stand it. My skin's raw . . . it's bad enough . . . don't move. You're making it land on me."

"What?"

"Everything . . ." she looked up at him. "See it . . . it's killing me." And she raised her hand to show him."

"I don't see anything."

"See . . . that," She pointed to a little speck. "It's drilling into my flesh. I can feel everything . . . it's all digging in . . . don't move . . . if I don't move . . . it'll stop . . . it's got to."

She shivered uncontrollably. The tears streamed down her face and she began to whimper. "Make them stop it. Make them stop."

"I don't know how."

"They're killing me!"

"Jeska, Jes—"

"Stop it! No . . . not that—stop!"

"Jes, what's wrong?"

"No . . . no . . . ! Stop it . . . don't burn me. No!" Her whimpering turned into howling.

"Jeska!" He grabbed her shoulders. Her pupils were huge. Gino shook her. She no longer responded to his touch. "Look at me, look at me."

Suddenly, the sound stopped. Gino wrapped his arms around her and held her. She was cold to the touch. He knew she was gone, but he rocked her like a baby.

"Jes," he whispered over and over again.

When Gino woke up, the zoo was darker. His head felt as if it were splitting open. He got up slowly and walked over to the cage. He placed his hand up to the bars. The leopard backed away and watched.

Gino held steady as the cat, tired of the diversion, went back to pacing. Gino, too, turned away.

Walking on to what was scheduled to be the last of his appointments, he kept thinking of Jeska. He remembered every detail of this dream. It was one of the dreams he lived every night. But this wasn't just a dream; it was real . . . not some nightmare to be shooed away in the light of day. It'd happened and there was no going back to save her. He couldn't deny it even when he'd poured the kerosene and torched the center. He knew he could only try to save himself, but he still had attempted to appease his vengeful nature.

Though this episode held no happiness, as long as he remembered; he knew he was alive. If he held on to his own thoughts, he might have a chance . . . to survive.

Gino breathed deeply and closed his eyes.

The building at 407 Main was one of the last of its kind: a beautiful stone mansion isolated on the shore. He rang the doorbell and waited. Over the intercom, a mechanical voice droned, "Enter." The door opened.

In the entryway, every inch of wall, floor, and ceiling were covered in a deep, rich mahogany. Even the massive staircase seemed to be carved out of a single piece of wood. Gino moved quickly into the building.

The same cold voice droned, "On the table to your left you'll find a passcard. Please put it on."

Gino did so.

"Mr. Smith, take the stairs to the third floor. Once there, enter the door to the library. It'll be the only open door you'll encounter. If you should veer off course, you'll be corrected."

The smell of rancid furniture polish only added to Gino's problems. His brain was pounding and his stomach starting to churn.

When he reached the third floor, he was ready to pass out. He pulled a pack of cigarettes from his jacket. He leaned back against the banister. His hands were shaking as he put a cigarette in his mouth. He started toward the open door as he searched his pockets for a match. Not finding one he cautiously took out his lighter, lit his cigarette, and slid the lighter back in his pocket.

He inhaled the smoke deeply as he strolled into the library. He was greeted by the sight of more wood. The huge library was lined on two sides with maple bookshelves; the shelves were overflowing with books, old and new. A lot of chairs and sofas were situated throughout the room. At the far wall were two ornately carved doors. In front of this wall was a desk; and behind that desk was an ancient gentleman.

"Mr. Smith," he boomed, "nice of you to come. Do sit down."

Gino came in and sat in an old chair.

"Do you have the envelope?"

"Yes, sir." He got up and placed the envelope on the desk.

"Thank you very much," he said as he opened it. "I'm pleased to know you do such good work . . . it's so very rare these days to find . . . oh, do forgive me, I didn't introduce myself. I'm Mr. Byrne."

"Mr. Byrne?"

"Right, as I was saying . . . someone who's willing to work and knows how to follow instructions. You have integrity. It's good to find someone with integrity, so few are blessed with such traits."

"Sir?"

"Never mind, my boy . . . you've done well," he mumbled. "You've come through with flying colors."

Mr. Byrne leaned forward and confided, "I'd like to offer you a job. You could work directly for me."

"Well, uh—"

"You don't have to answer right this minute," he chuckled. "I understand you'll need time to think. Nothing should be rushed into . . . nothing that counts. Take your time. Sleep on it."

"Thank you, sir" said Gino. He got up to leave. Mr. Byrne handed him a new envelope.

"And if you don't accept, I might still throw some business your way. You can call me any time, my number's there, along with your bonus. Good night, son."

"Thank you," Gino hurried from the room. He wanted to sprint down the stairs, but he knocked a long ash from his cigarette and walked.

When he reached the first floor, the intercom crackled, "Remove the card and place it on the table."

Gino ripped the card from his lapel and tossed it on the table. The door swung open and he left.

"Jeska! No!" he cried. He bolted up and his brain exploded with excruciating pain. His teeth were trying to wiggle free. Gino clamped his hand over his mouth. He struggled to remain conscious. He had dreamed again. This time his two dreams had fused. Jeska had become a part of the unreality. He thought maybe this was a sign: their dream was becoming his own.

"Money" he said out loud.

Well . . . I could always use the money, but . . . always a but. But what . . . but this could be too dangerous. And dangerous ain't smart.

He went to the Zone to think. This had been his kingdom. He felt secure here among his own kind. He felt closer to Jes here.

He found a phone in a corner coffee shop. He dialed the number Mr. Byrne had given him. The old man answered on the second ring. "Yes."

"Mr. Byrne, it's Mr. Smith."

"Oh, Mr. Smith, been expecting your call. I was just discussing your situation with a few acquaintances. Everyone's pleased with your progress."

"I can't take the job."

"That's too bad. We had high hopes for you, but I

do understand your reluctance to tie yourself down. I only hope that we'll work together in the future. A few of my colleagues would be interested in meeting you."

"Well, I don't think that's possible."

"Pity, but we do understand. Commitments can be so costly, but I'm sure we'll get together soon."

"Thanks, but—"

"Keep an open mind, Mr. Smith. Things have a way of changing before our eyes . . . overtaking you when you least expect it."

"I hope not."

"All we ask is that you're openminded."

His head was pounding savagely. Gino slammed the phone down.

For close to an hour, Gino wandered through the streets. He finally knew that he needed to find Parks. After checking out quite a few establishments, he headed for the Good Moves Saloon. Parks was slumped over the bar.

"Parks."

"Huh . . . leav' me . . . 'lone . . . ain't bothering nobody," he slurred.

"Parks," Gino tapped the man on the shoulder.

Peering up, Parks started laughing. "What ya know, Gino? How's my buddy? Can I . . . uh . . . buy you a drink?"

"No, thanks. But I need something."

"Don't we all."

"Some info."

"Uh, information . . . well, that'll cost ya . . . but seeing as you're such . . . a . . . good pal, I'll give ya a rate."

"How much?"

"Not much I promise . . . not much . . . with the bundle you got—"

"How much!?"

"Well, still talkative." He turned to the bartender and shouted, "Hey, I need a refill."

"How much?"

"Uh, that depends."

"On what?"

"Depends . . . on what ya wanna know . . . and more importantly, depends on who's . . . all affected."

"Which means?"

"Which means, it depends."

"Which means, you're drunk. Tomorrow when you sober up, I expect to see you."

"Right, pal," replied Parks. He laughed to himself.

"At 10 a.m."

"10 a.m.," he repeated. "Anything you say."

"At the zoo, at the lion house. And you won't be late."

"Right, Gino," he nodded.

Gino placed his hand on Parks' wrist and squeezed slightly. He looked him in the eye and said, "I know you won't disappointment me."

"Of course not . . . I . . . I'd never do that."

Parks was a little early; he seemed hung over. Gino sat on the lion house steps, tossing something shiny in the air.

"Have a seat."

"No, thanks. Don't think I could get up from there."

Gino leaned back and said, "Suit yourself."

"What . . . what do you need?" he said nervously.

"Some information on ByrneCorp."

"You're kidding?"

"No."

"ByrneCorp, no, I don't think so—"

"Parks, I'll pay—"

"Brother, you haven't got enough."

"I'm serious."

"You gotta death wish, but I don't." He turned away.

"You aren't going anywhere." Gino leapt up to stop him. He dropped his lighter.

"Listen, ya don't mess with the big boys . . . 'cause if you do . . . you're gone, not even a memory. They'll make you disappear . . . not just now, but all the way back. . . you wouldn't have even been a gleam in your daddy's eye after they get through with you."

"Tell me what you know."

"I just did."

Gino held Parks by the collar and dragged him around the building to the leopard cage. The cat stalked back and forth. He whispered, "Tell me everything."

"You've got the wrong guy . . . I don't know nothing."

"Tell me," he snarled as he seized Parks' throat.

"Really . . . I don't know anything." Gino slammed him against the bars. The leopard backed away and roared.

"Shit, man . . . don't do this . . . I don't know nothing. I . . . I—"

The cat roared again and moved forward. Parks felt the animal's breath on his back.

"Tell me."

"Oh, God . . . uh, oh no . . . oh, God . . . uh, they . . . they paid me. They paid me to find you."

"For the job?"

"No! They wanted you . . . so, I, uh . . . uh found you. I've been following you . . . since uh, before . . . before the fire."

"You can't have—"

"Yes, it's been easy—for the most part. They gave me this." He pulled a little brown metal box from his coat.

Gino snatched it. The box contained a miniature screen where a light pulsed on and off. "This?"

"Yeah, a tracking device . . . it works on chips and, uh, uh those Y-sensors."

Gino released him. "Go call your boss."

"What?"

"Call him."

"You're crazy. I don't wanna die."

"Either way, you're dead. Tell him I want to meet him."

"I ain't doing it."

A switchblade was shoved against his throat. "Well, then, you've got a choice. Die now or die later."

Three hours later, Gino sat with his back against the cage. Occasionally, the cat brushed against the bars. The feel of its warm fur was reassuring to him. The security patrols had been paid off for the night.

He waited in silence; he waited for the dream.

The earth trembled and he stood bathed in a white light. He heard the rumbling grow closer and louder, but he turned to face it.

Pain shot through his skull like a runaway locomotive. But he stood firm.

The invisible blades roared overhead.

And silence fell.

He strained to see.

Nothing but white light all around.

Alone, but Jes was there. He couldn't see her, but her voice echoed, ". . . to the wind . . . to the sky."

He awoke from his daydream with a dull headache. Gino stood up and took Parks' tracker and smashed the lock off the cage. He opened the door and sat back down.

The leopard leapt from the cage. It marked off its

new territory around Gino and lay down beside him. It was dark before Parks' boss arrived. Dressed in gray, Mr. Taylor strolled up.

"Mr. Taylor, good of you to come."

"Mr. Smith."

"Cut the crap. You know who I am, you've always known. I think it's about time to tidy up."

Taylor squatted down. "Maybe it is. This project didn't turn out the way we planned. But on the whole, pretty good research.

"You're different, Gino. Extraordinary . . . Mr. Byrne's special case."

"How so?"

"One of the few long-term projects. You might say he raised you," he smiled, " . . . and in a sense—he has. He's always had a power over you. He instilled a sense of what's really important.

"Not directly, of course. But he's not without influence."

"What the hell for?"

"Because he owns you. You're his creation. He's given you things since you were five. Not money . . . but people. People . . . your mother; clients in your sordid career; the women you've loved. Everything for a purpose."

"You're full of shit."

"Only you developed a little off the mark and he had to correct it. So up pops Doc Dryden and his bag of tricks. He tried his best, but still you fought back. A little surgery, an implant here and there and you were susceptible to a little dream therapy. It might have worked too, but Jeska screwed that up."

"I don't believe this."

"You should, it's all true. He was so proud of you. Pity, you could have been a great triumph."

Gino stroked the leopard's head. "I sort of thought

you'd feel a little less than charitable." The cat went to sleep.

"Sorry," he said as he pulled out a gun.

Closing his eyes, Gino whispered, "Wind and sky."

A sharp blast of air pushed past and the helicopter began its requiem again.

Power. He envisioned thousands of blades piercing a body: spine was chopped in two; skin mutilated, bones split, fingers severed. Legs amputated at the ankle, at the knee, then at the hip.

Flesh pulled away from muscle; muscle torn from tendons; teeth smashed, eyes and ears gone.

Nothing intact.

Raw, mangled nerve endings dangled like live wires downed by a massive storm.

Nothing, but pain.

When he opened his eyes, what was left of Mr. Taylor lay at his feet. The cat still slept at his side.

Power. The vision was real: creation outshines creator.

He rocked back and forth with the cat's head nestled in his arms and thought he could be a god.

And he walked away. . . .

STANDING ORDERS

by Barry N. Malzberg

This is Luke Christmas, the President. The standing orders are in effect. President today, Secretary of Defense yesterday, Health and Welfare tomorrow. Then recycle and switch. Being President is the most fun of all, the day he looks forward to. With luck it happens twice a week unless they call off the Cabinet meetings on sudden notice and herd them all into the dayroom for extra thorazine and career planning. Luke had been afraid that they would pull one of those switches today. They hadn't done it in a while, but here it is Wednesday and the Cabinet meeting seems to be going off without a hitch. Luke is having a good time, here in simulation therapy. That is what they call it in their charts and summaries. Luke has a better name for it, though. He calls it playing President. (Or playing Secretary of Defense, whatever.) It is about as good as it is likely to get for him. Luke knows that the future is nothing he can count on. Sometimes the drugs take hold and sometimes they do not. Sometimes he thinks he has the situation licked and other times he feels like an old loony in a ward somewhere, playacting power fantasies. Up and down, in and out. But today is a good day. Luke feels solid, all the way through and the Cabinet is listening to him with unusual intensity. They are paying attention and well they should. He is, after all, the President.

So here is Luke Christmas talking to the Secretary

of Defense, the Secretary of State, the National Security Adviser, and so on and so forth. "We have to
take a strong line," he says. "We are coming into a
new game plan, a new universe altogether. A new
millennium coming up. Everything is going to change
in the two thousands, you know? Different times, different rules." He twirls the belt on his bathrobe, flaps
it around, shows the three hundred and sixty degree
angle which represents the Earth moving around the
Sun. "Get it?" Luke says. "Everything is going into
a different orbit. So what do you think down there?
Is the Argentine situation under control?"

Argentina has been a son of a gun recently. Rebels,
revolutionaries, struggles among the loyalists, a Presi-
dential assassination, the succession of the widow to
the unfilled term, a panic when flood relief (*flood relief in Argentina?*) went astray and slipped into Bolivia
instead. Bolivia, Argentina, Nicaragua, Brazil: all of
these people and places were in tumult and it was
hard to sort them out. Still, you had to keep them
separate in your mind, the President thought. That
was part of the job. Every third day, anyway. "So
what do you hear?" he says.

The National Security Adviser breaks the silence,
looks over his shoulder, then stares at the President.
"Borders," he says, "they're infiltrating borders. It
has to do with the sheep."

"Sheep? Whose borders? What infiltration?"

"Well," the Adviser says, "we're working on this.
We're trying to figure it out. It's not easy. We get
conflicting reports."

Luke Christmas stared at his counselor, then looked
up and down the table. "Hard to sort out," he said,
"well, it's a confusing business. Are there any other
comments?"

Carmen, the chairman of the Joint Chiefs of Staff
today says, "We're having a little trouble with that

situation in Montana. It looks like we're going to have to have a full mobilization there, try to control the situation." She shakes her head, looks toward the door. "I don't want to be too specific," she says. "You know what I mean."

Luke knows what she means. The reactor has been firing out of control for some weeks now. They cannot seem to control the chain reaction and the burn is moving inexorably through the earth, threatening to break free in Helena or some place like that. It is a situation with which he had to contend when he was Defense and he had no answers then; it certainly hasn't improved. "Well," Luke says, "if we have to call out the troops, we'll just do it, I guess. Keep it under control any way you can. I don't think there's much we can do."

The chairman nods vigorously. "I know," Carmen says, "Still, you have to try, right? We're all trying." There are little murmurs up and down the table. It is agreed that everyone is doing his or her best according to the parameters of the situation anyway, and no one should be unduly criticized. After a while the nods and mumbles subside and the Cabinet and sub-Cabinet officers look expectantly at Luke again. That is the problem with being President. It has its power and prerogatives, sure, but you have to *run* these things. But what if you don't feel like running them? What if you've had enough of this already and you have other things on your mind? It isn't all simulation therapy. Behind this masking, Luke knows that there are some real problems: the terrible family stuff and so on and the question of drug maintenance which is, when you think about it, delusory because how long can you use drugs to avoid a situation which just gets worse and worse if you didn't believe that you could deal with it. Things could just get worse and worse, and that was for sure.

Anyway. Luke felt the disinterest coming over him. Sometimes it happened just that way. You were at the center of things, simulating like a son of a bitch, and then you just wanted *out*. "Well," he said, "I guess that's all of it, if no one has anything to add. We'll proceed with the agenda in the usual way. Things should be much calmer by tonight, don't you think?"

They seem to think so. They look at him with rounded, glaring Keane eyes, the big eyes of drug-induced accommodation and Luke supposes that he is looking back on them in the same way. They must be some bunch in this dayroom, sitting among the checkerboards and pingpong tables, doing simulation therapy, acting out power politics when most of them are so drugged, so filled with grief, that without the support of the situation they would probably be stretched out on the floor, twitching. "I think we'll adjourn now," Luke says. "Is that all right? What does everyone think? We have this busy day ahead, dealing with our own stuff, isn't that so?" Everyone seems to think that is so. Luke picks up the gavel which they gave him and pounds it once on the table. Sometimes it is fun to be formal even though he is sure that a gavel hasn't been used by any President other than he in all the years that simulation therapy has been going on here. Shrugging, gossiping, his Cabinet shuffles away, turning to give respectful nods, then leaving Luke standing alone in the dayroom. Dr. Williams waits until all of them are out, then comes through the side door and comes right up to Luke, dealing with him in that engaging, Williamesque way which Luke has always found so heartening and yet at the same time so irritating. "You did very well," Dr. Williams says. "We felt that you showed some real control, Luke."

"Well, thank you," Luke says. Really, what can he say? He is not sure he knows any way to deal with the shrink, even after all these months. You always have to be on guard with your doctor, but then again Williams is as engaging as a puppy, seems to want to be on informal terms. A strange reversal. Isn't it usually the shrink who is distant? "Well, sure," Luke says, vaguely, "sure thing. I'm doing the best I can."

"And a very neat job of it, too," Williams says. He is a short, intense man with twinkling eyes—eyes very different from the dull-eyed, big-eyed bunch with whom he does most of his business—and a brisk manner, but Luke suspects that there is something very wrong with Williams inside, something deep and tragic, maybe something as troubling as whatever is inside Luke himself. "Well," Williams says, "what do you say we go back to the Oval Office now?"

"Well, sure," Luke says, humoring him. "Whatever you say, it's all right with me."

"We can lay out some more of the day's events, you have a speech to the National Council of Churches at eleven, and then there's the Medal of Freedom ceremony in the Rose Garden at three. In between, you can have a really nice lunch. We're going to have sausages today, maybe some pastry, too. How does that sound?"

"Oh, good," Luke says. "It sounds good." Williams' hand is on his arm, guiding him. They move through the dayroom and into an empty anteroom, once an electroshock parlor Luke guesses, which serves as the Oval Office. "Now, Mr. President," Williams says, "why don't you just sit down and have a little rest while we get your schedule going. How will that be?"

"Fine," Luke says. "That will be fine." He is tired from that Cabinet meeting and no kidding. It may not seem like much on the outside, but there is a lot of responsibility there and one slip, a single slip could bring down the target bombs on your head. There is tension all through him. Sometimes it is very hard to remember that this is just a dayroom and he is in simulation therapy, damned if sometimes it doesn't feel real. *"Right* back," Williams says. He moves away, leaving Luke alone in the Oval Office which is not, now that he looks around, really very big. They could do better than this even though if they took away that old electroshock machinery here, it probably would be a little bigger. Well, maybe a lot bigger.

Anyway, the Cabinet meeting is over and now there will be only ceremonial stuff and sausages and maybe pastry for lunch and the Rose Garden. The worst part of the day is behind him, Luke thinks, and tomorrow he can go back to Health and Welfare again which involves a lot less strain. Still, it would be nice if Williams did not cut out on him like this all the time and if Carmen had more of a definite plan instead of just talking about heavy mobilization. Signs of panic there.

Luke goes over to the window, looks down upon the grounds surrounding, listens to the sounds of the milling crowd in the distance. Certainly a lot of people in this place, more than you would think just looking at it. Doing simulation therapy of their own. Luke thinks about this and that, thinks of all the good and bad points about simulation therapy, waiting for Williams to come back. Where is Williams? He has promised to be back soon. But the gray-bearded, twinkly-eyed, undependable little fuck simply won't show and the sounds of the crowd in the distance are unpleasantly louder. It's the damndest thing. Luke has the intimation that in just a few minutes he'll be hearing gunfire. How about that, gunfire? It's remarkable the ends to which they'll sometimes take this kind of thing to provide realism. Luke waits and waits for Williams to come back, to tell him what the next thing to do will be, but there's no sign of him and after a time, Luke feels a sudden certainty that the guy isn't going to come back after all. What the hell is with him? What is going on in this place anyway? There are sounds in the dayroom, suddenly, which he does not like.

Here is Luke Christmas. He is President of the United States today. He wants to turn and tell them that this was not so yesterday and it will not be so tomorrow, simulation therapy will pass the baton to someone else, but as they come through the door, they do not seem inclined to listen. They do not seem to be interested in any aspect of Luke's intelligence. Here they are. "I think that I will skip lunch. I don't want to go to the Rose Garden. I think I need a lot more medicine now," Luke says very quietly in a bleak and mouselike little tone, barely audible to the hulking forms, some of them from Montana, who lay enormous hands on his wrists, seem to have enormous plans for him. Uncontrolled chain reaction, Luke Christmas thinks. There goes Luke now. He is gone. They are definitely takng him away and there is no Cabinet to help him out. There is *nothing* to help him out, as Luke in his secret heart has always feared.

COMING OF AGE

by Susan Casper

The grass was still thin and brown from the heat of the summer, and the girl's feet had left a bald patch of earth, tracing a path as she played a solitary game of ball. A few steps east—toss, catch; toss, clap, catch—and she reached the edge of the woods. A few steps west—toss, slap shoulders, catch; toss, whirl hands, catch—and she was up against the wire fence that marked the border of a neighboring farm. Her head buzzed with the chant she sang silently: *A mimsy, a clapsy, I whirl my hands to bapsy* . . . She was careful to see that her lips did not move; careful to give no outward sign.

From deep inside the shadow of the porch, Margaret could feel the eyes of the old woman upon her like a leash, pulling her back every time she neared the boundaries. Eyes that never left her, not even to check the deft needlework upon which the gnarled hands were at work. She was used to the eyes. They had been on her for thirteen years, come October. *Touch my knee, touch my heel, touch my toe* . . . As she threw the ball up into the air, the heel of her shoe caught in the stiff cotton fabric of her dress, and she fell to the ground. The ball came down on her shoulder, and bounced away. Cautiously, careful not to rip the dress, she scrambled to her feet and started chasing after the ball, then pulled up short. It had come to rest in the dead leaf-mulch just inside the edge of the forest. Apprehensively, she glanced back at the porch. She bit her lip.

"Margaret!"

"But, Aunt Lilly, my ball . . ."

"If you're careless with things, you lose them. You know that." The voice was almost a whisper, so soft that Margaret had to strain to hear it. But she heard it, all right. She had heard it all her life. She would always hear it. She stared wistfully after her toy. It was so close, only a few yards away, but for her it might as well have been in another world. It was lost to her now, as so much had already been lost in her young life, things closing in and in until it sometimes seemed that there was nothing left in the universe except this ramshackle old house, this bare and dusty yard, the surrounding wall of somber forest, the ever-watchful eyes of the old woman.

"That place is choked with evil, child. Surely you can't be thinking of going *in* there. Christian folk should stay out of that evil place. And you, especially *you*—you must *never* go in there. Do you hear?"

Margaret continued to stare stubbornly back at the shadow where the old woman sat, but then she sighed, and her shoulders slumped in resignation. She knew that the ball would not be replaced, but she knew, too, that it was better not to argue with *that* voice.

"Come along, child," the old woman said at last. "Time to go in." The voice was still soft, but the tone was now conversational rather than commanding. "I was never fond of the way you play with that thing, anyway. There's something almost pagan about those motions you go through. *You*, who should be the *most* careful. Where did you learn that game, anyway?"

There was no response. Margaret did not know where she had first learned the game—it seemed like she had always known it. She covered her lack of answer by walking back to the house, head bent, her thick brown braid slapping against her back with every step.

"You've got to remember, now, that all the praying in the world isn't going to save you from turning out just like your mother if you don't keep God in your heart. *Avoid even the appearance of evil.* It says so right in the Bible."

Again, Margaret bit her lip, but this time to hold back the words she dared not say. The old woman rose with more agility than her appearance would have suggested, and Margaret followed her into the house. The front room was always in shadow, blocked from the sun by the big covered porch; a gloom that was emphasized by the deep browns and greens in which it was furnished. There were two wall hangings. One was a "miracle" picture of Jesus, with eyes that could be either open or closed depending upon your angle of vision. The other was an oiled photograph of Margaret's grandfather in uniform, taken in Europe during the Second World War. It was inscribed "To my sister Lillian, until we meet again—Ben." He had a wonderful face, warm and friendly—Margaret often wished that she could have known him.

The room's only other decoration was a large rosewood cross on the fireplace mantle, and it was before this that the old woman paused and bowed her head in prayer. "Dear Lord, bless this house and all who dwell within. Cast Your benevolent gaze upon this poor wretched child of sin and save her from the evil of her mother's ways. Help her to accept You into her heart . . ."

Margaret had assumed an attitude of prayer, but she refused to listen to what the old woman was saying. Her eyes were open—just the tiniest bit, but enough to see the numerous tiny cracks in the white enamel paint on the fireplace columns; her mind drew glorious pictures with the lines. Pictures of forbidden places, forbidden things. She knew she was an un-grateful child; willful, covetous, and doomed to suffer the same fate as her mother. She knew because the old woman had *told* her so, told her again and again, every night for years. Still, even though the old woman was very good, pious and upright and self-sacrificing, and Margaret's mother had been a bad woman, an evil woman, sinful as Satan himself, still, somehow it was her *mother's* face that she wanted to see. She longed to know her mother, to feel the soft and tender touch of her hand—for it *had* been tender. Of that one thing, Margaret was sure.

". . . that she may grow up among the paths of righteousness, if it be Your will. Amen."

"Odd men," Margaret mumbled, and looked up into the ice-blue gaze of the old woman. It was what she always said, though she dreaded the day when it would actually be heard.

"Come, child. You can do your studies while I cook lunch."

Margaret followed her into the kitchen, pulled a worn, leatherbound Bible from the shelf, and slid onto her stool. This was the only room in the house that Margaret actually liked. It was spotless, though the stove and refrigerator had yellowed with age. The table was butted up against a window that admitted the sun-sweetened breezes and a view of an untended field that ran riot with clover and Queen Ann's lace and dandelions all summer long. She allowed herself only the briefest of glances, then pulled at the long red ribbon that marked her place in the book.

"Woe to her that is filthy and polluted, to the op-pressing city," she read, her voice too loud in the si-lent room. *"She obeyed not the voice; she received not correction; she trusted not in the Lord; she drew not near to her God."*

The old woman was making a soup—vegetables in

a tomato stock. Bland. Spices were a concession to worldly pleasure, and therefore, sinful. Margaret was so tired of that same soup. She paused to pour herself a cup of water and continued working her way through Zephaniah and Haggai and the first few chapters of Zechariah, until her tongue felt thick and she stumbled over the words, drawing a sharp look from the old woman. There was a pleasant memory of other books, interesting and colorful, and a room full of other children, and a blonde lady with very red lips. But that was a long time ago. School was an evil place, where she had been taught to condone sin and pay heed to the snares and delusions of Satan. . . .

Suddenly, Margaret felt trapped. The smell of the simmering broth was making her ill, her belly ached as if it were about to burst, and she felt so weak that she could barely hold on to the book on her lap. Yet, instinctively she held her tongue and did not ask to be excused. She watched the old woman's wizened hand clamped firmly on the handle of the wooden spoon, the prominent blue veins rippling under the pale parchment skin. One . . . two . . . three . . . four times, the spoon slowly circled the pot. Around and around . . . The book inched over the stiff cotton skirt, across the bare skin of her knees, but Margaret never noticed that it was slipping from her hands until it hit the floor with a loud and ominous *clap*.

The old woman whirled around, wooden spoon in hand, splattering soup across the stove. "So *this* is how you show your respect for the Good Book? You—" Then she paused, and her expression changed. "You're not feeling well, are you?" she asked slowly, almost reluctantly. But it was not concern that showed on her face—it was terror. "What's wrong with you, child. Speak up."

Margaret tried to explain, though it was an effort even to speak. There was a long, heavy silence.

"So it's happening, is it?" the old woman said at last. "Let me see your underpants." The dark stain frightened Margaret. She couldn't understand what was happening to her. How could she have soiled her pants without even knowing it. But the old woman's reaction was so strange that it frightened Margaret even more.

The old woman just stared at Margaret for a *long* time. Stared at her as if she had never seen anything quite like her before.

"So now you are a woman," she said bitterly. There was another brief pause. "And *still* full of sin and degradation," She spat out the words. "Your mother came to womanhood unrepentant and she was accursed. *Accursed!* Take your lesson, child, while there is still time. This may be your last chance. This may be the last night left to save your soul." The old woman's eyes were blazing and wild, her hands were curled into claws, and when she began to speak again, she punctuated each word with a savage blow from the spoon upon Margaret's arms. "Take your lesson, girl! Take your lesson! The evil is in your blood! It's in your *blood,* and you must fight it every second, or succumb! Go to your room and get down on your *knees!* Kneel and *pray*! Pray for forgiveness with all your heart! Pray that a child born in *sin* of a wicked woman, a child with evil in her blood, might still be allowed to find salvation. Pray!" She pushed the sobbing child toward the stairs.

Almost in a trance, Margaret ascended the steps, turned down the hallway and entered her room. Though her legs ached miserably and the tears burned hot behind her eyelids, she ignored the tiny bed with its chipped and peeling iron bedstead, and knelt before the picture of Jesus that sat atop the plain oak bureau. A moment later she heard the door being pulled shut behind her and the frightening click of the key being turned in the lock.

Margaret stared at the sad, kindly eyes of the Christ. She knew that she was not a *good* girl. Sometimes, without her even *thinking* about it, the most depraved things just seemed to pop out of her mouth. She had evil thoughts, sometimes. She had even lied to the old woman. But she *wanted* to be good . . . for Him. She wanted to pray for him to help her to be good, but her mind refused to focus on anything but the darkening bruises on her arms, and the pain, and the strange and frightening thing that had happened in the kitchen. And when the prayers did come, they were not for forgiveness. "Dear God, please, *please* help me!" she heard herself saying, horrified, but unable to stop. "Please take me *away* from here! Take me away!" The tears came then, and she leaned her head against the coolness of the wood and let them flow.

Shadows crept through the second story window, dimming the room to darkness. The old woman did not come to get Margaret for supper, nor were there any sounds downstairs that she could hear. Margaret didn't care. Her limbs, tired before, were now so weak that she couldn't even lift her body, as though her very bones had become soft. She huddled miserably against the oak bureau, watching the tops of the trees rustle in the gentle wind; a deeper blackness in the moonlight veil of night.

Then the strangeness in her body intensified. A sharp pain ran the length of her arm, as though all of the muscles had knotted up at once. Nausea shot through her, and pain like a red-hot knife. Her skin felt as if it were on fire, and her heart lurched and pounded as if it were about to burst from her chest.

She was dying! Terror washed over her like a wave, leaving her too frightened even to cry. She was going to die, locked up in this cramped and suffocating little room that she'd hated ever since she could remember. She tried to pull herself to her feet, but her legs gave out under her and she fell to the floor.

She writhed on the floor, lost in terror and strangeness, her muscles knotting and unknotting along the length of her body, the dust of the old wooden floorboards clogging her nose, in her mouth the brassy taste of blood—

Blood. The evil was in her blood.

Her hands curled shut and refused to open. She felt her legs draw up, knees touching her stomach. Her spine arched. Somehow, she was on all fours now. Her head bowed until her face almost touched the floor. She was panting in fear. Her muscles writhed like worms.

The evil was in her *blood*. She couldn't fight it anymore—

Suddenly, everything changed, like a window being thrown open somewhere deep inside her. All at once, she could *hear,* hear *everything* with stunning clarity, for miles around, it seemed—hear the old woman muttering frightened prayers as she knelt in the parlor below . . . hear the scurry of a field mouse in the attic above . . . hear the flapping of an owl's wings as it hunted through the forest . . . hear the shrill deathcry of its prey . . . barking on the far edge of the woods, a dog . . . somewhere far beyond that the sound of a freight train moving through the night. . . . And the *smells,* dozens of them, many more than she could possibly identify, sharp, oily, pungent, sweet, sour, rank, mouth-watering, smells so vibrantly powerful that they seemed to grab hold of her senses and shake them.

The world seemed to open up around her, the night unfolding like a flower. The night was suddenly *alive* around her, full of motion and mystery, smells and sounds. . . .

The moon was coming up, the hunter's moon, full and beautiful, framed in the dusty old window. She pressed her face against her shoulder and felt, not the silken smoothness of skin, but the husky rasp of fur against fur. All at once she understood and her heart surged with joy.

She rolled effortlessly to her four feet, reveling in her strength, the fluid ease of her motions, and threw herself at the window. She crashed through it in a spray of glass and rolled down the sloping roof in a controlled fall, easily leaping the last few yards to the ground.

Then the black, living earth was under the naked pads of her feet, the dew-soaked grass caressing her flanks, the night air flowing like silk around her.

Behind her, lights were coming on in the ruined old house, and she could hear the shrill, hysterical voice of the old woman calling to her, calling her to come back, but, howling in triumph and joy, she was already gone—into the deep woods, running easily between the trees, the house falling away behind her and vanishing, the old woman's voice fading behind, the night opening up before her with all its endless possibility and promise. . . . Free. Free! FREE! She was FREE!

At last she had come of age, and she was free to seek her heritage.

WAIFS AND STRAYS

by Charles de Lint

Do I have to dig,
Do I have to prod;
Reach into your chest
And pull your feelings out?
　　　　—Happy Rhodes, from "Words
　　　　　Weren't Made for Cowards"

1

There's a big moon glowing in the sky, a swollen circle of silvery-gold light that looks as though it's sitting right on top of the old Clark Building, balancing there on the northeast corner where the twisted remains of a smokestack rise up from the roof like a long, tottery flagpole, colors lowered for the night, or maybe like a tin giant's arm making some kind of semaphore signal that only other tin giants can understand. I sure don't.

But that doesn't stop me from admiring the silhouette of the smokestack against that fat moon as I walk through the rubble-strewn streets of the Tombs. I feel like a stranger and I think, *That moon's a stranger, too.* It doesn't seem real; it's more like the painted backdrop from some '40s soundstage, except there's no way anybody ever gave paint and plywood this kind of depth. We're both strangers. That moon looks like it might be out of place anywhere, but I belonged here once.

Not anymore, though. I'm not even supposed to be here. I've got responsibilities now. I've got duties to fulfill. I should be Getting Things Done like the good little taxpaying citizen I'm trying to be, but instead I'm slumming, standing in front of my old squat, and I couldn't tell you why I've come. No, that's not quite right. I know, I guess; I just can't put it into words.

"You've got to see the full moon in a country sky sometime," Jackie told me the other day when she got back from her girlfriend's cottage. "It just takes over the sky."

I look up at it again and don't feel that this moon's at all diminished by being here. Maybe because in many respects this part of the city's just like a wilderness—about as close to the country as you can get in a place that's all concrete and steel. Some people might say you'd get that feeling more in a place like Fitzhenry Park, or on the lakefront where it follows the shoreline beyond the Pier, westward, out past the concession stands and hotels, but I don't think it's quite the same. Places like that are where you can only pretend it's wild; they look right, but they were tamed a long time ago. The Tombs, though, is like a piece of the city gone feral, the wild reclaiming its own—not asking, just taking.

In this kind of moonlight, you can feel the wilderness hiding in back of the shadows, lips pulled in an uncurbed, savage grin.

I think about that as I step a little closer to my old squat and it doesn't spook me at all. I find the idea kind of liberating. I look at the building and all I see is a big, dark, tired shape hulking in the moonlight. I like the idea that it's got a secret locked away behind its mundane facade, that's there's more to it than something that's been used up and then just tossed away.

Abandoned things make me feel sad. For as long as I can remember I've made up histories for them, cloaked them in stories, seen them as frog princes waiting for that magic kiss, princesses being tested with a pea, little engines that could if they were only given half a chance again.

But I'm pragmatic, too. Stories in my head are all well and fine, but they don't do much good for a dog that some guy's tossed out of a car when he's speeding through the Tombs, and the poor little thing breaks a leg when it hits the pavement so it can't even fend for itself—just saying the feral dogs that run in these streets give it half a chance. When I can—if I get to it in time—I'm the kind of person who'll take it in.

People have tried to take me in, but it never quite works out right. Bad genes, I guess. Bad attitude. It's not the kind of thing I ever worried about much till the past few weeks.

I don't know how long I'm standing on the street, not even seeing the building any more. I'm just here, a small shape in the moonlight, a stray dream that got lost from the safe part of the city and found itself wandering in this nightland that eats small dreams, feeds on hopes. A devouring landscape that fed on itself first and now preys on anything that wanders into its domain.

I never let it have me, but these days I wonder why I bothered. Living in the Tombs isn't much of a life, but what do you do when you don't fit in anywhere else?

I start to turn away, finally. The moon's up above the Clark Building now, hanging like a fat round flag on the smokestack, and the shadows it casts are longer. I don't want to go, but I can't stay. Everything that's important to me isn't part of the Tombs any more.

The voice stops me. It's a woman's voice, calling softly from the shadows of my old squat.

"Hey, Maisie," she says.

I feel like I should know her, this woman sitting in the shadows, but the sense of familiarity I get from those two words keeps sliding away whenever I reach for it.

"Hey, yourself," I say.

She moves out into the moonlight, but she's still just a shape. There's no definition, nothing I can pin the sliding memories onto. I get an impression of layers of clothing that make a skinny frame seem bulky, a toque pulled down over hair that might be any color or length. She's dressed for winter though the night's warm and she's got a pair of shopping bags in each hand.

I've known a lot of street people like that. Hottest day of the summer and they still have to wear everything they own, all at once. Sometimes it's to protect themselves from space rays; sometimes it's just so that no one'll steal the little they've got to call their own.

"Been a long time," she says and then I place her.

It's partly the way she moves, partly the voice, partly just the shape of her, though in this light she doesn't look any different from a hundred other bag ladies.

The trouble is, she can't possibly wear the name I call up to fit her because the woman it used to belong to has been dead for four years. I know this, logically, intellectually, but I can't help trying it on for size all the same.

"Shirl?" I say. "Is that you?"

Shirley Jones, whom everybody on the street knew as Granny Buttons because she carried hundreds of

them around in the many pockets of her dresses and
coats.

The woman on the street in front of me bobs her
head, sticks her hands in the pockets of the raincoat
she's wearing over all those layers of clothing, and I
hear the familiar rattle of plastic against wood against
bone, a soft *clickety-clickety-click* that I never thought
I'd hear again.

"Jesus, Shirley—"

"I know, child" she says. "What am I doing here
when I'm supposed to be dead."

I'm still not spooked. It's like I'm in a dream and
none of this is real, or at least it's only as real as the
dream wants it to be. I'm just happy to see her.
Granny Buttons was the person who first taught me
that "family" didn't have to be an ugly word.

She's close enough that I can see some of her features now. She doesn't look any different than she did
when she died. She's got the same twinkle in her
brown eyes—part charm and part crazy. Her coffee-
colored skin's as wrinkled as a piece of brown wrap-
ping paper that you've had in your back pocket for a
few days. I see it isn't a toque she's wearing, but that
same almost conical velour cap she always wore, her
hair hanging out from below in hundreds of unwashed,
uncombed dreadlocks festooned with tiny buttons of
every shape and description. She still smells the same
as well—a combination of a rosehip sachet and
licorice.

I want to hug her, but I'm afraid if I touch her she'll
just drift apart like smoke.

"I've missed you," I say.

"I know, child."

"But how . . . how can you *be* here . . . ?"

"It's like a riddle," she says. "Remember our treasure hunts?"

I nod my head. How can I forget? That's where I

first learned about the freebies you can find in behind the bookstores, where I was initiated into what Shirley liked to call the rehab biz.

"If you cherish something enough," she told me, "it doesn't matter how old, or worn, or useless it's become; your caring for it immediately raises its value in somebody else's eyes. It's just like rehab—a body's got to believe in their own worth before anybody can start fixing them, but most people need someone to believe in them before they can start believing in themselves.

"You know, I've seen people pay five hundred dollars for something I took out of their trash just the week before—*only* because they saw it sitting on the shelf of some fancy antique shop. They don't even remember that it once was theirs.

" 'Course the dealer only paid me fifty bucks for it, but who's complaining? Two hours before I came knocking on his back door, it was sitting at the end of the curb in a garbage can."

Garbage days we went on our treasure hunts. Shirley probably knew more about collection days than the city crews did themselves: when each borough had its pick up, what the best areas were depending on the time of the year, when you had to make your rounds in certain areas to beat the flea market dealers on their own night runs. We had dozens of routes, from Foxville down into Crowsea, across the river to Ferryside and the Beaches, from Chinatown over to the East End.

We'd head out with our shopping carts, sensei bag lady and her apprentice, on a kind of Grail quest. But what we found was never as important as the zen of our being out there in the first place. Each other's company. The conversation. The night's journey as we zigzagged from one block to another, checking out this alleyway, that bin, those dumpsters.

We were like urban coyotes prowling the city's streets. At that time of night, nobody bothered us, not the cops, not muggers, not street toughs. We became invisible knights tilting against the remnants of other people's lives.

After Shirley died, it took me over a month to go out on my own and it was never quite the same again. Not bad, just not the same.

"I remember," I tell her.

"Well, it's something like that," she says, "only it's not entirely happenstance."

I shake my head, confused. "What are you trying to tell me, Shirley?"

"Nothing you don't already know."

Back of me, something knocks a bottle off a heap of trash—I don't know what it is. A cat, maybe. A dog. A rat. I can't help myself. I have to have a look. When I turn back to Shirley—you probably saw this coming—she's gone.

2

Pride goes before the fall, I read somewhere, and I guess whoever thought up that little homily had her finger on the pulse of how it all works.

There was a time when I wouldn't have had far to fall; by most people's standards, at seventeen, I was already on the bottom rung of the ladder, and all the rungs going up were broken as far as I'd ever be able to reach. I lived in a squat. I made my living picking garbage and selling the better stuff off to junk shops and the fancy antique places—only through the back door if you would, yes it's a lovely piece but terribly worn, sorry that's my best offer, many thanks and do come again. I had a family that consisted of a bunch of old dogs so worn out that nobody wanted them, not to mention Tommy who's—what's the current eu-

phemism? I lose track. Mentally handicapped, I guess
you'd call him. I just call him Tommy and it doesn't
matter how dim the bulb is burning in behind his eyes;
like the dogs, he became family when I took him in
and I love him.

I never thought much about pride back in those
days, though I guess I had my share. Maybe I was
just white trash to whoever passed me on the street,
but I kept myself cleaner than a lot of those paying
taxes and what I had then sure beat the hell hole I
grew up in.

I hit the road when I was twelve and never looked
back because up until then family was just another
word for pain. Physical pain, and worse, the kind that
just leaves your heart feeling like some dead thing
caught inside your chest. You know what pigeons look
like once the traffic's been running over them for a
couple of weeks and there's not much left except for
a flat bundle of dried feathers that hasn't even got
flies buzzing around it anymore?

That's like what I had in my chest until I ran away.

I was one of the lucky ones. I survived. I didn't get
done in by drugs or selling my body. Shirley took me
in under her wing before the lean men with the flashy
suits and too much jewelry could get their hands on
me. Don't know why she helped me—maybe when
she saw me she was remembering the day she was just
a kid stepping off a bus in some big city herself.
Maybe, just looking at me, she could tell I'd make a
good apprentice.

And then, after five years, I got luckier still—with
a little help from the Grasso Street Angel and my own
determination.

And that pride.

I was so proud of myself for doing the right thing:
I got the family off the street. I was straightening out
my life. I rejoined society—not that society seemed to

care all that much, but I wasn't doing it for them anyway. I was doing it for Tommy and the dogs, for myself, and so that one day maybe I could be in a position to help somebody else, the way that Angel does out of her little storefront office on Grasso, the way that Shirley helped me.

I should've known better.

We've got a real place to live in—a tenement on Flood Street just before it heads on into the Tombs, instead of a squat. I had a job as a messenger for the QMS—the Quicksilver Messenger Service, run by a bunch of old hippies who got the job done, but lived in a tie-dyed past. Evenings, four times a week, I was going to night school to get my high school diploma.

But I just didn't see it as being better than what we'd had before. Paying for rent and utilities, food and for someone to come in to look after Tommy, sucked away every cent I made. Maybe I could've handled that, but all my time was gone, too. I never really saw Tommy anymore, except on the weekends and even then I'd have to be studying half the time. I had it a little easier than a lot of the other people in my class because I always read a lot. It was my way of escaping—even before I came here to live on the streets.

Before I ran away, I was a regular at the local library—it was both a source of books and refuge from what was happening at home. Once I got here, Shirley told me about how the bookstores'd strip the covers off paperbacks and just throw the rest of the book away so I always made sure I stopped by the alleys in back of their stores on garbage days.

I hadn't read a book in months. The dogs were pining—little Rexy taking it the worst. He's just a cat-sized wiry-haired mutt with a major insecurity problem. I think someone used to beat on him which made me feel close to him, because I knew what that was

all about. Used to be Rexy was like my shadow; nervous, sure, but so long as I was around, he was okay.
These days, he's just a wreck because he can't come
on my bike when I'm working and they won't let me
bring him into the school.

The way things stand, Tommy's depressed, the
other dogs are depressed, Rexy's almost suicidal, and
I'm not in any great shape myself. Always tired, impatient, unhappy.

So I really needed to meet a ghost in the Tombs
right about now. It's doing wonders for my sense of
sanity—or rather lack thereof, because I know I
wasn't dreaming that night, or at least I wasn't asleep.

3

Everybody's worried about me when I finally get
home—Rexy, the dogs, Tommy, my landlady Aunt
Hilary who looks after Tommy—and I appreciate it,
but I don't talk about where I've been or what I've
seen. What's the point? I'm kind of embarrassed
about anybody knowing that I'm feeling nostalgic for
the old squat and I'm not quite sure I believe who I
saw there anyway, so what's to tell?

I make nice with Aunt Hilary, calm down the dogs,
put Tommy to bed, then I've got homework to do for
tomorrow night's class and work in the morning, so
by the time I finally get to bed myself, Shirley's may-
be-ghost is pretty well out of my mind. I'm so tired
that I'm out like a light as soon as my head hits the
pillow.

Where do they get these expressions we all use,
anyway? Why out like a light and not on like one?
Why do we hit the pillow when we go to sleep? Logs
don't have a waking/sleeping cycle, so how can we
sleep like one?

Sometimes I think about what this stuff must sound

like when it gets literally translated into some other language. Yeah, I know. It's not exactly Advanced Philosophy 101 or anything, but it sure beats thinking about ghosts which is what I'm trying not to think about as I walk home from the subway that night after my classes. I'm doing a pretty good job, too, until I get to my landlady's front steps.

Aunt Hilary is like the classic tenement landlady. She's a widow, a small but robust gray-haired woman with more energy than half the messengers at QMS. She's got lace hanging in her windows, potted geraniums on the steps going down to the pavement, an old black and white tabby named Frank that she walks on a leash. Rexy and Tommy are the only ones in my family that Frank'll tolerate.

Anyway, I come walking down the street, literally dragging my feet I'm so tired, and there's Frank sitting by one of the geranium pots giving me the evil eye—which is not so unusual—while sitting one step up is Shirley—which up until last night I would have thought was damned well impossible. Tonight I don't even question her presence.

"How's it going, Shirl?" I say as I collapse beside her on the steps.

Frank arches his back when I go by him, but deigns to give my shoulder bag a sniff before he realizes it's only got my school books in it. The look he gives me as he settles down again is less than respectful.

Shirley's leaning back against a higher step. She's got her hands in her pockets, *clickety-clickety-click*, her hat pushed back from her forehead. Her rosehip and licorice scent has to work a little harder against the cloying odor of the geraniums, but it's still there.

"Ever wonder why there's a moon?" she asks me, her voice all dreamy and distant.

I follow her gaze to where the fat round globe is ballooning in the sky above the buildings on the opposite side of the street. It looks different here than it did in the Tombs—safer, maybe—but then everything does. It's the second night that it's full and I find myself wondering if ghosts are like werewolves, called up by the moon's light, only nobody's quite clued to it yet. Or at least Hollywood and the authors of cheap horror novels haven't.

I decide not to share this with Shirley. I knew her pretty well, but who knows what's going to offend a ghost? She doesn't wait for me to answer anyway.

"It's to remind us of Mystery," she says, "and that makes it both a Gift and a Curse."

She's talking like Pooh in the Milne books, her inflection setting capital letters at the beginning of certain words. I've never been able to figure out how she does that. I've never been able to figure out how she knows so much about books because I never even saw her read a newspaper all the time we were together.

"How so?" I ask.

"Grab an eyeful," she says. "Did you ever see anything so mysteriously beautiful? Just looking at it, really Considering it, has got to fill the most jaded spirit with awe."

I think about how ghosts have that trick down pretty good, too, but all I say is, "And what about the curse?"

"We all know it's just an oversized rock hanging there in the sky. We've sent men to walk around on it, left trash on its surface, photographed it and mapped it. We know what it weighs, its size, its gravitational influence. We've sucked all the Mystery out of it, but it still maintains its hold on our imaginations.

"No matter how much we try to deny it, that's where poetry and madness were born."

I still don't get the curse part of it, but Shirley's already turned away from this line of thought. I can almost see her ghostly mind unfolding a chart inside her head and plotting a new course for our conversation. She looks at me.

"What's more important?" she asks. "To be happy or to bring happiness to others?"

"I kind of like to think they go hand in hand," I tell her. "That you can't really have one without the other."

"Then what have you forgotten?"

This is another side of Shirley I remember well. She gets into this one hand clapping mode, asking you simple stuff that gets more and more complicated the longer you think about it, but if you keep worrying at it, the way Rexy'll take on an old slipper, it gets back to being simple again. To get there, though, you have to work through a forest of words and images that can be far too Zen deep and confusing—especially when you're tired and your brain's in neutral the way mine is tonight.

"Is this part of the riddle you were talking about last night?" I ask.

She sort of smiles—lines crinkle around her eyes, fingers work the pocketed buttons, *clickety-clickety-click*. There's a feeling in the air like there was last night just before she vanished, but this time I'm not looking away. I hear a car turn onto this block, its headbeams washing briefly over us, bright light flicker, then it's dark again, with one solid flash of real deep dark just before my eyes adjust to the change in illumination.

Of course she's gone once I can see properly again and there's only me and Frank sitting on the steps. I forget for a moment about where our relationship stands and reach out to give him a pat. I'm just trying to touch base with reality, I realize as I'm doing it, but that doesn't matter to him. He doesn't quite hiss as he gets up and jumps down to the sidewalk.

I watch him swagger off down the street, watch the

empty pavement for a while longer, then finally I get up myself and go inside.

4

There's a wariness in Angel's features when I step into her Grasso Street office. It's a familiar look. I asked her about it once and she was both precise and polite with her explanation: "Well, Maisie. Things just seem to get complicated whenever you're around."

It's nothing I plan.

Her office is a one-room walk-in storefront off Grasso Street, shabby in a genteel sort of a way. She has a rack of filing cabinets along one wall, an old, beat up sofa with a matching chair by the bay window, a government surplus desk—one of those massive oak affairs with about ten million scratches and dents—a swivel chair behind the desk and a couple of matching oak straightbacks sitting to one side. I remember thinking they looked like a pair I'd sold a few years ago to old man Kemps down the street and it turns out that's where she picked them up.

A little table beside the filing cabinets holds a hot plate, a kettle, a bunch of mismatched mugs, a teapot and the various makings for coffee, hot chocolate, and tea. The walls have cheerful posters—one from a travel agency that shows this wild New Orleans street scene where there's a carnival going on, one from a Jilly Coppercorn show—cutesy little flower fairies fluttering around in a junkyard.

I like the one of Bart Simpson best. I've never seen the show, but I don't think you have to to know what he's all about.

The nicest thing about the office is the front porch and steps that go down from it to the pavement. It's a great place from which to watch the traffic go by, vehicular and pedestrian, or to just hang out. No, that's not true. The nicest thing is Angel herself.

Her real name's Angelina Marceau, but everyone calls her Angel, partly on account of her name, I guess, but mostly because of the salvage work she does with street kids. The thing is, she looks like an angel. She tries to hide it with baggy pants and plain t-shirts and about as little make-up as you can get away with wearing and still not be considered a Baptist, but she's gorgeous. Heart-shaped face, hair to kill for—a long, dark waterfall that just seems to go forever down her back—and soft warm eyes that let you know straightaway that here's someone who genuinely cares about you. Not as a statistic to add to her list of rescued souls, but as an individual. A real person.

Unless she's giving you the suspicious once-over she's giving me as I come in. It's a look you have to earn, because normally she'll bend over backwards to give you the benefit of the doubt.

I have to admit, there was a time when I'd push her, just to test the limits of her patience. It's not something I was particularly prone to, but we used to have a history of her trying to help me and me insisting I didn't need any help. We worked through all of that, eventually, but I keep finding myself in circumstances that make her feel as though I'm still testing the limits.

Like the time I punched out the booking agent at the Harbor Ritz, my first day on the job at QMS that Angel had gotten me.

I'm not the heartstopper that Angel is, but I do okay in the looks department. My best feature, I figure is my hair. It's not as long as Angel's, but it's as thick. Jackie, the dispatch girl at QMS, says it reminds her of the way they all wore their hair in the sixties— did I mention that these folks are living in a time warp? I've never bothered to tell them that the sixties have been and gone, it's only the styles are making yet another comeback.

Anyway, my hair's a nice shade of light golden brown and hangs halfway down my back. I do okay in the figure department, too, though I lean more toward Winona Ryder, say, than Kim Bassinger. Still, I've had guys hit on me occasionally, especially these days since I don't put out the impression that I'm some assistant baglady-in-training anymore.

The Harbor Ritz booking agent doesn't know any of this. He just sees a messenger girl delivering some documents and figures he'll give me a thrill. I guess he's either hard up, or figures anyone without his equipment between their legs is just dying to have him paw them, because that's what he does when I try to get him to sign for his envelope. He ushers me into his office and then closes the door, leans back against it and pulls me toward him.

What was I supposed to do? I just cocked back a fist and broke his nose.

Needless to say, he raised a stink, it's his word against mine, et cetera, et cetera. Except the folks at QMS turn out to be real supportive and Angel comes down on this guy like he's some used condom she's found stuck to the bottom of her shoe when she's walking through the Combat Zone. I keep my job and don't get arrested for assault like the guy's threatening to do, but it's a messy situation, right?

The look Angel's wearing says, "I hope this isn't more of the same, but just seeing you kicks in this bad feeling. . . ."

It's not more of the same, I want to tell her, but that's about as far as my reasoning can take it. What's bothering me isn't exactly something I can just put my finger on. Do I tell her about Shirley, do I tell her about the malaise I've got eating away at me, or what?

I'd been tempted to bring the whole family with

me—I spend so little time with them as it is—but settled on Rexy, mostly because he's easier to control. It's hard to think when you're trying to keep your eye on six of them and Tommy, too.

Today I could be alone in a padded cell and I'd still find it hard to think.

I take a seat on the sofa and after a moment Angel comes around from behind her desk and settles on the other end. Rexy's being real good. He licks her hand when she reaches out to pat him, then curls up on my lap and pretends to go to sleep. I know he's faking it because his ears twitch in a way they don't when he's really conked out.

Angel and I do some prelims—small talk which is always relaxed and easy around her, but eventually we get to the nitty-gritty of why I'm here.

"I've got this problem," I say, thinking of Shirley, but I know it's not her. I kind of like having her around again, dead or not.

"At work?" Angel tries when I'm not more forthcoming.

"Not exactly."

Angel's looking a little puzzled, but curious, too.

"Your grades are good," she says.

"It's not got anything to do with grades," I tell her. Well, it does, but only because the high school diploma's part and parcel of the whole problem.

"Then what *does* it have to do with?" Angel wants to know.

It's a reasonable request—more so because I'm the one who's come to her, taking up her time. I know what I want to say, but I don't know how to phrase it.

My new life's like a dress I might have wished after in a store window, saved for, finally bought, only to find out that while it's the right size, it still doesn't quite fit right. It's the wrong color. The sleeves are too long, or maybe too short. The skirt's too tight.

It's not something Angel would understand. Intellectually, maybe, but not how I feel about it. Angel's one of those people that sees everyone having a purpose in life, you've just got to figure out what it is. I don't even know where to begin figuring out that kind of stuff.

"Nothing really," I say after a few moments.

I get up suddenly, startling Rexy who jumps to the floor and then gives me this put-upon expression of his that he should take out a patent on.

"I've got to go," I tell Angel.

"Maisie," she starts, rising herself, but I'm already heading for the door.

I pretend I don't hear her. I pretend she's not following me to the street and calling after me as I head down the block at a quick walk that you might as well call running.

I'm not in good shape, I realize. Angel's the only person I know that I could have talked with about something like this, but I couldn't do it. I couldn't even start.

All I felt like doing was crying and that would really have freaked her because I never cry.

Not where people can see.

5

"So what are you really doing here?" I ask.

We're sitting on a bench in the subway station at Williamson and Stanton, Shirley and I, with little Rexy sleeping on the toes of my running shoes. We're at the far end of the platform. It's maybe ten o'clock and there's hardly anybody else down here with us. I see a couple of yuppies, probably coming back from an early show. A black guy in a three-piece checking out papers in his briefcase. Two kids slouched against a wall, watching a companion do tricks with her skateboard that bring her perilously close to the edge of the platform. My heart's in my throat watching her, but her friends just look bored.

I wonder what they see when they look down this way. A bag lady and me, with my dog dozing on my feet, or just me and Rexy on our own?

Shirley's gaze is on the subway system grid that's on the opposite side of the tracks, but I doubt she's really seeing it. She always needed glasses but never got herself a pair, even when she could afford them.

"When I first got to the city," she says, "I always thought that one day I'd go back home and show everybody what an important person I had become. I wanted to prove that just because everyone from my parents to my teachers treated me like I was no good, didn't mean I really was no good.

"But I never went back."

Ghosts always want to set something right, I remember from countless books and stories. Revenge, mistakes, that kind of thing. Sometimes just to say good-bye. They're here because of unfinished business.

This is the first time I ever realized that Shirley'd had any.

I mean, I wasn't stupid, even when I was twelve and she first took me in under her wing. Even then I knew that normal people didn't live on the streets wearing their entire wardrobe on their backs. But I never really thought about why she was there. She always seemed like a part of the street, so full of smarts and a special kind of wisdom, that it simply never occurred to me that she'd been running away from something, too. That she'd had dreams and aspirations once, but all they came to was a homeless wandering to which the only end was a mishap like falling down the stairs in some run-down squat and breaking your neck.

That's what your life'll be like, I tell myself, if you don't follow through on what Angel's trying to do for you.

Maybe. But I'd respected Shirley, for all her quirks, for all that I knew she wasn't what anybody else would call a winner. I'd just always thought that whatever she lacked, she had inner peace to make up for it.

I slouch lower on the bench, legs crossed at the ankles, the back of my head leaning against the top of the bench. I'm wearing my fedora and the movement pushes it forward so that the brim hangs low over my eyes.

"Is that why you're back?" I ask Shirley. "Because you still had things left to do here?"

She shrugs, an eloquent Shirley-gesture, for all the layers of clothes she's wearing.

"I don't really feel I ever went anywhere or came back," she says.

"But you died," I say.

"I guess so."

I try a different tack. "So what's it like?"

She smiles. "I don't really know. When I'm here, I don't feel any different from before I died. When I'm not here, I'm . . . I don't know where I am. A kind of limbo, I suppose. A place where nothing moves, nothing changes, months are minutes."

I don't say anything.

"I guess it's like the bus I never took back home," she adds after a moment. "I missed out on wherever it was I was supposed to go, and I don't know how to go on, where to catch the next bus, or if they're even running any more. For me at least. They don't leave a schedule lying around for people like me who arrive too late.

"Story of my life, I guess."

I start to feel so bad for her that I almost wish she'd go back to throwing cryptic little riddles at me the way she'd done the first couple of times we'd met.

"Is there anything I can do?" I say, but the subway roars into the station at the same time as I speak, swallowing my words with its thunder.

I'm about to repeat what I said, but when I turn to look at Shirley, she's not there any more. I only just make it through the doors of the car, Rexy under my arm, before they hiss closed behind me and the train goes roaring off again into the darkness.

The story of her life, I think. I wonder, what's the story of mine?

6

I should tell you about Tommy.

He's a big guy, maybe six feet tall and running close to a hundred and eighty pounds. And he's strong. He's got brown hair, a dirtier shade than mine, though I try to keep it looking clean, and guileless eyes. He couldn't keep a secret if he knew one.

The thing is, he's simple. A ten-year-old in an adult's body. I'm not sure how old he is, but the last time I took him in for a checkup at the clinic, the doctor told me he was in his early thirties, which makes him almost half again my age.

When I say simple, I don't mean stupid, though I'll admit Tommy's not all that bright by the way society reckons intelligence. I like to think of him as more basic than the rest of us. He's open with his feelings, likes to smile, likes to laugh. He's the happiest person I know, which is half the reason I love him the way I do. He may be mentally impaired, but sometimes I figure the world would be a better place if we all maintained some of that sweet innocence that makes him so endearing.

I inherited Tommy the same way I did the rest of my family: I found him on the streets, abandoned. I worried some at first about keeping him with me, but when I started asking around about institutions, I realized he'd have something with me and the dogs that he couldn't get anywhere else: a family. All a guy like Tommy needs is someone willing to put the time into loving him. You don't get that in places like the Zeb, which is where he lived until they discharged him so that someone with more pressing problems, read money, could have his bed.

One of the things I hate about the way my life's going now is that I hardly ever see him any more. Our landlady knows him better than I do these days and that's depressing.

The day after I talk to Shirley in the subway, I get off early from work. There's a million things I should be doing—like the week's grocery shopping and research for a history essay at the library—but I decide the hell with it. It's a beautiful day, so I'm going to pack up a picnic lunch and take the family to the park.

I find Tommy and Aunt Hilary in the backyard. She's working on her garden, which for a postage-sized tenement lot is a work of art, a miniature farm and English garden all rolled into about twenty square feet of sunflowers, rosebushes, corn, peas, every kind of squash, tomatoes and flowerbeds aflame with color and scent. Tom's playing with the paper people that I cut out of magazines and then stick onto cardboard backings for him. The dogs are sprawled all over the place, except for Rexy who's dogging Aunt Hilary's heels. You don't understand how apt an expression like that is until you see Rexy do his I-always-have-to-be-two-inches-away-from-you thing.

Tommy looks up when he hears the dogs starting

to yap, and suddenly I'm inundated with my family, everybody trying to get a piece of hello from me at the same time. But the best thing is seeing that kind of sad expression that Tommy's wearing too much these days broaden into the sweetest, happiest smile you can imagine. I don't figure I've ever done anything to deserve all this unadulterated love, but I accept it—on credit, I guess. It makes me try harder to be good to them, to be worthy of that love.

I've got the trick down pat by now, ruffling the fur of six dogs and giving Tommy a hug without ever letting anybody feel left out. Aunt Hilary's straightening up from her garden, hands at the small of her back as she stretches the kinks from her muscles. She's smiling, too.

"We had a visitor," she tells me when the pandemonium settles down into simple chaos.

Tommy's leading me over to the big wooden tray on a patch of grass to show me what his paper people have been up to while I was gone this morning, and the dogs sort of mooch along beside us in an undulating wave.

"Anybody I know?" I ask Aunt Hilary.

"I suppose you must," my landlady says, "but she didn't leave a name. She just said she wanted to drop by to see how your family was making out—especially your son."

I blink with surprise at that. "You mean Tommy?"

"Who else?"

Well, I guess he is like my kid, I think.

"What did she look like?" I ask, half-anticipating the answer.

"A bit like a homeless person, if you want to know the truth," Aunt Hilary says. "She must have been wearing three or four dresses under her overcoat."

"Was she black?"

"Yes, how did you—"

"Hair in dreadlocks with lots of buttons attached to them?"

Aunt Hilary nods. "And she kept fiddling with something in her pockets that made a rattly sort of a sound."

"That's Shirley," I say.

"So you do know her."

"She's an old friend."

Aunt Hilary starts to say something else, but I lose the thread of her conversation because all I'm thinking is, I'm not crazy. Other people *can* see her. I was being pretty cool whenever Shirley showed up, but I have to admit to worrying that her presence was just the first stage of a nervous breakdown.

Suddenly I realize that I'm missing everything my landlady's telling me about Shirley's visit.

"I'm sorry," I tell her. "What did you say?"

Aunt Hilary smiles. She's used to my spacing out from time to time.

"Your friend didn't stay long," she says. "She just told Tommy what a handsome young man he was and patted each of the dogs with utter concentration, as though she wanted to remember them, and then she left. I asked her to stay for some lunch, or at least a cup of tea, because she looked so—well, hungry, I suppose. But she just shook her head and said, 'That's very kind of you, but I don't indulge anymore.' " Aunt Hilary frowns. "At least I think that's what she said. It doesn't really make a lot of sense, when you consider it."

"That's just Shirley," I tell her.

I can tell Aunt Hilary wants to talk some more about it, but I turn the conversation to my plan for an outing to the park, inviting her along. She hasn't got the time, she says—is probably looking forward to a few hours by herself, is what I hear, and I don't blame her—but she gets right into helping me get a knapsack of goodies organized.

We have a great day. Nothing's changed. I've still got to deal with my malaise, I've still got the ghost of a dead friend hanging around, but for a few hours I manage to put it all aside and it's like old times again.

I haven't seen Tommy this happy since I can't remember when and that makes me feel both glad and depressed.

There's got to be a better way to live.

7

I decided it's time to get some expert advice, so the next day I call in sick at work and head off down to Fitzhenry Park instead.

Everybody who spends most of their time on the streets isn't necessarily a bum. Newford's got more than its share of genuinely homeless people—the ones who don't have any choice: winos, losers, the hopeless and the helpless, runaways, and far too many ordinary people who've lost their jobs, their homes, their future through no fault of their own. But it's also got a whole subculture, if you will, of street musicians, performance artists, sidewalk vendors and the like.

Some are like me: they started out as runaways and then evolved into something like when I was making cash from trash. Others have a room in a boarding house or some old hotel and work the streets because that's where their inclination lies. There's not a whole lot of ways to make a living playing fiddle tunes or telling fortunes in other outlets; and the overhead is very affordable.

Fitzhenry Park is where a lot of that kind of action lies. It's close to the Combat Zone, so you get a fair amount of hookers and even less reputable types drifting down when they're, let's say, off-shift. But it's also close to the Barrio, so the seedy element is balanced out with mothers walking in pairs and pushing strollers, old women gossiping in tight clusters, old men playing dominoes and checkers on the benches. Plus you get the lunch crowds from the downtown core which faces the west side of the park.

The other hot spot is down by the Pier, on the lakefront, but that's geared more to the tourists and the cops are tight-assed about permits and the like. If you're going to get arrested for busking or hawking goods from a sidewalk cart or just plain panhandling, that's the place it'll happen.

The kind of person I was looking for now would work the park crowds and I found him without hardly even trying. He was just setting up for the day.

Bones is a Native American—a full-blooded Kickaha with dark coppery skin, broad features and a braid hanging down his back that's almost as long as Angel's hair. He got his name from the way he tells fortunes. He'll toss a handful of tiny bones onto a piece of deerskin and read auguries from the pattern they make. He doesn't really dress for the part, eschewing buckskins and beads for scuffed old workboots, faded blue jeans and a white T-shirt with the arms torn off, but it doesn't seem to hurt business.

I don't really hold much with any of this mumbo-jumbo stuff—not Bones' gig, nor what his girlfriend Cassie does with Tarot cards, or Paperjack's Chinese fortune-telling devices. But while I don't believe that any of them can foretell the future, I still have to admit there's something different about some of the people who work this schtick.

Take Bones.

The man has crazy eyes. Not crazy, you better lock him up kind of eyes, but crazy because maybe he sees something we can't. Like there really is some other world lying draped across ours and he can see right into it. Maybe he's even been there. Lots of times, I figure he's just clowning around, but sometimes that dark gaze of his locks onto you and then you see this seriousness lying behind the laughter and it's like the Tombs all over again—a piece of the wilderness biding on a city street, a dislocating sensation like not only is anything possible, but it probably is.

Besides, who am I to make judgments these days? I'm being haunted by a ghost.

"How do, Maisie?" he says when I wheel my mountain bike up to the edge of the fountain where he's sitting.

I prop the bike up on its kickstand, hang my helmet from one of the handlebars and sit down beside him. He's fiddling with his bones, letting them tumble from one hand to the other. They make a sound like Shirley's buttons, only more muted. I find myself wondering what kind of an animal they came from. Mice? Birds? I look up from his hands and see the clown is sitting in his eyes, laughing. Maybe with me, maybe at me—I can never tell.

"Haven't see you around much these days," he adds.

"I'm going to school," I tell him.

"Yeah?"

"And I've got a job."

He looks at me for this long heartbeat and I get that glimpse of otherness that puts a weird, shifting sensation in the pit of my stomach.

"So are you happy?" he asks.

That's something no one ever asks when I tell them what I'm doing now. I pick at a piece of lint that's stuck to the cuff of my shorts.

"Not really," I tell him.

"Want to see what Nanabozo's got in store for you?" he asks, holding up his bones.

I don't know who Nanabozo is, but I get the idea.

"No," I say. "I want to ask you about ghosts."

He doesn't even blink an eye. Just grins.

"What about them?"

"Well, what are they?" I ask.

"Souls that got lost," he tells me, still smiling, but serious now, too.

I feel weird talking about this. It's a sunny day, the park's full of people, joggers, skateboarders, women with baby carriages, a girl on the bench just a few steps away who probably looks sexy at night under a streetlight, the way she's all tarted up, but now she just looks used. Nothing out of the ordinary, and here we are, talking about ghosts.

"What do you mean?" I ask. "How do they get lost?"

"There's a Path of Souls, all laid out for us to follow when we die," he tells me. "But some spirits can't see it, so they wander the earth instead. Others can't accept the fact that they're dead yet, and they hang around, too."

"A path."

He nods.

"Like something you walk along."

"Inasmuch as a spirit walks," Bones says.

"My ghost says she missed a bus," I tell him.

"Maybe it's different for white people."

"She's black."

He sits there, not looking at me, bones trailing from one hand to the other, making their tiny rattling sound.

"What do you really want to know?" he asks me.

"How do I help her?"

"Why don't you try asking her?"

"I did, but all she gives me back are riddles."

"Maybe you're just not listening properly," he says.

I think back on the conversations I've had with Shirley since I first saw her in the Tombs a few nights ago, but I can't seem to focus on them. I remember being with her, I remember the feeling of what we talked about, but the actual content is muddy now. It seems to shift away as soon as I try to think about it.

"I've really seen her," I tell Bones. "I was there when she died—almost four years ago—but she's back. And other people have seen her, too."

"I know you have," he says.

I don't even know why I was trying to convince him—it's not like he'd be a person that needed convincing—but what he says, stops me.

"What do you mean?" I ask. It's my question for the day.

"It's in your eyes," he says. "The Otherworld has touched you. Think of it as a blessing."

"I don't know if I like the idea," I tell him. "I mean, I miss Shirley, and I actually feel kind of good about her being back, even if she is just a ghost, but it doesn't seem right somehow."

"Often," he says, "what we take from the spirit world is only a reflection of what lies inside ourselves."

There's that look in his eyes, a feral seriousness, like it's important, not so much that I understand, or even believe what he's saying, but *that* he's saying it.

"What. . . ?" I start, but then I figure it out. Part of it anyway.

When I first came to the city, I was pretty messed up, but then Shirley was there to help me. I'm messed up again, so. . . .

"So I'm just projecting her ghost?" I ask. "I need her help, so I've made myself a ghost of her?"

"I didn't say that."

"No, but—"

"Ghosts have their own agendas," he tells me. "Maybe you both have something to give to each other."

We sit for a while, neither of us speaking. I play with the whistle that hangs from a cord around my neck—all the messengers have them to blow at cars that're trying to cut us off. Finally, I get up and take my bike off its kickstand. I look at Bones and that feral quality is still lying there in his grin. His eyes seem to be all pupil, dark, dark. I'm about to say thanks, but the words lock up in my throat. Instead I just nod, put on my helmet and go away to think about what he's told me.

8

Tommy's got this new story that he tells me after we've cleaned up the dinner dishes. We sit together at the kitchen table and he has his little paper people act it out for me. It's about this Chinese man who falls down the crack in the pavement outside Aunt Hilary's house and finds himself in this magic land where everybody's a beautiful model or movie star and they all want to marry the Chinese guy except he misses his family too much, so he just tells them he can't marry any of them—not even the woman who won the Oscar for her part in *Misery*, who for some reason, Tommy's really crazy about.

I've got the old black lab Chuckie lying on my feet, Rexy snuggled up in my lap. Mutt and Jeff are tangled up in a heap on the sofa so that it's hard to tell which part of them's which. They're a cross between a German Shepherd and who knows what; I found Jeff first and gave the other old guy his name because the two were immediately inseparable. Jimmie's part dachshund, part collie—I know, go figure—and his long,

furry body is stretched out in front of the door like
he's a dust puppy. Patty's mostly poodle, but there's
some kind of placid mix in there as well because she's
not at all high-strung. Right now she's sitting in the
bay window, checking the traffic and pretending to be
a cat.

The sad thing, Tommy tells me, is that the Chinese man knows that he'll never be able to get back
home, but he's going to stay faithful to his family
anyway.

"Where'd you get that story?" I ask Tommy.

He just shrugs, then he says, "I really miss you,
Maisie."

How can I keep leaving him?

I feel like a real shit. I know it's not my fault, I
know I'm trying to do my best for all of us, for our
future, but Tommy's mind doesn't work very well considering the long term and my explanations don't really register. It's just me going out all the time, and
not taking him or the dogs with me.

There's a knock on the door. Jimmie gets labori-
ously to his feet and moves aside as Aunt Hilary
comes in. She gives her wristwatch an obvious
look.

"You're going to be late for school," she says, not
really nagging, she just knows me too well.

I feel like saying, fuck school, but I put Rexy down,
shift Chuckie from my feet and stand up. Six dogs and
Tommy all give me a hopeful look, like we're going
out for a walk, faces all dropping when I pick up my
knapsack, heavy with school books.

I give Tommy a hug and kiss then make the good-
bye rounds of the dogs. They're like Tommy; long
term means nothing to them. All they know is I'm
going out and they can't come. Rexy takes a few hopeful steps in the direction of the door, but Aunt Hilary
scoops him up.

"Now, now, Rexy," she tells him. "You know Margaret's got to go to school and she can't take you."

Margaret. She's the one who goes to school and works at QMS and deserts her family five days and four nights a week. She's the traitor.

I'm Maisie, but I'm Margaret, too.

I say good-bye, trying not to look anyone in the eye, and head for the subway. My eyes are pretty well dry by the time I get there. I pause on the platform. When the southbound train comes, I don't get off at the stop for my school, but ride it all the way downtown. I walk the six blocks to the bus depot.

I get a piece of gum stuck to the bottom of my sneaker while I'm waiting in line at the ticket counter. I'm still trying to get it off with an old piece of tissue I find in my pocket—not the most useful tool for the job—when the guy behind the counter says, "Next," in this really tired voice.

Who's he got waiting at home for him? I wonder as I move toward the counter, sort of shuffling the foot with the gum stuck on it so it doesn't trap me to another spot.

"How much for a ticket?" I ask him.

"Depends where you're going."

He's got thinning hair lying flat against his head, parted way over on the left side. Just a skinny little guy in a faded shirt and pants that are too baggy for him, trying to do his job. He's got a tic in one eye and I keep thinking that he's giving me a wink.

"Right," I say.

My mind's out of sync. Of course he needs the destination. I let my thoughts head back into the past, looking for the name of the place I want, trying to avoid the bad times that are hiding there in my memories, just waiting to jump me, but it's impossible to do.

That's another thing about street people, whether they put the street behind them or not: the past holds pain. The present may not be all that great, but it's usually better than what went before. That goes for me, for Shirley, for pretty well everybody I know. You try to live here and now, like the people who go through twelve-step, taking it day by day.

Mostly, you try not to think at all.

"Rockcastle," I tell the guy behind the counter.

He does something mysterious with his computer before he looks up.

"Return or one-way?"

"One-way."

More fiddling with the computer before he tells me the price. I pay him and a couple of minutes later I'm hop-stepping my way out of the depot with a one-way ticket to Rockcastle in my pocket. I sit on a bench outside and scrape off the gum with a popsicle stick I find on the sidewalk, and then I'm ready.

I don't go to my class; I don't go home either. Instead I take the subway up to Gracie Street. When I come up the steps from the station I stand on the pavement for a long time before I finally cross over and walk into the Tombs.

9

The moon seems smaller tonight. It's not just that it's had a few slivers shaved off one side because it's waning; it's like it got tamed somehow.

I can't say the same for the Tombs. I see kids sniffing glue, shooting up, some just sprawled with their backs against a pile of rubble, legs splayed out in front of them, eyes staring into nothing. I pass a few 'bos cooking god knows what over a fire they've got rigged up in an old jerry can. A bag lady comes lurching out between the sagging doors of an old

office building and starts to yell at me. Her voice
follows me as I pick a way through the litter and
abandoned cars.

The bikers down the street are having a party. The
buckling pavement in front of their building has got
about thirty-five chopped-down street hogs parked in
front of it. The place is lit up with Coleman lights and
I can hear the music and laughter from where I'm
sitting in the bay window of my old squat in the Clark
Building.

They don't bother me; I never exactly hung out with
them or anything, but they used to consider me a kind
of mascot after Shirley died and let the word get out
that I was under their protection. It's not the kind of
thing that means a lot everywhere, but it helped me
more than once.

No one's taken over the old squat yet, but after five
months it's already got the same dead feel to it that
hits you anywhere in the Tombs. It's not exactly dirty,
but it's dusty and the wind's been blowing crap in off
the street. There's a smell in the air; though it's not
quite musty, it's getting there.

But I'm not really thinking about any of that. I'm
just passing time. Sitting here, waiting for a piece of
the past to catch up to me.

I used to sit here all the time once I'd put Tommy
to bed, looking out the window when I wasn't reading,
Rexy snuggled close, the other dogs sprawled around
the room, a comforting presence of soft snores and
twitching bodies as they chased dream-rabbits in their
sleep.

There's no comfort here now.

I look back out the window and see a figure coming
up the street, but it's not who I was expecting. It's
Angel, with Chuckie on a leash, his black shadow
shape stepping out front, leading the way. As I watch
them approach, some guy moves from out of the shad-

ows that've collected around the building across the street and Chuckie, worn out and old though he is, lunges at him. The guy makes a fast fade.

I listen to them come into the building, Chuckie's claws clicking on the scratched marble, the leather soles of Angel's shoes making a scuffly sound as she comes up the stairs. I turn around when they come into the squat.

"I thought I'd find you here," Angel says.

"I didn't know you were looking."

I don't mean to sound put off, but I can't keep the punkiness out of my voice.

"I'm not checking up on you, Maisie. I was just worried."

"Well, here I am."

She undoes the lead from Chuckie's collar and he comes across the room and sticks his face up against my knees. The feel of his fur under my hand is comforting.

"You really shouldn't be out here," I tell Angel. "It's not safe."

"But it's okay for you?"

I shrug. "This was my home."

She crosses the room as well. The windowsill's big enough to hold us both. She scoots up and then sits across from me, arms wrapped around her legs.

"After you came by the office, I went by your work to see you, then to your apartment, then to the school."

I shrug again.

"Do you want to talk about it?" she asks.

"What's to say?"

"Whatever's in your heart. I'm here to listen. Or I can just go away, if that's what you prefer, but I don't really want to do that."

"I. . . ."

The words start locking up inside me again. I take a deep breath and start over.

"I'm not really happy, I guess," I tell her.

She doesn't say anything, just nods encouragingly.

"It's. . . . I never really told you why I came to see you about school and the job and everything. You probably just thought that you'd finally won me over, right?"

Angel shakes her head. "It was never a matter of winning or losing. I'm just there for the people who need me."

"Yeah, well, what happened was—do you remember when Margaret Grierson died?"

Angel nods.

"We shared the same postal station," I tell her, "and the day before she was killed, I got a message in my box warning me to be careful, that someone was out to do a serious number on me. I spent the night in a panic and I was so relieved when the morning finally came and nothing had happened, because what'd happen to Tommy and the dogs if anything ever happened to me, you know?"

"What does that have to do with Margaret Grierson?" Angel asks.

"The note I got was addressed to 'Margaret'—just that, nothing else. I thought it was for me, but I guess whoever sent it got his boxes mixed up and it ended up in mine instead of hers."

"But I still don't see what—"

I can't believe she doesn't get it.

"Margaret Grierson was an important person," I say. "She was heading up that AIDS clinic, she was doing things for people. She was making a difference."

"Yes, but—"

"I'm nobody," I say. "It should've been me that died. But it wasn't, so I thought well, I better do something with myself, with my life, you know? I better make my having survived meaningful. But I can't cut it.

"I've got the straight job, the straight residence, I'm going back to school and it's like it's all happening to someone else. The things that are important to me— Tommy and the dogs—it's like they're not even a part of my life any more."

I remember something Shirley's ghost asked me, and add, "Maybe it's selfish, but I figure charity should start at home, you know? I can't do much for other people if I'm feeling miserable myself."

"You should've come to me," Angel says.

I shake my head. "And tell you what? It sounds so whiny. I mean there's people starving not two blocks from where we're sitting, and I should be worried about being happy or not? The important stuff's covered—I'm providing for my family, putting a roof over their heads and making sure they have enough to eat—that should be enough, right? But it doesn't feel that way. It feels like the most important things are missing.

"I used to have time to spend with Tommy and the dogs; now I have to steal a minute here, another there. . . ."

My voice trails off. I think of how sad they all looked when I left the apartment tonight, like I was deserting them, not just for the evening, but forever. I can't bear that feeling, but how do you explain yourself to those who can't possibly understand?

"We could've worked something out," Angel says. "We still can."

"Like what?"

Angel smiles. "I don't know. We'll just have to think it through better than we have so far. You'll have to try to open up a bit more, tell me what you're *really* feeling, not just what you think I want to hear."

"It's that obvious, huh?"

"Let's just say I have a built-in bullshit detector."

We don't say anything for a while then. I think about what she's said, wondering if something could be worked out. I don't want special dispensation because I'm some kind of charity case—I've *always* earned my own way—but I know there've got to be some changes or the little I've got is going to fall apart.

I can't get the image out of mind—Tommy with his sad eyes as I'm going out the door—and I know I've got to make the effort. Find a way to keep what was good about the past and still make a decent future for us.

I put my hand in my pocket and feel the bus ticket I bought earlier.

I have to open up a bit more, I think, looking at Angel. What would her bullshit detector do if I told her about Shirley?

Angel stretches out her legs, then lowers them to the floor.

"Come on," she says, offering me her hand. "Let's go talk about this some more."

I look around the squat and compare it to Aunt Hilary's apartment. There's no comparison. What made this place special, we took with us.

"Okay," I tell Angel.

I take her hand and we leave the building. I know it's not going to be easy, but then nothing ever is. I'm not afraid to work my butt off; I just don't want to lose sight of what's really important.

When we're outside, I look back up to the window where we were sitting. I wonder about Shirley, how's she's going to work out whatever it is that she's got to do to regain her own sense of peace. I hope she finds it. I don't even mind if she comes to see me again, but I don't think that'll be part of the package.

I left the bus ticket for her, on the windowsill.

10

I don't know if we've worked everything out, but I think we're making a good start. Angel's fixed it so that I've dropped a few courses which just means that it'll take me longer to get my diploma. I'm only working a couple of days a week at QMS—the Saturday shift that nobody likes and a rotating day during the week.

The best thing is I'm back following my trade again, trash for cash. Aunt Hilary lets me store stuff in her garage because she doesn't have a car anyway. A couple of nights a week, Tommy and I head out with our carts, the dogs on our heels, and we work the bins. We're spending a lot more time together and everybody's happier.

I haven't seen Shirley again. If it hadn't been for Aunt Hilary telling me about her coming by the house, I'd just think I made the whole thing up.

I remember what Bones told me about ghosts having their own agendas and how maybe we both had something to give each other. Seeing Shirley was the catalyst for me. I hope I helped her some, too. I remember her telling me once that she came from Rockcastle. I think wherever she was finally heading, Rockcastle was still on the way.

There isn't a solution to every problem, but at the very least, you've got to try.

I went back to the squat the day after I was there with Angel, and the bus ticket was gone. Logic tells me that someone found it and cashed it in for a quick fix or a bottle of cheap wine. I'm pretty sure I just imagined the lingered scent of rosehip and licorice, and the button I found on the floor was probably from one of Tommy's shirts, left behind when we moved.

But I'd like to think that it was Shirley who picked the ticket up, that this time she got to the depot on time.

SUGGESTION

by Rod Serling

I wouldn't have done what Harvey Hemple had asked me to do, if he hadn't hassled the hell out of me—pleading and begging and dressing up the goddamned thing as if I were the only human being on the planet who could give him peace of mind.

Hemple wasn't really a bad guy—just an uncomfortable combination of much too much aggressiveness tacked on to what must have been a draining, bleeding sense of inferiority. He was narrow shouldered, big nosed, jug-eared, and when he put on those Edwardian clothes of his, he looked like the sort of store manikin you might find in a very cheap department store—one that couldn't afford a professional window dresser.

It began at Lucille Novotny's cocktail party. Lucille was on the broad-hipped side of thirty, with a flat chest, a thirty-seven inch waist and legs by Steinway; all you could think of was a pasty white tube of toothpaste squeezed at the top. She wrote copy at the agency where Hemple and I both worked, and she was a gushy, really unpalatable broad who had come from Upstate New York direct from an across the tracks Polish community in a small town, obviously planning to spend the rest of her life trying to overcompensate for the humbleness of the beginning. She affected a clipped, precise British way of speech that was constantly intruded upon by unconscious and unbidden Slavic overtones. She littered her language with private girl's school bon mots like "barf" and "groovy" and "right on" which fit her like panty hose fit a squid. Her cocktail parties were protracted disasters that everybody showed up at because they didn't want to hurt her feelings. It was a bunch of incompatible people who had seen too much of each other at the office, forced to extend the particular day's association impressed into the social service of over-strong drinks and synthetic camaraderie. So we had stood around that night producing brittle, artificial laughter and equally brittle and artificial conversation. And it was Lucille, herself, damn her, who, after seeing a third of the guests leave after about a half hour, had fixed a witch's eye on me and brightly and loudly announced that I would now do my hypnosis act.

Well, I *do* hypnosis, but strictly as a gag and really not very seriously at all. I can put people under and occasionally can get a posthypnotic, and more than once I've accomplished regression or some kind of return to an earlier life. But, as I say, it was strictly a party gig and then only when I was sufficiently bagged to throw over a natural reticence and shyness of my own.

Lucille clapped her hands and banged on the bar and announced in that phony Joan Crawford voice of hers that Peter Connacher—me—would now entertain the assemblage with some mystifying mesmerizing. And who would be the first subject? The first volunteer? Well, of course, it was Harvey Hemple. He had been standing in the corner with a five foot, nine inch blonde, already mesmerized by her cleavage. It was really almost masochistic the way Harvey always targeted in on the lady least likely to give him a tumble—figuratively, or mattress-wise. The blonde was no exception. She did everything but yawn in his face, while he flitted around her like a suicidal moth, spewing out mispronounced French, trying to be witty and suave, miserably, humiliatingly conscious that he looked and sounded like an impotent poodle trying to make it with a St. Bernard. The saddest thing about the predictable and too-often-played scene was that Harvey was quite aware of the fact that he was striking out and all that remained was to find a way to bow out gracefully and save as much of his pinched little face as he could.

At the sound of Lucille's announcement, he whirled away from the blonde, held up his hand, and in his semi-falsetto voice shouted out, "Me! I want to be the one hypnotized!"

That undernourished chimp grin of his, built out of nerves and tension and insecurity was plastered all over his face as he approached me in the center of the room, and his eyes darted left and right as he responded to the less-than-excited applause. He sat down on the sofa, facing me, loosening his big four-in-hand tie and looking up at me expectantly.

Bored drinkers crowded around, grateful for the distraction; grateful for *any* distraction.

"Go ahead," Lucille Novotny urged me, hitting the vowels hard like Lawrence Welk, and momentarily forgetting the fake, superimposed culture that propped up her language like jerry-built stilts.

So what could I do? There was the piano-legged, fever-eyed hostess desperate to keep things moving; and there was poor Harvey Hemple seeking, if not immortality, at least a couple of minutes of not fusing with the wallpaper and taking on a focalized identity of his own.

I remembered thinking at the time that Harvey would make a perfectly lousy subject for hypnosis. He was too damned tense, too preoccupied with himself, too uptight.

Oh, God, how wrong I was!

I looked down into that eager, painfully homely little face, now shining with excitement and expectation, and I also remembered thinking that I'd give him about three minutes and if he didn't respond by then I'd call it a wash, apologize, and get the hell out. Harvey was the insult added to Lucile Novotny's injuries.

"All right, Harv," I intoned. "Now close your eyes and relax. That's right, just relax. Keep your eyes closed. You're getting very tired . . . very drowsy . . . very sleepy, Harv. You're falling asleep."

His little calf eyes fluttered for a second or two and then closed.

"Now, Harvey," I continued softly, "you're falling asleep. You're relaxing and it's beautiful. Just beautiful, Harv. That drowsy feeling is just what you needed."

There were a couple of snickers from the group and they crowded around closer. This would, of course, be just great for Harvey—because he needed attention like most men needed eggs to go with their bacon. But I suddenly realized, looking down at him, that he was quite unaware of anyone else. He had responded to suggestion almost immediately. The eyes were, indeed, closed and there was no feigning. Harvey *was* falling asleep. There was no flutter in the eyelids and his body was totally relaxed. His breathing was slower but more regular. And, as fate would have it, this poor little bastard whose ambitions and thyroid left his talent behind at the starting gate, turned out to have one particular strength. He was the most suggestible subject of hypnosis I'd ever seen.

"Harvey," I said, getting more interested, "raise your right arm, Harvey."

He did so.

"Now try to lower it, Harvey."

The arm started to lower.

"Harvey," I interrupted, "you can't lower it any-more. It's chained to the ceiling. You simply can't lower it."

A look of strain showed on his face and then some perspiration. His arm shook as he gave it a good college try with maximum effort—but it stayed suspended in midair.

At this point Lucille's cocktailers were hooked. Hypnosis, in social situations, is a kind of freak show. It's a promise of watching an acquaintance make an ass out of himself or at least do things he wouldn't ordinarily do. I had no intention of embarrassing Harvey because his whole bloody life was an embarrassment. I thought I'd just run him through some fundamental paces then snap him out of it and forget it.

"Now open your eyes, Harvey," I ordered. "I want you to clasp your hands like this." I put my hands together in front of him, fingers interlocked. "Now look at my eyes, Harv. Clasp your hands tight."

I reached over and took hold of his hands, pulling them forward until they were extended, then I squeezed his fingers together. "Make them real tight, Harv. As tight as you can. That's it. Tight—real tight. Now your fingers are all locked together."

I saw his hands quiver as their grip on each other became more solid.

"That's it, Harvey," I said. "Tighter and tighter now. Your fingers are sticking together more and more. They're becoming more and more tightly clasped. They're sticking together. They're getting really stuck. They're locked, Harv. Your hands are stuck fast. You can't take them apart. Now in a minute I'm going to tell you to pull them apart but you won't be able to. You can't pull your hands apart. Try, Harv. Try—but you won't be able to."

There was no fear in Harvey's now open eyes but

there was strain and tension as he tried to pry his fingers apart. He pulled and yanked until the veins bulged out on his temples and his eyes looked glassy.

"That's all right, Harvey," I said. "You can take them apart now."

Slowly his hands and fingers seemed to relax and fell to his sides. The depth of his trance state was phenomenal.

For the next few minutes, after awakening him, I had him stiffen, kneel, crawl, search for gold, sing a song, and then let him go back to sleep.

The fascinated idiots standing around us had a couple of dozen suggestions as to intriguing exercises—most of them immoral. Normally—or at least, so it is said—a subject under hypnosis will perform no act that his normal nature would rebel at. But in Harvey's case, I wasn't so sure. He seemed so completely susceptible to command that there was really no assurance that if I'd ordered him out the window, three stories down to the street, he wouldn't comply.

Just why I came up with the next bit, I'll never really know. But I happened to see the half filled highball glass in Lucille's hand. I wasn't thinking, really. It just came to me that with anyone as suggestible as Harvey, you could practically go the route. You could put him off on some misty limbo of the subconscious, and only guess at just how completely he'd accept the fantasy.

I held up Lucille's glass and I said to Harvey, "Harv—open your eyes, please."

His eyes opened, staring at me.

I pointed to the glass. "This is a mug of boiling hot, scalding water."

Harvey's eyes looked bland and neutral.

"Harvey," I ordered, "put your fingers in this mug. And remember—it's scalding hot."

Harvey reached across with his right hand, stuck

two fingers in the ice-filled glass, let out a little gasp of pain, then quickly pulled them out.

I don't give a damn if no one believes this. I really don't. But I swear to God, I saw it. Harvey's fingers were covered with thick, white blisters stretching from nails to knuckle joints.

Lucille's guests loved it. They loved it like kids love a horror show—part an overwhelming fascination, and part an ice cold chill of apprehension. Something was going on that they couldn't fathom. But what should have stopped me there—but didn't—was the fact that I didn't understand it either. Here was the mind taking over completely the functions of the body. Brain cells were telling the flesh, a body length away, that boiling hot liquid had attacked skin and skin, in turn, had to react.

I don't think anyone in the room quite understood the implications of what had happened. Just as I don't suppose the ticket buyers to a freak show really ever give a thought to the psychology of the tattooed man or what it is that motivates him to cover up his humanity with red and blue ink and sentence himself to the status of freak for the rest of his life.

I should have realized then that I had left the road with the signposts and was stumbling off into a wilderness beyond that was one half quicksand and the other a mine field.

What I'd intended to do at that point was simply to run through a few more pretty fundamental demonstrations—having the subject rise, then feel that he was falling, or else follow me and then make him believe he was forced to walk backwards—just a few relatively simple suggestions that are interesting to watch and kind of fun, but which carry with them no particular risk. This is what I'd *planned* to do. But Lucille and her drinking buddies would have no part of it.

Some mini-skirted broad from the Accounting Office started to make noises that we should make Harvey think he's Mark Anthony entering the boudoir of Cleopatra. And Lucille, with much heavy breathing, concurred that this would be a kick.

Another Account exec started to ootz me to plant a suggestion that I should wake Harvey up, but give him a posthypnotic that whenever somebody claps his hands, Harvey would imagine himself a big stallion and the first girl he met would be a filly in heat.

All of them—every damned one of them—with flushed face, alcohol-bright eyes, and a bottom-line insensitive cruelty had some other small item of clinical advice as to how we could turn Harvey into a side show and do whatever raunchy, dirty little thing their own subconscious desperately wanted, but couldn't climb over the wall of convention to do themselves.

And while they were shouting at me and giggling at me and panting out rotten little X-rated suggestions— I took a long look at Harvey. I saw him at that moment as I'd never seen him before. He wasn't just Harvey the Klutz, the self-deluded Lothario, the sad little swinger who could find no one to swing with. He was just a guy. A discontented, unhappy, small man who held on to a deadly, dull life with the dirty end of the stick, destined to be nobody, do nothing, and live and die with no other distinction than that at the art of losing, he was very successful.

And while I was staring at his ugly little face in repose, the Lucille Novotny Marching Chowder and Stick a Needle into a Buddy's Back and Humiliate the Hell Out of Him Club kept up a running barrage of suggestions on how to spice up an evening.

"Make him take off his clothes."

"Make him go to the bathroom."

"Give him a posthypnotic that he's a monkey trying to open up a banana with his hand bandaged."

"Make him do something exciting, Pete," Lucille Novotny ordered, exasperated and subconsciously battling convents, Catholicism, and thirty years of suppressing a marching parade of sexual fantasies that perched outside of her bedroom door, forbidden to come in, but oh, so desperately desired.

It wasn't that I particularly liked Harvey Hemple. He was a drag, a bore, a self-deluded horse's ass, and a pain to be with. But he'd already paid his dues for his self-delusions. He'd paid for them with much too much loneliness—more than men should have to live with. So I thought at that moment I'd give him a break. I'd turn my back on this pack of lusting, would-be voyeurs and I'd give Harvey a ticket to his own private and personal fantasy with a door locked to the outside. I'd let him hallucinate and have fun doing it, but provide no windows for the cocktail peeping Toms to leer.

I bent down over the sleeping figure and I said, softly, "Harvey—you're in a place . . . a special place . . . where you've always wanted to be. It's a nice place. A friendly place. A place you think about a lot."

I saw some kind of movement behind the closed eyes and there was just a barely perceptible nodding of the head.

Lucille and her buddies started to complain that this act wasn't fair. They wanted something spectacular. They wanted something that came without clothes and with humiliation. But then they stopped their yapping because very slowly both of Harvey's hands were raised and the fingers clutched something in mid-air—something, of course, invisible.

From deep in his throat came a sound. First it was as if he was just clearing his throat and then the sound took on some kind of form. It was the kind of loud hum that a kid uses when he's playing airplanes.

And then it hit me, as it did a couple of others—that's precisely what Harvey was doing. He was flying an airplane. He was banking and winging over, diving down toward the ground then zooming upward, looping and then shooting skyward, and all the time there came this deep chest low roar of the engine noise, manufactured in the pistons of his chest and in the factory of hallucinations that was his mind. And while we were watching, his eyes opened and there was the look of eagles. There was the keen, probing expression of the trained pilot as he jetted across the sky.

It figured, of course. A jet pilot. That would be Harvey Hemple's deep-rooted wish and layered-over dream to be the one thing he could *never* be. He would never have the skill, the coolness, the nerve, the intelligence, or the physical makeup to fly an airplane. And because it was the totally unattainable item on the agenda of his destiny, it was the first thing he thought about in his subconscious. It was lyrical and poetic and romantic. Harvey Hemple, jet pilot! Harvey Hemple with the silver wings, the slouch cap, the earphones; Harvey Hemple, the conqueror of the far-out air.

And while we all watched, Harvey Hemple flew his jet back and forth across a mystical sky, diving through clouds and then pulling back on the imaginary yoke to send his aircraft whistling upward into a deeper blue. Upward. Still upward. His enclosed fists rested against his stomach. The imaginary plane was sitting on its tail, absolutely vertical and still climbing.

And then, as we all watched, it happened.

A sudden look of bewilderment clouding his eyes. Then confusion and doubt. And then fear. Fear that picked up Harvey Hemple in a giant, iron fist and squeezed him dry. For a moment he looked like a frozen tableau, sitting there on a couch, his back pressed tightly against a cushion, his face raised toward the ceiling, fists still clenched at his stomach, holding onto the make believe controls of an aircraft. For just one additional moment, wild, frightened eyes scanned what must have been an altimeter, an airspeed indicator, and whatever other dials there were to register and document distance, time, fuel consumption, engine status and all the other clues that tell a man how safely he's defying the laws of gravity. And then very slowly, while Harvey's hum turned into an inhuman thin wail of sound, his head bent forward, following the direction of his clenched fists, then the trunk of his body also bent over and it was like watching a perfect pantomime of a man in a cockpit of a plummeting aircraft.

Down, down, down,

He was falling.

Illusion. Dream sequence. A pantomime of fantasy played out in an apartment house on a living room sofa.

But the reality was eerie and astounding.

For on Harvey Hemple's face could now be seen the flush-pulled distortion of negative G-forces; a horror-mask of distended lips, popping eyes, bulging cheekbones, as the flesh was tightened to a breaking point by gravity's screaming protest.

The ear-piercing whine of Harvey's voice simulating a jet's descent literally enveloped the room. And the drinkers, Lucille and those thrill-seeking cocktail-swigging animals, began to realize they were getting much too much thrill for their money and started to back away.

Later . . . weeks later . . . months later . . . when in nightmares they would recall this scene, they'd be thankful they *had* backed away.

For over Harvey's scream, and over my own shouted commands for him to "wake up" and "stop falling"—commands which hypnosis rejects as point-

less. You don't scream at a subject. You tell him he's
able to do something—not that he's forced to. But
by that point, while watching Harvey's face turn into
something close to a Halloween hell, it was too late
to try to move in to his fantasy. He was beyond any
external suggestion. The plane of his special and private world was unreachable from where I or anyone
else stood.

And then it happened.

I felt something wet—like a moistened switchblade—
slash across my cheek. I heard screams from all
around the room. And then I looked down at what
had been Harvey Hemple.

He was on the floor, crunched together like a kneeling Buddha—his clothes smoldering. *Smoke spiraled
up from burnt hair; blackened stumps stuck out from
charred sleeves; his legs, smelling of burnt flesh, stuck
out at crazy and impossible angles.*

*Harvey Hemple had crashed. He was the burnt,
blackened, crushed, battered victim of metal hitting
earth at the speed of sound.*

There was an autopsy. There were hours and days
and weeks of questioning by the police. There was a
total, unbelieving rejection of everything said to the
authorities by the guests at Lucille Novotny's cocktail
party. And finally they put a tag on a manila folder
that read: "Hemple, Harvey. Suicide. Self-immola-
tion." Then they stuck the folder in a big file—the
carded graveyard where statistics take the place of
corpses.

And as for myself: I don't hypnotize anymore. I
discreetly stay away from cocktail parties of any sort.
I'm always afraid that at some given, dull moment,
when the bourbon and martinis cease doing their job
of palliating the unbearable dullness and despair of

humans who can't hack it, somebody might look across the room at me and say, "We will now be entertained by some mystifying mesmerizing from Peter Connacher."

Forget it.

Peter Connacher has retired from the entertainment business.

Peter Connacher no longer puts the ring of suggestion through the nose of some unwary subject.

He doesn't because quite obviously a subject can turn into a victim.

Now I stay home a lot and I do my drinking in solitary, and very reflective privacy.

That may not guarantee my longevity.

But at least I'll remain sane.

DAW

Don't Miss These Exciting DAW Anthologies